*To Pat –
all the best –
Enjoy –*

THE MEDAL

a novel

*Believe &
have faith –*

Kerriann Flanagan Brosky

*Kerriann Flanagan Brosky
12/7/13*

OTHER BOOKS BY KERRIANN FLANAGAN BROSKY

Huntington's Hidden Past
Huntington's Past Revisited
Ghosts of Long Island: Stories of the Paranormal
Ghosts of Long Island II: More Stories of the Paranormal
Delectable Italian Dishes: For Family and Friends,
with Sal Baldanza

www.KerriannFlanaganBrosky.com
www.PadrePioMedal.com

Cover Photo by Randy Radke at The Saltair Inn - www.SaltairInn.com
Cover and Book Design by Karl W. Brosky
Author Photo by Thomas Decker Studio at Sagamore Yacht Club - Oyster Bay, NY
Hair Stylist - Joseph Crocilla - Gizay Michaels Salon

First published by Dog Ear Publishing
4010 W. 86th Street, Ste H
Indianapolis, IN 46268
www.DogEarPublishing.net

ISBN: 978-1-4575-1400-5
ISBN: 978-1-4575-1402-9 (eBook)

Printed in the United States of America

Praise for The Medal

"Why do bad things happen to good people? Does one's misfortune mean that God overlooks us, or even worse, does God sometimes punish us? Could a family tragedy lead to a greater blessing in disguise? In *The Medal*, Bethany does a tremendous amount of soul searching in her attempt to answer these very questions.

Bethany's fate as caretaker for her ailing father seems grim at first, but as she struggles to regain her faith, she finds that her Life Plan has much more in store for her than the situation in which she has found herself. The reader is initially saddened by Bethany's frustrating predicament, but then her steady, spiritual evolution becomes absolutely mesmerizing! Why do certain people begin to appear in her life? What messages do they bring? In modern times, can we still believe in miracles?

"The Medal encourages all of us to think about the lessons God intends us to learn, if we are to find profound meaning in the "cards we are dealt" in this lifetime. Ultimately, life is not just about sickness and health, or even life and death. It's about how we choose to take this journey, when to decide to take a leap of faith, and when we allow ourselves to open up to those we can *trust* and *love* along the way."
   – *Richard Scheinberg, LCSW, BCD-author of Seeking Soul Mates, Spirit Guides, and Past Lives*

"Inspiring and faith filled – *The Medal* brings us along one woman's journey as she navigates life's heartaches eventually finding her way back to her own heart — and true faith, with a little help from a cannoli eating angel, proving that even God has a sense of humor!"
   – *Danielle Campbell, Journalist & Anchor, News 12 Long Island*

"Engaging, original and inspirational…this beautifully written novel tells the tale of a daughter's care-giving journey with honesty, warmth and love. This novel will make any parent gleam with pride.

Bethany's journey of caring for her father with progressive multiple sclerosis, hits home with so many people who care for those with a progressive chronic illness. A beautiful story told with warmth and love that is sure to resonate with people of all faiths."
   – *Pamela J. Mastrota, President & CEO National Multiple Sclerosis Society, Long Island Chapter*

"*The Medal* takes a fresh look at a controversial religious figure, while presenting a deeper message that things are sometimes more than they appear. Brosky presents a wonderful, historical and thought provoking story about Padre Pio through the eyes of an unconventional messenger who has a unique vernacular and style all his own... an angel who speaks in tongues - with a Brooklyn-Italian accent. The result is an inspirational, modern-day-tale of faith, spirituality, and history.

A powerful, thought provoking, and moving journey in search of the modern day miracle. *The Medal* will have you believing."
  – Chris Collora, Reporter, Long Island Online News

"*The Medal* so accurately portrays the feelings that family members often feel when faced with caring for a loved one. It was so easy to see that Bethany loved her father, and was willing to do whatever it took to make his life comfortable. While we see this we also see Bethany as someone who is stressed and unsure of whether life is passing her by. I could easily understand her feelings of resentment toward her brother, and really enjoyed the way the author allowed us to see Steven's side. I thought that Rob played a pivotal role in helping to take care of John. There is also another side to this story: it is how someone named Jimmy tries to help Bethany find her faith again. It was so easy to envision Jimmy, as a husky Italian who loved eating cannolis. Even though the main characters in this story are Catholic, a faith I know very little about, I was still able to easily connect with the faith-based messages woven into the story. I thought the author's notes at the end of the story explaining who Padre Pio was, really contributed to the story.

The Medal is a story about finding faith when all faith is gone, and how there is a higher power if only we believe. The author's descriptions of faith were amazing, and allowed me to learn quite a bit about Catholic Faith. A story that is very easy to connect with whether you are Catholic or not, because many of us are dealing with taking care of loved ones and struggling with faith."
  – Five Stars - Brenda C. for Readers Favorite

"*The Medal* is a highly well-written book that features a family's love for each other and what they do in the face of impending death. The dialogue among the book's characters is realistic and the characters themselves are believable and three dimensional. The excellent storyline follows Bethany's eventual return to religion and her gradual acceptance of her father's fate. The character of Jimmy will be a delight to all readers. *The Medal* is a book that should be on the top of readers' lists everywhere. "

  – Five Stars - Alice D. for Readers Favorite

Acknowledgements

To my editor, Erin Brown. For your superb editorial skills and your unfailing guidance in seeing this project through.

To Jean Cody. For your contributions to this book, and for having more faith in me than I sometimes have in myself. Thanks for believing.

To Richard Schoeller. For giving me the encouragement I needed to go on. You're messages from the other side have been invaluable to me. You have been such a positive influence in my life.

To Suzanne N. For being my sounding board. Thanks for your support.

To Laurie "LJ" King. The journey has been long and you always managed to lift me up when I needed lifting. It was great having someone to share both the good and the bad on the ever-changing road of literary life. I never would have made it through without you, beach girl.

To my mother, Deanna Flanagan. Thank you for giving me wings which allowed me to be creative and to follow my dreams. Thank you for believing in this book, and for allowing me to bring this story to life.

To my sons, Ryan and Patrick. You have seen the ups and downs. I hope it has taught you to persevere and to follow your own dreams in life. Anything is possible if you put your mind to it.

To my husband Karl. I am the luckiest person in the world to have a husband who is as supportive as you. You never once gave up on me, and you pushed forward and stepped up to the plate when I had very little left in me. Words cannot express how grateful I am.

To my family and friends in spirit. Daddy and Julie, your love and encouragement guided me through this project. You have proven life does go on after death.

To Johnny. You told me years ago I would be writing this story. It's all been because of you. You taught me to always have faith, no matter how bad things get.

Lastly, to Saint Pio who I believe encouraged me to write this book. You have changed my life forever.

For Johnny Ambrosio
who brought Padre Pio into my life,
and who encouraged me to write this book.
Thanks for giving me faith.

Preghi, speranza e non si preoccupi.
Fidi di della qualitá infinita del dio onnipotente.
—Padre Pio of Pietrelcina

Pray, hope and don't worry.
Trust in the infinite goodness of almighty God.

PART I

One

Bethany held the pastry bag tightly as she skillfully created an assortment of lavender colored flowers made from Royal icing. She took a step backwards to examine her work. *A few more here* she thought, as she slowly spun the elaborate wedding cake. She had been working on the masterpiece for hours. The cream colored fondant which engulfed the rich chocolate sponge cake was perfectly smooth, and served as a platform for the delicate, sugary flowers. "Not bad," Bethany said.

Opening the door of the walk-in refrigerator, Bethany carefully rolled the enormous cake inside. "All set for tomorrow," she said as she closed the door. She went around the commercial kitchen and cleaned up. Neatness and organization in the kitchen were key. She quickly finished and looked at the clock hanging above the sink. She had better get home. She never knew what she'd be walking into. For the first time in a while, she was feeling relaxed and she hoped that nothing would disrupt this temporary moment. With some sense of dread, she unbuttoned the knots of her chef's coat and hung it on a nearby hook. She then went around the bakery making sure everything was locked. The bakery had been closed for nearly forty-five minutes. She had sent the shop's manager Alison home earlier. Bethany turned off the overhead chandeliers and then made her way back into the kitchen. After giving one last look around, she headed out the back, shutting the heavy steel door.

Even though it was early evening, the SUV was stifling hot when Bethany opened the door and got in. The summer so far, had been brutal. She took a deep breath before starting the ignition. "So what do you have in store for me when I get home, God?" Bethany said, tempting fate. She took the quick trip down Woodbine Avenue, the narrow street that ran alongside Northport Harbor. Ornately decorated Victorian homes lined the other side of the street in the seafaring town, and offered spectacular views of both the harbor and the sunset. Bethany began to tense as she approached the turn up Hollow Lane where she lived. Slowly she drove up the winding hill where the 1860 Italianate lay waiting. She looked over the expansive backyard as she parked her black Chevy Tahoe in the circular driveway. How she wished to just go inside, pour herself a glass of wine and head back out to the Adirondack chair for a moment of relaxation. Despite the sultry heat, she longed for time spent outside alone. There was no such thing however, no matter how much she wished it. She gathered her bag and made her way up the brick path.

"Cherie, what happened?" Bethany asked upon entering the expansive kitchen. Cherie had on rubber gloves and was on her hands and knees cleaning up the remains of a broken potted plant. Pieces of the ceramic pot were scattered everywhere along the large tiled floor. A pool of yellow liquid ran parallel to the island which was located in the center of the country kitchen.

Bethany threw down her bag and keys upon the island and knelt down in her checkered chef's pants to help Cherie.

"No, no, no," Cherie protested, her voice still showing traces of her Jamaican roots. "I'll take care of it. Your daddy had an accident, that's all."

Bethany stood up a bit bewildered. "Did he fall?" She looked around the kitchen for her father's live-in aide. "Where's Rob?" she asked.

"He's taken him into the bathroom to clean him up." Cherie said, pointing with her gloved hand to the pool of yellow liquid along the floor. "Get me a bucket of hot water, will you?"

Bethany quickly went to the hall closet where cleaning supplies were kept. She grabbed an extra roll of paper towels, a bucket, and a mop. She filled the bucket with hot water and carefully carried it to Cherie who by now had picked up most of the ceramic pieces.

"I want to get this cleaned before it stains the tile," Cherie said grabbing the mop.

"I can take care of this, Cherie."

"Don't be silly. You just come home from work."

"Well what happened? What was he doing?" asked Bethany.

"Your daddy decided to go out on the porch. It's too hot out there. He wouldn't listen to me. He said he needed fresh air and couldn't stand one minute more of being inside," she explained. "I told him, 'Don't do it, Mr. Fitzpatrick....you'll be sorry' but he didn't listen."

"Where was Rob?"

"Rob went to pick up his medication in town. The pharmacist said he had it ready. As soon as he left, I see your daddy making his way to the porch. That's when I started yelling at him but he didn't listen. He can be stubborn, you know." Cherie mopped the tiles with the steaming water and sprayed it with disinfectant.

"How did he get over here?" Bethany asked, growing frustrated.

Cherie put the disinfectant on the counter and then rubbed her forehead with the back of her hand. Her ebony colored skin glowed as a bead of sweat rolled down the side of her head and onto her round, full cheeks. She felt the top of her coarse black hair to make sure it hadn't unraveled from its tight bun. She sighed and said, "He couldn't have been out there ten minutes when I see him come shuffling down the hall. I knew right away he was overheating, and just like the times he's had a fever, his body started shutting down. So I say to him 'Get right in here this minute and sit down before you fall down.' I knew he was in trouble, Bethany. I dragged a kitchen chair over, took the compress from the freezer, and poured him a glass of cold water. Just as I turn around from the fridge, I see the rubber stopper on the walker get stuck inside the leg of this table," Cherie said, pointing to the decorative side table that lined the wall by the stairs. "I knew he was going down. All his weight pushed forward and the walker didn't move. I couldn't get to him fast enough. I feel so terrible."

Cherie plopped herself on one of the stools lined up around the island, her rubber gloves still on her hands.

Bethany sat down next to her. "Is he alright?" she asked.

"I think so," Cherie answered. "Rob is checking him out now. His muscles will be aching tomorrow, that's for sure. But my mama always said that hurtin' a man's pride is the worst pain he can endure. Well, other than a hit to the you-know-what." She smiled and Bethany felt her pain lift just a bit.

"So he fell…did he hit his head?"

"No. I saw the whole thing. He tried to brace himself against the wall here by the stairs but missed. His arm came down on the plant and he went over the walker and landed on his side. I ran to him and that's when I noticed he'd wet himself."

Bethany took a deep breath.

"I know this is hard for you, Bethany. Thank heaven Rob walked through the kitchen door right then. I couldn't get your daddy up by myself. Your daddy insisted he was fine. Rob was not too happy with me for letting him go outside, but your daddy wouldn't listen, Bethany, he wouldn't *listen*," Cherie stressed, tossing her arms up in defeat. "You come home ten minutes ago you would have seen the whole thing."

"Don't worry about Rob," Bethany said putting her hand on Cherie's shoulder. "I'll talk to him. It wasn't your fault. I'll talk to my dad too. I don't know what he was thinking."

"He wanted to be outside, Bethany. He's locked away in this big old house. It's been hot as Haiti out there this summer. When was the last time he got to go outside? He misses it."

"I know, Cherie. It's terrible. I can't imagine what it's like."

"Well go check on him," Cherie said as she hopped off the stool. "I'll finish cleaning this stuff up."

Bethany walked down the long hallway, which ran the length of the massive main staircase. She turned left into the large parlor and then entered into the guest room which had become her father's bedroom when the stairs became too difficult for him. Her father was lying on top of the bed in a fresh pair of cool summer pajamas.

Rob was applying cold compresses and washcloths to his head and wrists. Bethany could see beyond them to the bathroom where her father's soiled clothes appeared in a heap on the floor. His walker stood next to the bed, and a rotating fan quietly moved back and forth causing John's graying hair to lightly blow.

"Hi, Beth," Rob said when he noticed her in the doorway. With the exception of John and Cherie, everyone else called her Beth. "He's going to be okay," Rob said. Rob had been Bethany's rock these last few years, and she had no idea what she would have done without him. In his late forties, Rob was tall and husky. He had dusty-blond hair and a short, grayish-blond beard and mustache which stood out against his weathered face. Like many people from the area, he was a man who enjoyed the sea and had spent many years of his life fishing and scuba diving.

"If he's able to get up tomorrow I may just take him down to the doctor to get an x-ray," he said. "He may have broken a rib when he hit the tile. He's in no condition to go now."

"Daddy, what were you thinking, going outside in this heat?" Bethany asked as she sat down next to him on the bed. She smoothed back his thin hair and smiled.

Too weakened to turn his head toward her, he quietly replied, "I haven't stepped foot outside for three weeks. I'm sick of being locked away in air-conditioning all day and night. I've only been out for my doctor's appointment. I haven't even been to church."

"I know it's been a lot, Dad," Bethany said, "but it's not safe out there with this heat wave. As soon as it breaks we'll get you to church; you'll be able to sit on the porch in the evenings with JJ and Max…just please, wait for this to be over. It's not worth it."

As if on cue, JJ and Max, the two tri-colored Collies, came bumbling into the room.

John said nothing and just continued to stare into space while Rob changed the compresses.

"Feeling better?" Rob asked. Without waiting for a reply he said, "You need to rest. We'll bring your dinner in here tonight."

Her father did not answer. Bethany knew he was not in a good way. She stood up next to Rob and looked down at her father, lying helpless with the compress on his head.

"If you need anything, Daddy, just buzz us, okay?" She put her hand over his and squeezed it gently before leaving the room with Rob.

"I'm sorry about this, Beth," Rob said quietly as they walked through the parlor to the hall.

"There's nothing to be sorry about," Bethany answered. "It's no one's fault. He's getting more stubborn it seems."

"You can't blame him, Beth."

"No, I don't at all, but he has to be sensible. Do you really think he broke a rib?" she asked, turning toward him.

"I think he may have."

"What happens then?"

"There's not much we can do. I'll wrap his side but he's going to be pretty uncomfortable for a while. It won't be easy for him to get around," said Rob as they reached the kitchen.

"Sit," Bethany said as she walked to the refrigerator and pulled out a bottle of chardonnay. "I'd offer you some..."

Rob waved his hand. "Thanks, but no thanks."

Cherie came through the kitchen via the dining room carrying the soiled clothes. Walking past them she said, "I'm goin' down to put on a load of laundry before I get out of here."

"Oh jeez, I'm sorry, Cherie. I left the clothes in the bathroom," Rob said as he rubbed his eyes with the palms of his hands.

"No worries. I've got it covered. You've been through enough with him." Cherie turned the corner by the long hallway and headed through the first door by the stairs.

"So..." Rob said, offering a tired smile as Bethany came and sat down next to him.

It seemed like something was on his mind so Bethany waited for him to begin. "I guess now is as good a time as ever to talk to you about some things," he started. "Your dad's been struggling a lot the past few weeks."

"It's been hot," Bethany said.

"That's true, but I think there is more going on here. I think the MS is starting to progress."

"But he just saw the doctor."

"Yes, but you know how they are. What are they going to say? 'You're getting worse, John. Sorry, there's not a whole lot we can do.' Your father already knows he's getting worse."

Bethany sat and thought for a moment. "What about that new medicine that's coming out. Couldn't that help him?"

"I asked the doctor about that," Rob replied. "He told us it hasn't been approved by the FDA yet, and even if it had been, your father is not a candidate for it."

"Why is that?" Bethany asked.

"He's too far along. The drug was created for people who were just diagnosed. Your father already has too much damage. You've got to remember Beth, that multiple Sclerosis is caused by damage to the myelin sheath. The myelin sheath is the protective covering that surrounds the nerve cells. Once these nerve cells are damaged, that's it. It can't be reversed," Rob explained. "The nerve impulses slow down or stop altogether. That's why MS affects so many parts of the body and why it's so debilitating. Everything gets shut down. It's a progressive, neurological disease."

"I know that the nerves are damaged by inflammation, but with all of the medical mumbo jumbo, I've never understood exactly how they got inflamed in the first place. Why can't they be uninflamed?" Bethany smiled weakly.

"Even in the worst moments you can make me laugh, Beth," said Rob. "The nerve damage is caused by inflammation. The inflammation is caused when the body's own immune cells attack the nervous system. "

"And the accident today? He must have been mortified."

"He was. I really felt bad."

"But he's not old, Rob. My God, he's not even sixty!"

"I know, Beth," Rob said, putting both his hands on her shoulders. "I know. It's the nature of the disease." He paused, letting her take that in. "I've been noticing other things, as I'm sure you have as well. He's been getting more spasms in his legs, which have been causing him pain. His balance is worse; he's complained of having numbness, his coordination is off."

Bethany had noticed all of these things but hadn't said anything. She was silently hoping that somehow it was temporary, a setback.

Deep down she knew, but didn't want to admit that he was, in fact, getting worse.

"This is what I propose. John's ready for the next step. He's going to hurt himself with the walker. I think he's almost at the point where he'll need a wheelchair full time."

"A wheelchair? In the house? He'll never go for that!"

Up until this point her father had only used a wheelchair briefly when going somewhere. It was a lightweight travel model which could easily fold up into a car.

"He'll need a more substantial chair."

"He'll never go for it," Bethany repeated, rising from the stool and folding her arms across her chest.

"He doesn't have a choice, Beth," Rob answered as Bethany paced the floor.

"I hate this," she said. "It isn't fair. It isn't right. Everything is going to be taken away from him. Everything. He's lost his wife, he's lost his health. Hell, I've given up my life as well!" Rob sat and listened, not having an answer for her.

"Have you talked to him about it yet?" she asked.

"No, I haven't. I wanted to talk to you first because we'll have to be on the same page with this. He's gonna fight it."

Bethany paced the floor again and then headed back towards her wine and quickly drank it down.

"Why is my life like this, Rob?"

Rob shook his head. "I don't know, Beth. I don't have an answer for you. I wish to God I did."

"So God hasn't listened to either of us then, has he?"

Two

Bethany's father did break two ribs in the fall, and just like Rob had predicted, he was quite uncomfortable for the first two weeks. Bethany decided it was best not to bring up the conversation about the wheelchair until he was feeling better. When she wasn't working, Bethany catered to her father's every need as best as she could. It was difficult for him to get around before the broken ribs; now he needed help with just about everything. Unfortunately that meant that his physical therapy had ceased for the time being. The lack of exercise made Bethany's father physically weaker, and it also depressed him because he had made so many friends at therapy and missed it socially. During the weeks of the heat wave, one of the therapists was nice enough to come and do exercises with him at home, since making the trip out was too taxing on him physically. Bethany was concerned that this latest incident would greatly set him back. He's a fighter, Rob would tell her, although she already knew that. Her father would not let this get the better of him, but for now he needed to rest.

By the third week there was some progress and her father felt more like himself. He was determined to get back into a routine, which meant going back to therapy. It had been convenient for Rob during that hot month in July when he didn't have to take John to therapy three times a week. It was often an undertaking getting John from point A to point B. Having the therapist come to the house made things much easier. Rob understood the importance of getting John out to socialize however. Seeing his buddies at therapy made all the difference in the world and not just to John either. The other patients came to know John as their friend, while others thought of him as a mentor. John was always very positive. He would see people in worse condition than himself, and he would go above and beyond for them. There was one gentleman he befriended in particular. He, like John, had MS, and it had progressed more quickly than John's. The man went through the motions of physical therapy, but mentally no one could get through to him. John, in his soft spoken ways, spent much time talking to him and encouraging him. After a while, the man's condition, as well as his attitude, began to change. The therapists would tell John he did wonders, that it was because of him the man was getting better. John, of course, would deny that he had anything to do with it. It was true though. John was an inspiration to those who worked with him and his fellow therapy patients. It would be good for all involved if John went back.

He improved even more after his first week back at therapy, more than both Rob and the therapists had expected, and John seemed to be on cloud nine.

"Look at you getting around," Bethany said to her father as she walked out onto the expansive porch of their home early one evening. He was standing with his walker at the edge by the steps watching JJ and Max having a tug-o-war with a long rope toy. Hearing his daughter's voice he slowly turned.

"Hello, Bethany," he said cheerily.

"It's good to see you up and about, and outside no less," Bethany remarked as she walked over and kissed her father on the cheek. "They look like they're having fun," she said, nodding towards the dogs.

"They've been at it for at least a half hour now," John said.

"Have you been out here standing the whole time?"

"Yes, I have," he said proudly. "Now that the heat wave is finally gone, a bit of a breeze is coming in off the water. And with my ribs almost healed, I feel like a new man."

Bethany smiled. Her father did seem much better. The days were getting cooler now that September had arrived, and she was always grateful that they lived high up on a hill not far from the Long Island Sound. It was amazing the difference in temperature when living by the water. It was just what John needed.

"Would you like me to help you get to the Adirondacks?" Bethany asked. "I'd love to sit with you for a while."

"What time is it?"

"A little after five."

"You're home early." John smiled.

"Yes, I am. Things were a little slow and I completed all my orders so I decided to call it a day and come home and see you," she said and smiled back as she re-twirled her blond hair into a soft ponytail.

"Who's closing up shop?"

"Alison. It wasn't a problem."

"Okay, then. Let's sit."

John took one hand off the walker and steadied himself against the tall, round column on the porch. When he was ready, Bethany removed the walker and brought it down the three steps and onto the lawn. Slowly and mechanically, John carefully placed his right leg on the step. Bethany stayed by his side ready to assist if needed. John was able to grab the banister with both hands, and then he lowered his left leg. As he did so, Bethany saw Rob appear on the porch ready to help. She gave him a wave and mouthed the words, "I've got it," sending him back inside. She turned to her father who had focused all of his concentration and efforts into getting down the three steps. When he got to the last one, Bethany was waiting with the walker. John kept his left hand on the railing, leaned forward, and then with his right hand reached out to Bethany for support. As he took the final step down, Bethany could feel his weight as he gripped her hand tightly. He removed his left hand from the rail and immediately latched onto the walker with both hands, letting out a sigh.

"Are you okay?" Bethany asked.

"Good as ever. Now let's get over to those chairs."

It took approximately five minutes to go about ten feet. It was always difficult for John to walk on grass because he couldn't shuffle along with his feet like he could inside. He not only had to lift his feet, but he had to lift the walker as well. He managed to do it though, and Bethany was proud of his progress. It had been about nine weeks since he had spent any time in his favorite spot. Once they reached the chairs, Bethany assisted her father once more until he was settled comfortably. Bethany reached down and carefully pulled John's left leg up and placed it on the wooden ottoman. Going around to the other side, she did the same with his right leg.

"Ah, very good," he said, satisfied. "It's wonderful to be sitting here, I have to say."

"I'm sure it is," replied Bethany. "It's been a long summer for you."

Her father sat silently for a minute looking out over the horizon. Because the Victorian home sat high upon the hill, it offered a wonderful vantage point. Tall oak trees which lined Woodbine Avenue, served as a picture frame around the view of the harbor, while an assortment of sailboats and small power boats rocked gently on their moorings. Seagulls in search of food squawked above, while others continuously dropped their finds against the rocks, hoping the hard shells would open revealing their meal. As one looked off to the right, the peaks of other Mansard-roofed Victorians could be seen amongst the Maples and Dogwoods. A gentle breeze captured the wafting scent of the briny sea. The sounds of Black Capped Chickadees filled the air, while brightly colored Cardinals poked from the delicate landscape surrounding the house. John believed the cardinal was a sign from his beloved wife, Victoria. It was always a playful joke when Victoria was alive, that Victoria lived in a Victorian. She had loved the old house, and the view and tranquility it had offered.

"You thinking about Mom?" Bethany asked.

John nodded. "We'd sit here for hours with a glass of wine. Any problems from the day would fade away. It's so peaceful."

Bethany undid the knotted buttons of her chef's coat and put her feet up. She could picture her parents there, and she felt that familiar pang in her heart.

"I know God had better plans for her," John said.

"Why is that?" Bethany asked, although she really didn't want to get into this.

"God always takes the good ones," he said, "and I don't mean that in a sarcastic way. He has some other purpose. I miss her so much, Bethany, more than you can imagine, but I know whatever she is doing, it must be wonderful."

Bethany turned and looked at her father who was still staring out into the distance.

"I don't understand, Daddy. Your wife was taken from you, you have this terrible disease...you don't deserve this. How can you say there is good in any of this? We've all suffered."

"First of all, Bethany, there is good in everything although we may not always see it."

"I just don't know how you can say that sometimes," Bethany said.

"Well, for one thing, if I was still working I wouldn't have had the time I have with you now," John replied, and then laughed. "Although I'm sure you're thinking we didn't *need* to spend quite *this* much time together."

Bethany smiled. "You know I love spending time with you, Dad. It just would be nice for us to actually do something together or go somewhere. You're so limited."

"But we do have quality time together. Look at us now."

"I don't know how you do it, Daddy," Bethany said, sitting back in her chair.

"Well one day when we're long gone we'll find out all the answers."

JJ and Max, tired from their round of tug-o-war, came around and settled in next to the chairs. JJ rolled on his side and lay panting next to Bethany, while Max insisted on getting pet on the head by John, who was happy to oblige. As they sat quietly with the dogs, Bethany wondered if now was the time to bring up her conversation with Rob. She made sure to approach the topic carefully.

"Daddy," she began, sitting back up in her chair again, "there is something else I've been meaning to talk to you about."

"Oh?"

"Yes. I've been doing a lot of thinking about your last fall. It's had me, and also Rob, a little concerned.

"Why is that?" he asked. "I was stupid, I got myself overheated; the walker got stuck in the leg of the table..."

"I understand all that, but it set you back for weeks. I'm really surprised you're doing as well as you are now, with the broken ribs and all."

"Okay."

"Well, I just don't want to see that happen again. You might not be so lucky the next time. What if you hit your head on the tile floor, or the corner of the counter? What if you broke your leg or your arm? Then what? Rob and I were thinking maybe it would be best if you started using a wheelchair around the house. You've adjusted to the one we keep in the car, and this one would be bigger and more comfortable for you. You'd be safe."

Bethany waited for her father to respond. Instead he just looked forward and didn't answer. "Daddy?"

"I do understand why you'd be worried," he finally began, "but what you don't understand is that once I commit to that, that's it. It's over. I wouldn't be walking anymore...ever."

"You would still get in and out of it if you wanted to sit in a regular chair for dinner, let's say."

"I would not be walking, Bethany."

"But are you really walking now?"

"Yes...yes, I am. I can't walk as well as you can, but for me it's okay. I'm still standing up and walking. I cannot have that taken away from me right now. I *will not* have it taken away from me. That's giving in. I have to live my life, Bethany. This is the life God has given me and I must make the best of it. How would you feel spending your whole life sitting? Greeting people when you're sitting and they're standing? I know it will come to that for me one day. How soon? I don't know. I am not blind to what's happening to me. Please understand that. I've gotten much worse since your mother died. I don't envision things being all that rosy in the future, but for now I'm making the best of it. I don't believe it's the time for me to be spending my life in a wheelchair. Hell, if it takes me ten minutes instead of five minutes to get to this old Adirondack chair, then I'll do it. What is life worth living for if I don't take hold of the little that's left in me?"

Bethany wasn't the least bit surprised by her father's statement; in fact she had almost expected it.

"I will also speak with Rob. I have a feeling he put you up to this, didn't he?" John asked.

When Bethany didn't reply, John said, "I thought so."

"He means well, Daddy, you know that, and yes, I have been concerned about you getting hurt again...really hurt."

"I will be fine, my dear Bethany. You'll see," John said patting her knee.

"How about this?" Bethany said. "Let's see how you do this winter. If you can get through the winter without much mayhem then we can reevaluate everything, and I won't bring up the wheelchair. If anything else happens, if you should fall again, I may not give you a choice. You can't keep getting hurt. I love you too much to see that happen, Daddy."

"And I love you too, Bethany. Your mother would be so proud of the woman you've become, let alone the best pastry chef on the North Shore."

"Well, I don't know about the best, but I am pretty good, aren't I?"

"Speaking of which, what do we have for dessert tonight?"

Three

J ohn Fitzpatrick did not take well to being told what to do. Almost as if in spite, he somehow managed to hold his own over the long winter. He would not resort to a wheelchair full time as long as he had something to do with it. His will was quite remarkable, and he managed to get around without falling. He continued his various routines of physical therapy, doctors' appointments, and church, and he made sure he behaved himself when dealing with Rob and Cherie. He didn't want them giving him a hard time either.

"Mind over matter," he would say to his daughter.

Bethany was unsure whether it was that or pure luck that seemed to make him better. Despite her strong Catholic background, Bethany had all but given up faith, so she doubted God had anything to do with John's change. After her mother's tragic death, Bethany questioned God as to why. They had been the epitome of the perfect family; happy and loving, generous, caring, religious. They had it all until John was diagnosed with a debilitating disease, and Mom was taken by God. *Why?* Bethany questioned over and over. Bethany's anger towards God grew even more when it was she, not her brother Steven, who had to give up her dreams to take care of their father. Regardless of the past, in this particular moment she was thankful that both her father's life and her own seemed a little easier. The doctors were also pleased, and they told John that his condition was stable. Not much had changed, and the progression had slowed.

Bethany knew not to get her hopes up. Things could change again quickly, but she kept her mind focused on her work at the bakery.

By the summer, Bethany, Rob, and Cherie began to notice signs of John slowing down again. Unlike the summer before, the temperatures had been unseasonably cooler this time around, so the heat could not be blamed for the recent changes in John's walking. As if that weren't bad enough, almost a year to the day, John had another accident which left him quite agitated.

Bethany was naturally upset when she came home and found out the latest news.

"What happened exactly?" she asked Rob.

Rob grabbed a bottle of water from the refrigerator and took a long swig. After setting it on the counter he said, "I was in here making his lunch when all of a sudden I heard him cursing. I go running down the hall, knowing it can't be good, and there he is, leaning on his walker, his left pant leg soaked and a puddle on the floor."

"Oh, brother," said Bethany, pulling out a kitchen stool and sitting down. "Then what?"

"I told him it was okay, but he snapped that he didn't want my sympathy."

"He said that?"

"Yep. I tried to calm him down, but he said that men his age weren't supposed to wet themselves. Then he actually took his fist and slammed it into his walker. I knew better than to say anything else. If it were me, I'd probably feel the same way."

"I feel just terrible for him. Things are bad enough," said Bethany.

"Tell me about it. Luckily, Cherie was here so she helped me get everything cleaned up so I could take care of John. When I was helping him put on another pair of pants he said he was completely humiliated. I felt so bad for him. I don't like seeing him lose his dignity any more than he does. He's exhausted, he's been having painful spasms…he's feeling defeated."

"This is so unfair," Bethany said. She put her head in her hands and wondered what else could go wrong. She knew she probably wouldn't have to wait long for an answer.

Part of her felt guilty, because Bethany was actually glad that she had not been there to witness it. It would have made matters much worse for her father, and she wasn't quite sure how she would have handled it. Like so many times before, she felt angry. Just that day at the bakery a woman a little younger than herself came in with her father and two small children. Bethany couldn't help but notice how the man, who appeared much older than her father, got around with such ease. Not only that, but he picked up one of the children so the little girl could get a better look at the cookies in the glass case. Bethany's father couldn't lift a thing, let alone a child. It wasn't fair. The scene had stayed with Bethany all day, and now she had come home to this.

She still believed that God was punishing her somehow; that he did not want her to be happy. She always imagined herself married and having a child or two. Under her present circumstances, Bethany felt it was impossible to have a relationship with a man. Even dating was a challenge. She had all but given up on the idea, despite the fact that she was only twenty-seven years old.

After dinner, Rob helped John settle into the parlor where John could listen to his audio books. Bethany, meanwhile, poured herself another glass of wine and leaned up against the kitchen counter feeling angry and exhausted. Within a few moments she could hear the sound of her father's book on tape, although it was too distant to make out the words. She took a sip of her wine and began cleaning up from dinner.

"Are you okay?" Rob said, poking his head into the kitchen.

"I'm fine," Bethany said, although not convincingly.

"I'll be down in an hour to put him to bed," said Rob. "You sure you're alright?"

Bethany simply nodded her head and continued to clean off the dishes while Rob made his way upstairs to his room. Max and JJ laid sprawled out on the kitchen floor, oblivious to any of the day's happenings. Clearing the mats off the table, Bethany stepped over the dogs and placed the mats neatly in a drawer in the island and thought how easy it was to be a dog. She lit a fragrant candle on the stove, turned off the overhead table light, and left the room with her wine glass in hand.

She could hear a conversation between two characters on her father's tape as she approached the parlor. There in the doorway, Bethany took a sip of wine, folded her arms, and leaned against the entryway. Her father had fallen asleep in his special lift chair. The lamp next to him was on and shone an eerie white cast over his face, making him look washed out and pale. He breathed softly, his lips slightly parted, and to Bethany he looked peaceful. But his illness made him appear much older than he really was. A tear ran down her face as she watched her father's knee jerk in a spasm. John was so exhausted that he slept through it. Bethany turned her attention to the many books which lined the walls of the parlor, all books John had read at some point. He loved to read and now even that had been taken from him. His sight had deteriorated somewhat over the years so he began reading large print books. Over the past several months, the books became too heavy for John to hold, and the pages too difficult to turn. Like most everything else, except the bathroom incident, he took it in stride.

What kind of life was this? She turned off the tape and sat on the couch across from her father and watched him as he slept. The house was quiet. She remembered how active it once was, filled with laughter and activity. There was always something cooking on the stove, and a roaring fire often burned in one of the many fireplaces. The neighborhood children practically lived at the Fitzpatrick house. It was like something out of the Judy Garland movie *Meet Me In St. Louis*, a household brimming with family and friends. Now it was just the two of them, struggling with what life had tossed them.

No longer could Bethany hold back her tears. With her hand covering her mouth, she cried silently for everything she had lost. She wanted her mother's comfort, and she wondered what life would have been like if her mother hadn't died. She wondered what life would have been like if her father wasn't sick. All the wondering in the world would not change the situation though. The worst part was that she knew things would only get worse. There was no cure for

MS and her father's condition was too far gone for medications to put him in remission. *What would become of him?* The MS, little by little, would take every last bit of life and dignity from her father—a long, slow battle, a long slow death. *How would she ever survive this?*

Knowing that Rob would be in soon to get her father to bed, Bethany wiped her eyes, picked up the wine glass she had placed on the end table, and left the room. Once in the kitchen she splashed cold water on her face. If she ran into Rob on the way up to her room she didn't want him to see that she had been upset. Rob was great to talk to, but right now, if she couldn't have her mother, she wanted to be alone.

Walking up the stairs she glanced in the hall mirror and paused. She felt she had aged beyond her years. Disgusted, she stopped in her father's old study and switched on the light. The study looked like that of a successful lawyer, dark mahogany wood furniture, law books lining the walls, encased in rich, dark shelving. She walked around the room and looked at everything as if she had never seen any of it before. She stopped and looked at his law degree, which was prominently displayed on one wall: John William Fitzpatrick, University of North Carolina, Chapel Hill. His specialty had been intellectual property law. Over the years he had been quite successful.

Bethany walked behind the massive desk and pulled out the big, leather chair and slowly sat down. She pulled the gold cord of the old fashioned, green banker's light, turning it on. From the chair she took another look around the room again. Finally, from the desk she picked up a framed photo of her parents who smiled happily from their boat docked in Northport Harbor. Bethany ran her finger over her mother's smiling face while another tear fell on her own. She held the photo to her chest and cried. Carefully placing the frame back on the desk, she picked up another, smaller photo of herself and her brother taken on a vacation back when she was twelve. *A lifetime ago.* She would do anything to go back to those perfect times if only for a moment.

Placing the photo back on the desk, Bethany let out a sigh and turned off the light. Quietly she got up from the chair and left the room. She thought about torturing herself further by entering her parents' bedroom, but she decided she'd had enough suffering for one day. She walked past the closed door and went to her bedroom. As she closed her door she heard Rob's door open, and then she heard his footsteps going down the stairs to take care of John.

She quickly changed and washed up thinking she'd get a good night's sleep. Knowing she'd regret it in the morning, Bethany cried herself to sleep anyway.

Four

In just a few short months, John became so weak that he could barely get around. The day had finally come when he was confined to a wheelchair most of the time. John didn't try to fight it. He had battled long enough and he knew there weren't any other options. A handicap ramp was installed at the back porch and John's bathroom became handicap accessible. As if there wasn't enough disruption in Bethany's life, running back and forth from the bakery and having to deal with workers left a toll on her. There was simply no place for her to go to relax and unwind; no space of her own to be alone.

"Bethany, I've noticed you've been really struggling with all that's been going on here," Rob said to her one night in the kitchen after he'd put John to bed. "I just want you to know that I understand what you're going through. I wish there was some way I could help you. I wish I could take some of your stress away."

Bethany stirred the coffee she had just poured. Without looking up at him she said, "There really isn't anything you can do. Believe me...I wish there was."

Rob sat on the stool, hands folded in his lap, and looked at her sympathetically. "Why don't you make some time for yourself. Go out, see your friends, do something crazy." Rob smiled and then let out a laugh trying to lighten the moment. Bethany glanced at him, smirked and rolled her eyes.

"What? What's wrong with that?" he said. "You've got to try and go out and live your life. I've got things covered here."

"I know you do, Rob," Bethany said as she took the stool next to him. "It's just...it's more of a guilt thing. I feel guilty leaving him. I'd feel guilty going out and enjoying myself. Hell, I don't even know if I'm capable of enjoying myself anymore. Isn't that nuts?"

"With everything you've been through, Beth, I don't think it's nuts, but you've got to try. You should at least make an effort. Never once has your father asked you to stay home or made you feel guilty. He's not that type of guy. You know that."

Bethany took a sip of her coffee and contemplated this. Deep down Bethany knew that Rob was right. She fully entrusted Rob with her father's care, so why couldn't she get out once in a while? Her father would be happy to see her doing something for herself.

"What are you thinking?" Rob asked when he didn't get a reply.

Spinning the stool to look at him she smiled. "I was thinking that maybe you're right. Maybe it would do me some good to get out."

Rob smiled back at her. "That's what I wanted to hear."

"I don't know what I'd do without you, Rob. You've helped me in so many ways."

"That's what I'm here for."

"No," Bethany chuckled. "You're here to take care of my father, not to be my therapist.

"You could say I'm a man of many talents then."

"Well, let's not inflate your head too much."

"If I could get a smile out of you then it's fine," Rob said as he gently placed his hand on Bethany's shoulder. "I'm beat. Your father's settled in for the night. I think I'll hit the sack too. Try to get some rest." He stood and pushed in the stool.

"I will. Thank you."

With a wave of his hand Rob left the kitchen.

By mid-November, Bethany gave in and made dinner plans with her two best friends, Sarah and Cassandra, whom she hadn't seen in quite some time. On the night she was heading out to see her friends she stopped by her father's bedroom.

It was only seven o'clock when Bethany entered, and like most nights, her father was already in bed. A month prior the beautiful, old guest bed was taken up to the attic to accommodate a hospital-type bed, which made it easier for Rob to assist John. The back of the bed came forward so John could go into a seated position. When Bethany came into the bedroom, John turned down the volume on the TV remote, looked at his daughter, and smiled. "Well don't you look beautiful?"

Bethany sat on the corner of the bed by his feet and tried to return his smile.

"You can do better than that, I'm sure," John said. "You should be happy you're going out. Have a wonderful time." He patted her knee. "I'm feeling okay. I have a program to watch. All is well."

"I just feel bad leaving you," said Bethany.

"Don't," he said. "Where are you ladies going to dinner?"

Bethany felt a twinge in her stomach. "Villa LaMarco." It had been her parents' favorite restaurant in town. John simply nodded, and she felt that old, guilty feeling again.

"Are you sure you'll be okay?" Bethany asked.

"Yes. I can buzz Rob if I need him."

With that, JJ entered the room and walked over to the bed and rested his long snout on top of John's legs.

"There you go. Now I have company." John smiled. "You go and have a great time. Say hello to Rocco for me."

Bethany got up and kissed her father on the cheek. "I love you, Daddy."

"I love you too, Bethany."

She turned and left the room. She forced herself to get into her car and drive into town.

When Bethany reached the restaurant her friends were seated at the small bar.

"Hey, how are you?" Cassandra said, throwing her arms around Bethany. "Okay, I hope. You're always on my mind." Cassandra had a smile that could light up a room. She had short blond hair that she didn't fuss much with, and she had an Ivory-soap-girl complexion, so she wore very little makeup. Sarah was beautiful, with long, wavy brown hair and dark eyes. Her makeup was perfectly applied and she was always done-up in the latest fashions. They had been friends since childhood.

"It's been so long I almost forgot what you looked like," Sarah said playfully as she pushed Bethany away to get a better look. "I've missed you, my friend." Sarah hugged Bethany and kissed her on both cheeks. "I have *so* much to tell you, it's incredible!" When the friends were through with their greetings, the bartender asked Bethany what she would like to drink.

"Margarita on the rocks...no salt," she replied.

"Well look who it is!" Bethany heard a man say loudly in broken English. "It's zhee best customer!"

She turned to see Rocco walking toward her with hands outstretched. It had been a while since she had seen him, and she noticed his hair had thinned and grayed.

"How's my girl?" he said loudly, wrapping his big arms tightly around her. "You look wonderful." Youthful memories flashed in Bethany's head. How many times had she come here with her family on special occasions? The dinner following her First Holy Communion had been here, her brother's high school graduation dinner. There were countless times. It was the longest running, family-owned restaurant in Northport, and the interior hadn't changed a bit.

"How is your father?" Rocco asked. Cassandra and Sarah stood by watching the exchange.

"It's been difficult the last few months," Bethany replied. "He said to say hello, by the way. He'd been doing so well and then all of a sudden...I don't know...he started getting really weak, he had a lot of trouble walking. The doctors say it's par for the course. He's in a wheelchair now."

"Oh my goodness...Mr. Fitzpatrick...he my best customer for years. I hate to see this. I will give you something special to take back to him. He will love it. Please tell him I was asking about him. And zhee bakery? How is that?"

"The bakery is doing quite well, thankfully." Bethany answered.

"Zhee best bakery and pastry chef in town." Rocco laughed loudly as he put his arm around Bethany. "All my customers who come in and rent the back party room…they all bring cakes that you made…magnificent and so delicious too." He laughed again. "Are you ladies ready? Come…I have your table set."

He motioned to the bartender to bring the drinks to the table. "Zhee next round is on me," he said as he pulled a chair out for Bethany at the corner table. "Very good," and off he went.

The waiter placed their drinks on cocktail napkins that he had just laid out. "I will be right back with your menus," he announced.

"He's a riot," Sarah said, referring to Rocco as she settled into her chair.

"He and my father would get into these long conversations all the time. Rocco really loves him," Bethany said.

"You have wonderful memories," added Cassandra.

Bethany changed the subject. "So what have you two been up to?" Bethany asked.

"Brian and I decided to surprise the kids and take them to Disney after Easter," Sarah announced. "We haven't gone in three years so we're really looking forward to it. We can really use a vacation too. It's been nonstop with the kids, their endless activities, Brian's job…" Sarah was a stay-at-home mother of three, and a few years older than Bethany. She was married to Brian who, a year prior, had become a partner at one of the large accounting firms. Sarah had left her career in banking once she had her first child. Although Brian worked long hours, Sarah didn't seem to mind much. She enjoyed having money and she spent her days volunteering up at school, shopping with her mom, or decorating their expansive Huntington Bay home.

Cassandra, who was a year younger than Bethany, was also married and had two children, a boy and a girl, who were also in grade school. Unlike Sarah, Cassandra lived a bit more modestly in a middle-sized home in Smithtown. She was married to a police detective who worked for the Emergency Services Unit in New York City, and she herself was an ESL teacher.

Each of the friends had grown up in Northport together, and although their lives were greatly different, they remained quite close despite not being able to get together that often. The three ladies talked a few minutes about Sarah's Disney plans as they perused their menus and ordered.

"Oh, I almost forgot to tell you," said Cassandra. "You'll never believe who I ran into at the mall recently."

"Who? Do tell." Sarah smiled.

"Remember that guy Arthur I dated?

"No...get out! Not him!" said Sarah.

"The nerdy guy from England?" Bethany asked. "The one you met in college? I thought he was going back to London after he graduated."

"Apparently he didn't. He found a good job in the city, and would you believe he met another English woman in a bar in Midtown. They ended up getting married and they moved out to Long Island."

"Oh my gosh. Where do they live? Do they have kids?" Sarah asked.

"A little boy. They live in Hauppauge not far from me. Can you imagine?" Cassandra laughed.

"Only you," said Bethany. "You run into everybody. But him?"

"I know. I don't know what I ever saw in him."

"It was his accent. You've always been a sucker for accents," Sarah said.

"This is true," said Bethany.

"Oh stop you two. There had to be something more than that at the time."

"Please...I doubt it. He was so boring and nerdy. How could you stand it?" asked Sarah.

"I had the kids with me when I ran into him," Cassandra said. "They said, 'Mommy, Mommy who was that man?' Luckily he was by himself. Talk about awkward."

The friends laughed as they reminisced about old times. When it was Bethany's turn to talk, she realized how little she had to say.

"So your dad's not doing too well?" Sarah asked cautiously.

"Not really," Bethany said, flattening the napkin in her lap.

"What's going on?" Cassandra asked.

Bethany filled them in on all the latest occurrences while they ate their appetizers.

"What do the doctors say about all of this?" Sarah asked. "Why did his condition change so suddenly?"

"They have no answers," Bethany replied. "The MS is progressing. They've tried him on some different medications but it doesn't help much."

"Is he still going to therapy?" asked Cassandra.

"Yes, but not as frequently. It's too tiring for him because he's weaker."

There was a pause in the conversation. Finally, Cassandra spoke. "And what about you, Beth? How are you holding up?"

"I don't really know actually. I never really have time to think about how I'm doing. It's draining. Even with Rob and Cherie it's a lot of work and a lot of worrying. It's a full time job tending to his needs and speaking with doctors, and then owning a business and working full-time on top of that..."

"I don't know how you do it," Sarah said. "You need a massage. Oh my gosh, I should arrange one for you! My girl is *the* best!"

"I don't know how I do it either," Bethany responded, starting to feel a bit bitter. "Unfortunately I don't have any time for myself, so a massage is out of the question." She tried to hold back her tears. She felt like a dam about to burst. Her friends lived such normal, happy lives. What had she done to deserve any of this?

Cassandra put her hand on Bethany's arm and tried to console her. "You have to make *some* time for yourself, honey."

Bethany quickly wiped away a stray tear and took a deep breath. Giving a fake smile, she put her chin up and said, "I'll be fine. It's just been a bad week, and I'm by myself. This is just not what I thought my life would be like. I really thought I would have at least gotten married by now. I'm not even dating." She wiped another tear from her face. She caught Sarah and Cassandra giving one another a look as if to say, *How can we possibly help her? This is terrible and so pathetic.*

There was no one who could help her, this much Bethany knew. She looked away from her friends and tried to compose herself when she noticed a man sitting alone at a table against the wall. He caught

Bethany's eye and looked at her for a moment while he ate from a huge bowl of spaghetti. The man had to have been in his late fifties, and Bethany couldn't help but wonder if that would be her one day, eating in a restaurant by herself. She tried to imagine his circumstances when her thoughts were interrupted by their entrees being served.

As the waiter put down the last dish, Sarah asked, "What about Father Michael? Have you tried talking to him?"

Father Michael was the pastor of St. Francis of Assisi RC Church down on Main Street. The Fitzpatricks had been very active in the parish early on, and Victoria and John became very close with Father Michael. He would often come to their house for dinner. Growing up, Bethany and her brother Steven had always enjoyed Father Michael's company, and they looked forward to his visits. He always had a funny joke to share, and he was more like a favorite uncle than a priest. He, like Bethany's parents, was a man of great faith and generosity.

"He's come many a time to visit my father and he's offered to talk to me, but it doesn't help much," Bethany said. "Everything Father Michael tells me, and I know he means well, just doesn't make sense. He talks about crosses to bear, our journey to heaven, how I'm serving God. It's a bit extreme, don't you think? Is trying to be a good person your whole life *not* a good enough way to serve God? I had to be given this?" Bethany threw the question out to her friends. "You're both good people. God hasn't punished you." Her friends shot glances back and forth again, and Bethany knew she was out of line. "I'm sorry," she said softly. "I know that sounded bad. I'd just like to know what I did to deserve this, and especially, what did my father do?"

Again, there were no answers so Sarah and Cassandra did their best to change the subject and happily chatted about the most trivial of events. Bethany stayed somewhat quiet. The weight she felt in her chest and in her heart was always present. Nothing could possibly take it away.

They finished up their meals and Bethany passed on dessert. Rocco offered to buy them after dinner drinks but Bethany insisted she had to get home and that she had a full day ahead at the bakery.

She hugged her friends goodbye as they told her to hang in there. What else could they say? Although she had been glad to see them, she felt somewhat relieved when the night was over. It had just been too difficult for her. She was too sensitive and she had too much on her mind.

"Let's get together after Christmas," Sarah said. "We'll have you both over. We'll laugh, we'll have a good time. You know my wine cellar is always stocked." She gave Bethany a wink.

"That sounds wonderful," Bethany said, although she didn't really mean it. With all that was going on in her life, how could she possibly think about Christmas?

"I'll keep you in my prayers," Cassandra said to Bethany.

The friends parted ways outside and Bethany headed back home, with nothing but dread in her heart.

Five

Bethany was out of the house early the next day. Her father was still sleeping and she knew Rob would take care of things. She had made some homemade muffins for them for breakfast, walked the dogs, and then quickly headed down to the bakery. She had a bunch of orders which needed to be filled, but also she simply didn't want her father to ask how her evening out went. Bethany had enjoyed seeing Sarah and Cassandra and she was grateful to be eating someone else's cooking, but she couldn't fully enjoy herself. For the first time she began to contemplate the fact that she may be clinically depressed. Nonetheless, she had to be strong. She convinced herself she'd snap out of it. She always had before.

Bethany unlocked the steel back door to Giovanni's Italian Bakery on Woodbine Avenue, which was located across from the town docks on picturesque Northport Harbor. Giovanni had been her mother's maiden name, and the bakery name was both a memorial and tribute. After all, it was Victoria Giovanni Fitzpatrick who first taught Bethany to cook. The bakery itself was quaint yet upscale. It had been Bethany's vision and creation, when she took over the Olde Town Bakery which had been there since her childhood. The space was large, so there was ample room for several small tables and chairs, which sat on a highly polished, small patterned black and white checkered floor. The long, glass bakery cases were outlined in wood, and were made from beautiful walnut. Antique chandeliers with mini lampshades hung from the gold-colored, ornately patterned tin ceiling. Outside, six small wrought-iron tables ran parallel to the large bakery window and offered a charming view of the harbor that her customers so appreciated. It wasn't just the view that kept customers coming back, it was Bethany's superb skills as a pastry chef which was really quite remarkable for her age. She had graduated from the Culinary Institute in Hyde Park, in Dutchess County, New York, at the top of her class. CIA was the world's premier culinary college. She specialized in cakes for all occasions, but she was also proficient at making Italian pastries, cookies, pies and breads. In the winter she set out old fashioned cauldrons brimming with steaming, homemade soups which were accompanied by homemade croutons left over from the bread from the day before. Sandwiches were sold year round on warm, crusty baguettes. Despite her difficult situation at home, she was able to make her bakery thrive.

It was Saturday morning, and she wanted to get the finishing touches done on yet another gorgeous wedding cake which had to be delivered to a catering hall in a few short hours. Bethany focused completely on her creation, one of the few things that she could focus on, and she was proud of the end results. Just as she was finishing up, Alison, Bethany's right hand, entered through the kitchen's back door.

"You're here early," Alison said as she unraveled the blue plaid scarf around her neck. Alison was tall and slender and somewhat boney, perhaps from being a strict vegetarian for most of her life. She had long, straight black hair which she always wore in a high ponytail for work, and her complexion was quite pale like a china doll. She was about the same age as Bethany. Alison was a single mother who came to the bakery shortly after the birth of her son three and a half years ago. She had practically begged Bethany for a job. Alison lived with her parents in Centerport, the next town over, and they helped raise her young son. When she met Bethany, Alison had both waitressing and food preparation experience, and Bethany felt sorry for her situation and hired her on the spot. She knew this young woman would commit to the job because of her responsibilities to her son, and Bethany liked her cheery personality right away. After training and then losing people, Bethany was pleased that Alison would be sticking around for a while. It was one weight off Bethany's shoulders anyway. The times Bethany had to leave the bakery abruptly to go to her father, Alison always had everything under control, which was a huge relief. Alison, along with a few part-time people, kept the bakery functioning so Bethany could concentrate on her pastry work and the business end of things.

"Wow, that's fantastic!" Alison said upon seeing the finished wedding cake. She was always enamored by Bethany's work. "Some lucky bride and groom," she continued, as she hung up her bag and jacket on a hook by the door.

"Thanks," Bethany said, taking a step back to study her three-tiered creation. The young bride and groom were beach lovers who were having their affair at a local catering facility which looked out over the Long Island Sound. They wanted their cake to be non-traditional, and they asked Bethany to create something with a 'sea' theme. So Bethany dyed the fondant a pale blue, and she created edible white seashells to go around each tier. White chocolate starfish were interspersed among the shells, while drapes of intricately folded white chocolate ribbons spilled over from the top tier. "I guess it came out okay," Bethany smiled.

Alison moved around the kitchen turning on ovens and the huge crocks for soup. She pulled an apron off the wall and then some batter from the refrigerator. Alison began preparing muffin tins, and then she efficiently poured the thick batter into the tins and popped them in the pre-heated oven. She then made her way to the front of the store and began turning on lights and uncovering items already behind the glass counters. While she did so, Bethany carefully rolled the huge cake into the walk-in refrigerator and began preparing bread dough as well as some Italian pastries for a retirement party. She would make extra since it was Saturday and the Italian pastries always went fast. By eight o'clock the doors of the bakery were opened and things were moving along.

Three hours later, the morning rush had ended and Bethany had finished baking her bread as well as filling her pastry order. She packed the pastries neatly in a box, and placed the remaining ones for the store on a long, narrow silver tray. Leaving the kitchen and holding the tray, she carefully bent over and placed the tray in one of the cool, glass cases in the main part of the bakery.

As she slid the door to the case shut and stood back up, she was taken by surprise when she saw a man sitting across the way from the counter. A shiver went down her spine. It was the same man who had been sitting alone at the restaurant the night before, and again she found him looking at her. He sat drinking a cappuccino and eating a cannoli. Their eyes locked again, but only for a second because Bethany quickly turned away. She walked around the back of the counter toward the cash register where Alison was ringing up a customer. When Alison was through with the transaction she turned to Bethany.

"What's up?" Alison asked.

Bethany turned and faced Alison so that her back was towards the man.

"Do you know who that guy is by any chance?" Bethany asked.

Alison peered over the counter nonchalantly. "Nope. Can't say I do," she said. "I've never seen him before today. Why?"

"Did you help him?" Bethany asked, ignoring Alison's question.

"Yeah, I did. He didn't say much, just that he wanted a cappuccino and a cannoli." Alison crossed her arms and leaned up against the countertop with the cash register. "Is everything okay, Beth?"

"I don't know. I guess so," Bethany said, glancing back over toward the man. "It's just…well, I was out with some friends last night at Villa LaMarco and he was there, a few tables away. He was eating alone. I've never seen him around town either, and now he's in my store."

"So? What's the problem?" Alison asked.

"Well, I know everyone around here. I've never seen him. I felt bad for him last night when I saw him eating alone. It got me thinking…" She glanced his way again. Alison waited patiently for her to continue. "I caught him looking at me, and now here he is in my store staring at me again. I just think it's odd."

"What? Do you think he's some kind of stalker or something?"

"No, no. I don't know, maybe I'm just going crazy. I'm making more of this than it is."

"I'm sure it's just a coincidence," Alison said. "Both times you saw him eating. He likes to eat, at least he *looks* like he likes to eat." She peered over the counter at the man. She paused for a moment, then continued. "Looks Italian to me. Italian restaurant, Italian bakery. Makes sense unless he likes you, of course." Alison smiled, trying to lighten things up.

"Please," Bethany said as she rolled her eyes. "I'm half his age. That's all I need. I guess you're right then. It's just a coincidence."

"I really think that's all it is," Alison said.

"Well let me know if he comes in again, will you?"

"You've got it."

Two customers entered the store as they finished up their conversation. Bethany headed back to the kitchen, but she turned one last time to look at the man. He was gone.

"How was your day?" John asked as Bethany arrived home from work. John was seated in his wheelchair at the kitchen table having dinner with Rob. Before Bethany had a chance to answer, John said, "I'm sorry we got started without you. I'm feeling a little tired and wanted to go to bed earlier."

"No worries," Bethany said, removing her jacket and placing it on the coat rack. She unbuttoned her chef's coat and bent over to pet the dogs who were happily wagging their tails.

"So your day was okay?" asked John again.

Bethany was flipping quickly through the mail: medical bills, utility bills, *MS Connection* magazine. Putting the pile down she turned around to face her father.

"It wasn't bad. I made a killer wedding cake, filled a bunch of orders, and the store was pretty busy all day so I can't complain." She went to the refrigerator and poured herself a glass of wine, which had become her normal routine now. She headed toward the kitchen table and sat down.

"This chicken marsala is delicious," announced Rob.

"It is wonderful," John said a bit weakly. "I'll have to give Rocco a call to thank him."

"He told me you'd love it," Bethany said. "How's the pasta?"

"Excellent," Rob said as he put another huge forkful in his mouth.

"I'm glad you're both enjoying it," said Bethany.

"Let me get you a plate. There's a ton here," Rob said as he started to get up from the table.

"No, please eat, Rob," Bethany said, putting her arm on Rob's to stop him. "I'm not hungry right now anyway. You can leave out the leftovers and I'll take care of them. I'll make myself a plate soon."

"How did you enjoy yourself last night?" her father asked.

"We had a very nice time," Bethany said as she thought back to her mood at the restaurant. She filled her father in on what was going on in her friends' lives when suddenly John dropped his fork, causing the marsala sauce to splatter around the table.

Bethany rushed to get the kitchen sponge. "I've got it." She came around behind her father and carefully cleaned up the mess. As she did so she watched her father struggle to pick up his water glass. His hand and the glass were shaking, and he was moving it towards his mouth very, very slowly. Bethany's first reaction was that he was going to drop the glass and spill the water. She went to reach for it.

"Do you want me to help you with that, Dad?" she asked.

"No, I've got it, thanks. It might take me a bit longer but I've got it."

Bethany watched as her father finally lifted the glass to his lips. She exchanged glances with Rob. Rob and Bethany had developed a keen sense of everything which affected John, and they both made mental notes of any new difficulties he might experience.

"You get some rest tonight, Daddy," Bethany said as she rubbed her father's back. "I'm going to go upstairs and wash up and get out of these clothes. I love you." She kissed his head.

"I love you too, baby," John said quietly as she left the room.

About forty-five minutes later Bethany came down in a comfortable pair of sweats and her fluffy slippers, her hair down and tucked behind her ears. Rob had covered the food with foil and placed it on the stove top. Bethany got a plate and served herself. Pouring a second glass of wine, she took her plate and went towards the microwave to re-heat the food. While it spun around, she grabbed a set of utensils from the drawer and went towards the kitchen table. Just as the microwave beeped, Rob came into the room.

"He's all set. He's in bed," Rob said. "He was really fatigued today, and he was complaining that his legs were really bothering him. He seems to be retaining some water. I think we should talk to the doctor about it."

"When is his appointment? Tuesday?"

"Wednesday, actually. They called and needed to change it."

Bethany didn't reply right away. She took her dinner out of the microwave and brought it over to the table and sat down.

"I can't stand watching how bad he's getting," she finally said.

"I know. Something's definitely going on."

Bethany stayed silent. No reply was needed. With Rob she could be this way. He was about the only one who truly understood both her situation and John's, and Bethany took some comfort in that.

"I'll be upstairs if you need me," said Rob. "I'm expecting a call from my sister upstate. When I'm through I'll take the dogs out for you, if you like."

"That would be great. Thanks." Bethany was tired after the long day and she didn't mind not going back out into the cold to walk the dogs. It was early November yet it seemed like late December, and Bethany hated the cold. Rob was great for so many things.

Rob made his way upstairs and all was silent. She sat by herself and ate, and the image of the man in the restaurant came back. She let out a sigh as she thought about the irony of it. Here she was sitting alone in her father's house on a Saturday night at eight o'clock. *I'm destined to be alone.*

She picked at her food and thought about Sarah and Cassandra. She knew what they were doing tonight. Sarah and her husband had tickets to a Broadway play. They were going to dinner first in New York City, and Sarah's mom was staying over to watch the kids. Cassandra and her husband were going to the movies with another couple. They had a steady babysitter and could go out as they pleased. Putting her fork down, she looked out the window into the darkness of the backyard, while tears ran down her face. She dumped her remaining meal into the trash, her appetite now gone.

"My life is pathetic," she said to no one. "Thanks, God."

Six

John woke up Monday morning with legs that looked like tree
trunks. He could not move them at all and he frantically buzzed
Rob on the intercom for help. Hearing the commotion, Bethany,
who had been preparing her morning cup of coffee, came running as
Rob came swiftly down the stairs.

"What is it, Dad?" Bethany asked breathlessly as she reached his
room. Rob followed behind.

"My legs," John said weakly. "Something's happened. I can't
move them at all."

Bethany quickly pulled off the blanket and sheet and gasped
when she saw the size of his legs.

"It's edema," Rob said. "He's retaining water. He needs to be
on something to reduce the swelling." He looked at John's face and it
appeared pale and clammy. "Get me a thermometer," he said to
Bethany.

Bethany entered John's bathroom and came back with a
thermometer she found in the medicine cabinet. Her heart was
racing. "He's so weak," she said softly to Rob.

He didn't answer. Instead, he stuck the thermometer in John's
mouth and waited. "101.1. He has a fever," Rob said.

Bethany knew this was not a good thing. The fever would take every last bit out of her father. John would appear as if he were paralyzed, because the heat from the fever would in a sense, short-circuit his system. That coupled with the edema, Bethany knew the situation was not good.

"Hang tight, John," Rob said as he touched John's arm lightly. "Give me a minute to figure out what to do, okay? We'll get you taken care of. I promise."

"Okay," John said weakly.

Rob started walking towards the door, as he silently indicated to Bethany to follow. Once they were out of John's room Rob said, "He needs to be seen by a doctor. I think he has an infection. I can try, but I don't know if I can get him there by myself."

"I can help you," Bethany said.

"He's going to be dead weight, Beth. There's no way you'll be able to lift him with me." Rob put his hands on his hips. He looked down as he contemplated the best thing to do. "Listen," he said softly as he looked back at Bethany. "Our best bet is to call an ambulance and get him to the hospital so we can see what's going on. I don't think we have a choice. We'll never get him to the doctor by ourselves."

Bethany nodded in agreement although she wasn't happy about the decision.

"I need you to call his doctor and have him meet us at the hospital. Fill him in on what's going on. Can you do that?"

"Of course."

"I'll call the ambulance, and I'll get John together as best as I can," said Rob. "Were you off today?"

For a minute Bethany couldn't even recall what day it was. Finally realizing it was Monday she said, "Yes. The bakery is closed. I'm caught up with everything else down there. I was planning on taking the day anyway."

"Okay, good. Call Dr. Rosenberg and Dr. Melman. See who you can get a hold of." Rob took his cell phone off his hip and dialed 911.

Bethany went to the kitchen and called Dr. Rosenberg, John's neurologist. She knew that he would not attend to him at the hospital, but he needed to know what was going on. Next she called Dr. Melman, the general practitioner. He said he'd get to the hospital as soon as he could, and until then he'd be in contact with the attending physician.

Passing by her cold cup of coffee, Bethany took a step back and dumped it down the sink before heading back down the hall to John's room.

"How are things going?" she asked.

"I've got him all cleaned up and ready to go. The ambulance is on its way." said Rob.

"Okay. I called Dr. Melman and he's going to get to the hospital as soon as he can." Bethany stared at her father, lying in bed with his eyes closed, completely helpless. Her face could not hide her feelings.

"Be strong, Beth," Rob whispered in her ear.

"I'm tired of being strong," she said quietly. "I'm tired of it."

"Unfortunately you don't have a choice. I can't take care of both of you right now."

Within fifteen minutes the ambulance transport was at the house. Bethany watched as two EMTs, with the help of Rob, lifted her father onto the stretcher. They allowed Rob to stay with him on the way over to Huntington Hospital while Bethany followed behind. As she drove, she felt alone and scared. It took all she had just to focus on the drive there. Thankfully the emergency room was not busy. Rob went off with John while Bethany sat at the check-in station filling out paperwork and handing over insurance cards. When all was said and done, they allowed her in to see her father. The usual hospital chain of events took place, the waiting, the tests, the waiting again.

Finally Dr. Melman, a brown-haired man of average build and height, pulled open the privacy curtain in the makeshift room. His face and hair were boyish, despite the fact that he was probably in his late forties. He pushed away some long straight layers of hair that fell into his eyes as he conversed with John. The fluorescent light, which came from the box on the wall behind John's bed, cast a strange, greenish tint over Dr. Melman's face which Bethany couldn't help but notice. When he was through asking John questions, he checked the chart and then he turned toward Rob and Bethany.

"It's very common for MS patients to have lower limb edema, especially in those patients with reduced mobility," he began. "We have to try to get the edema under control because in some cases it can travel up around the heart." He paused momentarily and looked down at John to make sure he understood. "When people are healthy, the normal regulatory functions of the nervous system, as well as the endocrine system and the kidneys, help to maintain a functional water metabolic balance. It is this balance which prevents the occurrence of edema even with excessive water intake. In the case of your father," he said looking back at Bethany, "his disease prevents this balance."

"And what about the fever?" asked Rob.

"There is definitely an infection he's trying to fight. Let's start you with a round of antibiotics, John," he said, turning toward him again. "If it turns out to be viral, the antibiotics won't do a whole lot, and the infection will have to run its course. I'd also like to put him on anti-inflammatory pills," he said to Bethany and Rob, "and once we get things under control, we'll monitor the edema with water retention medication. For now he'll have to be admitted. I'll have the nurse put a pillow under his knees and we'll keep him comfortable." Putting a hand on John's shoulder, Dr. Melman turned and said, "They'll take good care of you here, John. I have rounds to make tomorrow so I'll check in on you." John did not answer.

"Thank you Dr. Melman," Bethany said as the doctor, clipboard in hand, turned to go. Another hour and a half went by before John was settled in a room on the second floor. He was put with a patient who looked well over ninety years old. If Bethany didn't know better, she'd think the man was already dead. He couldn't have weighed more than eighty pounds as he lay there sleeping with his mouth wide open, and alone. Although she felt sorry for the man, Bethany was upset that her father was sharing a room with him. The whole situation felt more like a nursing home, and it was quite depressing. She pulled the hospital curtain around to separate her father from the man. At least he could look out the window beside his bed.

She and Rob stayed to make sure John ate. The hospital food arrived and just the smell of it made Bethany's stomach turn. She removed the cover to find sliced turkey breast with congealed gravy, some overcooked canned string beans, some dried-out instant mashed potatoes, and a cup of applesauce in a plastic container with a foil top. Bethany sighed. It was amazing to her that the food was simply dropped off and left on the stand. Her father was clearly too weak to feed himself. What if she and Rob weren't there? Who would feed him? She looked around the curtain to see the older man still sleeping, his tray of food getting cold by his bedside.

Rob removed the utensils from the sterilized packaging. Bethany put her hand over his and said, "I'll do it. It's okay, Rob." Using the utensils, she began to cut John's dinner as if preparing it for a child, and then with everything she had left in her, Bethany carefully fed her father, a man who wasn't even sixty years old yet. It was hard to fathom such a thing. She thought about her mother, knowing that Victoria would have been much stronger than she. Bethany wondered if her mother was watching from wherever she was. Did she know the struggles they faced?

John ate only a small portion. When he was through, Bethany wiped his mouth and covered up the tray. She pushed aside the mayo stand containing the tray, and she stood up over her father. She was exhausted and knew that she and Rob should get back. He needed rest. She hated to leave him at the hospital, and a terrible sadness overcame her. John's eyes were closed, and he breathed softly. It struck Bethany that her father looked like he was closer to seventy-five years old. Sarah's father was the same age as John, born a month a part. Sarah's father played golf and tennis twice a week, traveled, and spent time with his wife, kids, and grandkids. Bethany hated herself for comparing, but how could she not? Her thoughts became ten times worse when a new nurse came on shift. When checking John's vitals, she told Bethany not to worry, that she would take good care of her grandfather.

"He's my father," Bethany said.

The nurse apologized and continued on with her duties. Bethany was scarred from the comment. Bethany said her goodbyes to her father, and then she and Rob headed home. On the way back, Bethany realized how very little she and Rob had eaten that day. They picked up a quick pizza along the way and brought it back to the house where the dogs were happily waiting.

While they ate, Rob went through the things Dr. Melman had told them and explained a little more to Bethany, whose head was already swimming. Besides dealing with the immediate issue of John being in the hospital, she also knew she had to call her brother in Colorado to fill him in, and she had work tomorrow besides.

Bethany and Rob discussed the next day's plan. Rob would head up to the hospital early so Bethany could start the day at the bakery. When things quieted, which was usually around one, Bethany would leave Alison in charge and she would make the fifteen minute drive to the hospital. She prayed there would be some improvement, and that maybe in a day John would be able to come home. Wishful thinking? Perhaps, but what was there actually to think about anyway?

By nine-thirty she sat down in her father's chair in the parlor and called her brother from the cordless phone.

"Hey, Steven," she said as her brother answered the phone.

"What's up? How's he doing?"

"Well, he's been admitted. He's on medication. They're trying to get his fever down as well as get rid of the edema. He's really weak."

"How are you holding up?" Steven asked. "You sound exhausted."

"I am," said Bethany. "It's mentally and physically draining. This hasn't been easy for me, you know. And I'm running the bakery at the same time."

"Rob's been helping out though, hasn't he?"

"Of course he is, Steven, but I still don't think you get it. Who do I have to lean on? You're the big brother. Remember you always used to stick up for me at school? Fight my battles when that jerk Derek tried to steal my books? I don't have that support anymore. It's so hard doing this by myself—running the household, being strong all the time, making decisions..."

Bethany couldn't help but give her brother a little guilt. For a moment there was silence between them. "Are you still there?" she asked.

"I'm here. I don't know what to say, Beth. I'm sorry. If you want I'll see what I can do and I'll try to come home. I don't know how many days I can keep taking off from work though. I've already used a bunch of personal days for Karen's fertility treatments. If it's not anything really serious..."

Bethany rolled her eyes while she twirled her hair with her left hand. "How am I supposed to know how serious it is? It's too early to tell, but the fact of the matter, Steven, is that Dad is getting worse. Much worse and it's taking its toll on me. I'll do anything for him, you know that, but I've given up everything it seems. I have no time to myself. I rarely go out. Do you forget what I gave up at graduation? I put in over thirteen hundred hours in the bakery alone. I graduated at the top of my class. I could've taken the job in Manhattan with acclaimed pastry chef Monique LaSalle. Mom was going to help me look for an apartment near the bakery on the Upper East Side. Do you remember this, Steven? I dreamed of working for her and of living in the city. Granted, Karen is from Colorado and you ended up finding a nice job there so she could move back, but sometimes I feel like when the going got tough with Dad, you were looking for any reason to move away."

"That's not fair, Beth. And we could never have anticipated what was going to happen to Mom. I was gone before any of that happened. Look...I know you're under a lot of stress, but you can't take it out on me. I don't like this situation any more than you do. You don't think I wish I could be there to help you?"

"Be careful what you wish for. Believe me, you wouldn't *wish* to be here if you really knew what it was like. Trust me."

Steven was silent again.

"Look, I'm really tired," Bethany said. "Please don't take everything I say to heart. I'm just at my wits end here, that's all."

"Well you may not believe me, but it's frustrating that I can't be there to help. And it's upsetting that I can't spend time with Dad like you can. Don't you think I would want to?"

Bethany thought about this for a moment. "I suppose." She continued to twirl her hair. "I'm sorry Steven. I didn't call to fight with you or get you upset. Please know that. I've been a bit moody these days. That's all."

"It's understandable. Don't shut me out though, you hear? You can pick up the phone and call me anytime. I want you to know I'm here for you if you need to talk or just to vent."

"You have your hands full with Karen. I don't want to burden you with more stuff. Besides, half the time I don't have a minute to do anything, let alone make a phone call just to complain. I'm going round the clock here."

"I know you are...and Beth...I'm sorry things didn't work out as planned as far as the job you wanted, and living in the city and everything, but you've done a damn good job at running your own bakery, especially for someone your age. It's unheard of."

Bethany thought about this. "I guess you're right, and what's in the past is in the past. No changing it now."

"I'm here. Remember that. If things get worse and you want me to come home, I'll make it happen."

"I don't want you to lose your job over it."

"I want to help."

"Thank you. I appreciate you saying that. I really do. I'll keep you posted on Dad, okay? I love you."

"I love you too, Beth. We'll get through this."

Bethany did not answer. Before she hung up she nodded to herself, somehow not quite believing it to be true.

Seven

John spent the rest of the week in the hospital and was ready to go into a rehabilitation center by Friday. His infection had cleared and the edema was greatly reduced. His doctors wanted him in rehab for a week so he would get sufficient physical therapy and monitoring of the edema. The rehab was located in Huntington, not far from the hospital.

Bethany tried her best to keep herself together. She was there with Rob when the transport came to take John from the hospital to the rehab. John, for the first time, seemed quite sad, and this made Bethany's stomach turn. She knew that he did not want to go. He wanted to be home in his familiar surroundings, spending time with his dogs and listening to his tapes. It broke Bethany's heart to send him somewhere else.

"It'll be okay, Dad," Bethany began, as John was being rolled out on a stretcher. "You need to be stronger before you can come home. You've been through a lot."

Her father simply stared upward, looking at the world from a new perspective. Once he was loaded in the transport Bethany added, "I'll be right behind you, Daddy. I'll be there with you when you arrive and we'll get you all set." Still, John said nothing. She watched as the EMTs strapped the stretcher into the vehicle and then closed the doors. She and Rob quickly got into Bethany's car and followed the transport over.

"I'm worried about him, Rob," Bethany said. "He's not right. I've never seen him this way."

"It's understandable, Beth," Rob said. "He knows things are changing in his body and he's getting a little worse. He just spent a week in the hospital and who knows how long he'll be in rehab. He's weak. It could take time."

"I know. It's just that I'm really dragging along myself. I feel like screaming, crying...I don't know..."

"You feel like you're trapped. You can't help your father and you can't change the situation. It's frustrating. I get it."

"I know you do. You're about the only one that does. I mean, I talk to Sarah and Cassandra, but they just don't understand. They don't know what to say. Sometimes I think they're uncomfortable. They can't relate at all. Nobody can. It's an awful feeling, Rob." Bethany glanced his way as she continued the drive.

"I hear what you're saying, but you know what? Everyone has his day. Everyone experiences difficult times in their lives at some point. You don't know what's in store for your friends down the road."

"This just seems endless to me. There is no good that can come out of it. He's never going to get better. He's never going to be cured. Don't get me wrong. I certainly don't wish anything bad on my friends, but I feel like my life is passing me by."

"All I can tell you is to try to hang in there. Take one day at a time and try not to project into the future. You don't know what can change."

Once they arrived at the rehab, it took about an hour for Bethany to get John settled in his room and fill out more paperwork. A friendly, late-to-middle-aged black man with one leg shared the room with John, and John was fortunate again to get a bed near a window, which looked out onto the beautiful property. Bethany hoped that maybe her father would talk to his new roommate. After all, John made friends easily. It wasn't like John to be so quiet, and Bethany wondered what was going on his head.

The next day was Saturday, another busy day, but Bethany made a point of getting up to the rehab by noon. Her father was given lunch, and although Bethany had to help him drink from a cup, he was able to use the fork and feed himself slowly. He needed to regain his strength and try to do things on his own to some extent. John was given a schedule for what therapy he would have for Saturday, and almost every hour was accounted for.

"They sure mean business," Bethany stated after looking at the schedule. "You'll be up and running in no time, and you'll be home before you know it." She tried to sound cheery despite John's silence. After two long hours she decided she had been away from the bakery for too long. Gathering her things, she kissed her father on the forehead and promised to be back by seven.

On the drive back, Bethany thought about going to church. It had to have been at least a year since the last time her father had begged her to go with him. Bethany doubted going to Mass would help her feel better, but she thought it was important to go and pray for her father. If she could get everything done at the bakery, she would hit the five o'clock Mass. She began making dough and batters for the next day despite being overwhelmed and preoccupied. With her mind not completely on her work, she was glad that she didn't have any special orders to deal with that weekend. She got done as much as possible and then left Alison to close up the bakery. She entered through a side door at St. Francis and made her way toward the back of the church where she ran into Father Michael.

"Beth!" Father Michael said happily. "I'm very pleased to see you here."

Bethany kissed him on the cheek and told him of the week's events. Father Michael was a very tall and slender man. He was about the same age as John, but he looked much older because what little hair he had on his head was prematurely dark gray. He listened to her intently as he pushed his thin, round eyeglasses further up his nose and then crossed his arms.

"You know I'm always here to talk to, Beth," Father Michael said as he placed his hand on her arm. "Know that God is with you just as much as he is with John, even if it doesn't appear that way sometimes."

Bethany nodded, not quite sure what to believe. Mass was about to begin, so Father Michael said his goodbyes and was on his way. Bethany picked one of the long, mahogany pews, knelt down on the red cushioned kneelers, and began to pray. She prayed for John as well as for herself, and she asked for forgiveness for not going to Mass. She hoped that taking care of her father would at least give her some favors with God even if she hadn't gone to church. The Mass began and Bethany found herself going through the motions until the readings and the Gospel caught her attention. They focused on the miracles Jesus performed on the sick and the dying. It was strange to her that all this time she had not gone to church, and now the focus of the readings was on curing the sick.

"The Gospel of the Lord," the priest said as he closed the Bible. "Praise to you Lord, Jesus Christ," the parishioners responded as they sat back down. The priest stood before the congregation. He gave them a minute to settle in, and then he began to give his homily.

"In today's Gospel reflection, Mark tells us of a leper who approaches Jesus and asks him for a cure," the priest began. "The leper, a man who was shunned from society, had enough faith to approach Jesus and kneel before him. The leper said to Jesus, 'Lord, if you want to, you can make me well again.' Jesus looked at the leper, a man no one would dare touch, and with an outstretched arm, Jesus touched the man. Jesus then said, 'Be well,' and immediately the man's leprosy was gone." The priest took a dramatic pause to let this statement sink in, and then he continued.

"This reminds us that God *will* help us in time of need. He is there. All we need to do is ask and have great faith. It calls to mind another story of Bartimaeus, the man who was born blind. Bartimaeus was sitting on the side of the road when he heard a crowd begin to form. The crowd began calling out, 'Jesus of Nazareth!' The blind man quickly got up and began screaming over the crowd, 'Jesus, Son of David, have pity on me.' The crowd at once tried to silence the man, telling him that Jesus would not do anything for him. No one could keep him quiet, however. Bartimaeus would not keep silent. He would not give up," the priest said, pausing again.

"Hearing the man, Jesus stopped and asked the blind man to come forward. As the crowd stepped away, Bartimaeus stepped forward. Jesus already knew the man's request, but he asked him anyway, 'What is it that you want me to do for you?' What happened next was Bartimaeus's final test in his belief, in his faith, and in his trust. Bartimaeus said to Jesus, 'Master, let me receive my sight.' He knew…beyond a shadow of a doubt…that Jesus could cure him. With that, Jesus placed his hands over the blind man's eyes and his sight was restored. So today, I leave you with this," the priest said, holding up his finger as he looked around at the parishioners, "Today, we have learned that Jesus is able to help us. He can deal with our problems. Do not doubt. Trust and believe like the leper and Bartimaeus. Whatever your difficulties are, trust in the power and in the glory of our Lord, Jesus Christ."

With that, the priest carefully stepped away from the pulpit and sat back down, giving everyone a moment to reflect.

A tear ran down Bethany's cheek. How many times had she asked Jesus for help? How many times was her request denied or left unheard? Why could Jesus not cure her father when he was a good, decent, and God-loving man? She was overcome with all sorts of emotions and could not respond to the rest of the Mass. Her thoughts ran wild, as did her feelings, from anger to sadness to angst. She left the Mass before Communion vowing never to step into church again.

51

Eight

Bethany cried on her way back from church. When she arrived home she found herself totally alone. Max and JJ were all she had to greet her, and they wagged their tails happily. Bethany plopped herself on the floor and let the collies surround and comfort her as she held them tight, her tears leaving wet spots on their fur. She did not know how to go on. Sometimes she wished she didn't have to, and she wondered if being dead was any better. She knew she needed help, but from whom and how? She considered therapy, but when would she possibly find the time?

Despite her despair, she was brought back to reality when she glanced up and saw that the clock read six-thirty. She had promised her father she would be there by seven and she'd also promised Rob she would relieve him. It was a Saturday night and even Rob had plans. What would she do after she left the rehab and came home? She started to sob again. She wondered what it would feel like to have a husband who would take care of her, who would listen and understand. She wondered what it would be like to dress up and go out to dinner with someone, to kiss children goodnight, to be able to come and go as she pleased. All she felt were the painful chains wrapped around her, getting tighter and tighter until she could not move or bear the pain any longer. She felt suffocated, like every last bit of life and happiness had been completely sucked from her flesh and blood. Is this what life was about?

She wiped her eyes and stood up. She took the dogs out and then went up to her room and did her best to try and fix her tired, swollen face as she thought about the Gospel and homily once again. With anger building up, she swung her arms around and screamed.

"There's no such thing as a damn miracle! Why are you punishing me, God? I hate you!" Bethany knew her words were harsh but she didn't care. Would God send her to hell? She already thought he had. *How much worse could it be?*

Bethany stormed out of the house and drove recklessly to Huntington. She arrived at the rehab quickly, but she sat in her car for a moment staring into the darkness. After a few minutes she took a deep breath and opened the car door, and then made her way to her father's room.

If her father noticed something didn't seem quite right with Bethany, he didn't say. She had not rehearsed what she would tell him if questioned. The gentleman next to John was asleep and was snoring loudly.

"Where's Rob?" Bethany asked, suddenly noticing he wasn't there.

"Oh, he just went to see if he could find somebody about the TV," he said weakly.

"What's wrong with the TV?" Bethany asked as she moved a chair closer to John's bed.

"It's been acting funny, and now it just went off. Doesn't matter. Not much on anyway. But Rob insisted on seeing what he could do."

With that, Rob walked in the room. "Oh, hi, Beth. You okay?" he said when he saw Bethany's face.

"Yes, yes, I'm fine, Rob," she said, standing and turning her face away. "I'm sorry I'm late. What did they say about the TV?"

"They'll try to switch it tomorrow. No one's around to do it now. I'm sorry, John," Rob said.

"It's okay. I was just telling Bethany there's nothing on anyway. I'll just rest for a while."

Bethany and Rob stood looking at John, helpless as to how to help him or cheer him.

"You go, Rob. I'm here now. I know you have plans," Bethany said. "Did he eat his dinner?"

"Yes, somewhat, but I don't think he cared for it too much." Rob chuckled.

"I am lying right here," her father said. "Why don't you ask *me* if I've eaten and what I think of the food?"

Bethany turned sharply with surprise. "I'm sorry, Dad. I didn't mean it like that."

Her father turned his head away from her and stared at the wall. It took all Bethany had not to burst into tears. She was so fragile now, and she had hurt her father's feelings. She nodded for Rob to get going; that she would deal with her father. Rob said goodbye and told John he'd see him tomorrow. Her father did not reply and kept staring at the wall.

"I'm sorry, Daddy," Bethany repeated softly as she sat back down in the chair. "I've had a difficult day. I wasn't thinking."

"The food is terrible," he said. "And they wonder why I'm losing weight. The food was bad enough in the hospital."

Bethany knew her father was spoiled. He enjoyed good food and had grown accustomed to his daughter, a professional chef, cooking all his meals.

"There's no one around right now that I can speak to about it. I'll talk to someone tomorrow and find out what your current restrictions are. I'll even see if I can sneak you in some things. I'll tell them I'm a chef and that I'll make everything according to their specifications."

"Well I better not be on any dietary restrictions when I get home," John said.

"I know you don't want to be here, Daddy. You're not ready to come home though."

He didn't reply. For the first time in her life, Bethany was at a loss as to what to say to her father. She had also never seen her dad this out of sorts, and it hurt her. He had always been so positive and happy even in difficult times. Then she remembered she had some things in her bag for him.

"I brought you some magazines," she said, handing him a copy of *Newsweek, People,* and *Time.* He didn't reach out to grab them, so she placed them on the rolling cart next to him. Bethany did her best to make small talk and told him things about the bakery, the dogs…anything she could possibly think of, but still, John didn't seem to care much and he said very little. By eight thirty she'd had all she could take. She kissed him goodbye, gave a forced smile, and left. She hurried to her car, ready to burst. As soon as she got in and closed the door she put her head against the steering wheel and cried as if her whole world was imploding, which it was. A good ten minutes passed. She was getting cold and felt a headache coming on. Bethany started the car's engine and drove back home to the empty house.

When Sunday morning rolled around, Bethany looked like she'd been hit by a Mack truck. At least that's what she thought. She wished for a day off. She didn't feel like working. This was one problem with having your own business. She left the house before running into Rob. He had agreed to spend some time with John on Sunday, and Bethany promised to visit in the evening after work.

"Gosh, Bethany, are you alright?" asked Alison as she arrived at the bakery. "You look terrible."

"Thanks," Bethany replied.

"Things aren't going so great with your dad, are they?" Alison asked while grabbing her apron from behind the counter.

"No, no they're not," Bethany replied, buttoning her chef's coat.

Alison looked at her for a moment. "I'm here if you want to talk," she said, and then walked away. What Bethany liked about Alison was that she knew when to speak and when to keep quiet, and she seemed to understand Bethany's situation a bit more than her friends. If the same conversation had gone down with Sarah, she would simply change the subject and talk about some happy thing going on in her life, thinking that would help cheer Bethany up and distract her. Bethany always walked away upset when these conversations occurred. Sarah just didn't get it. Maybe because Alison had her own difficulties in life, she could relate to Bethany a little more.

Bethany busied herself making muffins and breads, while Alison took care of the rest of the shop. Before long customers were flocking in as they always did after the Sunday masses. At eleven Alison poked her head into the kitchen. Bethany was bent over, a pastry bag in hand, and she was putting the final touches on a cake.

"He's here," Alison said.

"Who's here?" Bethany answered, not looking up from the cake.

"Your friend…the guy who eats a cannoli for breakfast."

Bethany immediately stopped what she was doing and stood up. "He's here again?"

"Yep. Same time every time too," said Alison as she stood in the doorway with folded arms.

"What do you mean 'same time every time?'" Bethany asked.

"He was in a few times last week. Eleven o'clock on the dot. You were out taking care of your father on the days he was here."

"What? And you forgot to tell me?"

"Beth, I was trying to run things around here. You were coming in and out. It slipped my mind. I only remembered when he came in just now. Why are you so obsessed with him?"

"I'm not obsessed with him," Bethany said. "There's just something about him…something odd, and it's creeping me out a bit."

"Why?"

"I don't know what it is. I can't place it. We know everyone in this town. Who is he? Where did he come from?" Bethany walked around Alison and into the bakery. She peered over the counter and saw him sitting at the same table as last time.

"People move into Northport all the time, Beth. Maybe's he's new around here," Alison whispered in Bethany's ear. "Do you want me to ask him?"

"No, no, don't do that…well, maybe. No, not now. Let's wait." At that moment the man looked up and stared straight at Bethany. A chill went down her spine as she broke the gaze. "I'm going back to finish the cake." She paused and looked back at the man who was taking his last bite of the cannoli. "Let's see if he comes in again."

Nine

Bethany was completely exhausted when she made her way back up to the rehab Sunday night. She wished for nothing more than to go home after work and relax in a hot bath with a glass of wine and a good book. Instead, she was cooking food to bring to her father. Neither her mind nor her body had any rest ever, it seemed. She wondered if she should eat before heading over, but she really had no appetite. When she did arrive, her father was very much the same way he had been the night before, which left Bethany upset and frustrated. She spent another hour and a half with him until she had nothing more to give.

At home Rob had taken the dogs out for a long walk, so at least that was one less thing to do. She could barely stand, let alone walk up and down the streets and hills with the dogs. She wasn't in the mood for conversation or for eating, so she went up to bed. It was a little after nine. She could have taken a bath, but she was even too tired for that. Bethany washed up, read a few pages of a book she'd begun months ago, and then she called it a night.

Bethany thought that a good night's sleep would have helped, but she woke up more irritable than ever. It was seven, and she showered and dressed. Although the bakery was closed, she had a lot of paperwork and bills to go through, and she had to start preliminary drawings on a very intricate wedding cake she needed for the following weekend. Before Bethany left the house, she prepared special baked oatmeal for her father, which was one of his favorites. She carefully wrapped it in foil so it would stay warm until Rob brought it up to John at eight. For herself, she prepared a quick egg and ate a yogurt while the egg was cooking. She thought about the day ahead, what she needed to do both at the bakery and with her father, and already she felt overwhelmed. She ate the egg without even realizing it. She left a note for Rob and headed out the door to her car.

When Bethany arrived at Giovanni's and made her way toward the back door, she stopped dead in her tracks. Sometime during the night, someone had spray-painted an expletive on her door.

"You've got to be kidding me!" she yelled. *Who would have done this?* There was very little crime in Northport, and she could count on one hand the number of times her store had been vandalized over the years. *Of all times for this to happen!* She didn't have time to paint the door, nor did she feel like being outside painting in the winter. She thought about her customers who had teenage boys. Maybe she could hire one of them to re-paint it. Bethany unlocked the vandalized door, turned off the alarm, and switched on the light. While she unraveled her wool scarf from around her neck, she wondered if she should call the police. She quickly changed her mind. She came here to work, not to spend the day talking to police officers and filing reports. They'd never find out who did it anyway, so what was the point? This was the least of her troubles.

"Just kick me when I'm down," she mumbled.

Bethany made her way around the kitchen taking care of her to-do list. She became agitated when she couldn't find the order for the wedding cake. She was usually very organized, but these days, who knew what she could have done with it. Her heart began to race.

"I've got to find it," she said as she searched madly around the kitchen. Bethany turned up nothing, and the volcano that had been building up inside her finally erupted. Bethany began tossing metal bowls, spoons, muffin tins—anything she could find—wildly around the kitchen. She ripped aprons and chef coats off hooks, she threw papers around and she screamed and cursed like a madwoman. Years of pent up anger and sadness exploded from every cell in her body. Her heart raced faster and she was lightheaded, but she didn't care. When she felt she had done enough damage, she fell to the floor and banged her fists into the tile. Her screams turned into uncontrollable sobs.

"Why? Why? Why?" she kept repeating softly. "What have I ever done?"

She sat in the mess she had created for about an hour, staring at absolutely nothing. It didn't matter; she simply didn't care about any of the consequences of her actions. Her head was pounding, though, and she wanted to take something for it. Bethany managed to get herself up. She searched through her bag for some Tylenol and headed to the bathroom. She stared at herself in the mirror before taking the pills, unsure of whom she was looking at. Her thoughts drifted to her mother. What would she have thought of Bethany now? The good, happy child who never did anything wrong. What had happened to her? What had she become? Her mother had been a strong woman. Seeing her daughter like this would have been extremely disappointing, or so Bethany thought. *Could she see me now? From wherever she may be?*

Bethany cleaned up her face and fixed her hair. When she left the bathroom and saw the mess she had made, she let out a deep sigh. Without another tear or moment of anger, she began the daunting task of cleaning up. It took well over an hour to wash everything and put it all back in place. She was glad that nothing sustained any real damage. She was thirsty after the whole ordeal, so she went out into the main part of the bakery to get a bottled water from the refrigerated case. When she opened the door and grabbed the bottle, she had the overwhelming sense that someone was standing behind her. She turned quickly, dropped the water, and let out a short scream.

"Holy shit!"

"Shit ain't holy," the man replied.

Bethany's heart was pounding out of her chest.

"How did you get in here?" she asked angrily.

"Through the door," he replied. "It was open. I'm sorry...I didn't mean to scare you."

59

Bethany stood in utter disbelief that this man—the same man she had seen eating alone in the restaurant, and the same man who had been coming into her shop for cannolis—had somehow gotten into her locked bakery.

"What do you want?" she asked. "The bakery is closed."

"The door was unlocked," he said. "Go and take a look."

Without taking her eyes off him she walked sideways toward the front door. Sure enough it was unlocked.

Impossible. Bethany was positive that the door had been locked. She knew she was losing it, but she'd never forget to lock up the bakery. In fact, she was certain she did because she remembered fumbling with the keys and dropping them when she went to leave the night before.

She stood near the door in case he was a madman. This way she could run out quickly.

"I don't understand this," she said. "I know I locked this door,"

The man didn't answer. He looked at her sympathetically and waited for her to calm down.

"I'm sorry," he repeated. "I didn't mean to frighten you. I really didn't, if you know what I'm sayin'."

He never moved. He gave Bethany her space, as she evaluated him and the situation.

"What do you want?" Bethany asked for the second time.

"I just wanna talk to you about somethin'," he answered.

"Talk? You came here to talk? Look, I'm going to leave here and call the—"

"Do you believe in miracles?" the man asked.

"Excuse me?" Bethany asked. *What is going on here?*

"I asked, do you believe in miracles?"

Bethany stood motionless. Maybe she'd had a breakdown after all. Maybe she was hallucinating or going insane. *Miracles?*

"Why are you asking me that?"

"Do you believe in miracles?" he repeated.

Bethany paused for a moment, unsure of how to answer or if she should at all. Finally she said hesitantly, "I don't know. Maybe they existed when Jesus was alive, but I guess...no, I don't believe miracles happen anymore."

"My name is Jimmy. Do ya mind if we sit down? I promise you, I'm not a bad guy."

Against her normal instincts, something beckoned Bethany to have a seat at one of the small tables. Part of her thought that this was ludicrous. She did not know this man from a hole in the wall. He could be a nutcase. But something told her otherwise, that or maybe she really was going insane.

He pulled out the chair across from her and sat down. This was the first time Bethany actually saw him up close, and there was something…something about his face that seemed different. He was American, and his voice was something out of a movie, reminiscent of a Brooklyn-born Italian. She figured him to be about fifty-five years old. He had light brown hair that was carefully slicked back. He was tall, a little over six feet, and slightly overweight. He wore black pants, a black button down shirt, and a brown leather jacket. What struck her most were his skin and his eyes. Unlike many Italian Americans, his skin was not dark, in fact it was quite pale, and his eyes were a rich, baby blue. She found she could not look him straight in the eyes because something about them made her feel as if he could look deeper inside her. He was intimidating to say the least. She felt exposed and somewhat vulnerable, and had to look away from his face.

Jimmy folded his hands together on the table, and leaned forward. "Have ya ever heard of Padre Pio?" he asked.

"Padre Pio? No. I haven't," Bethany replied softly. "What does this have to do with me?"

"Well, Padre Pio had the stigmata…the five wounds of Jesus Christ."

Why is he telling me this?

"The stigmata?" she asked.

"Padre Pio, born Francesco Forgione in the southern Italian village of Pietrelcina, was born on May 25, 1887. His parents were peasant farmers and they were very poor. You know what I'm sayin'? When he was fifteen years old he entered the novitiate of the Capuchin Friars. He was very religious, even as a child. By 1910 he was ordained a priest. Eight years later, after offering his daily Mass, he received the stigmata on his hands, his feet, and in his side. He bore the wounds for fifty years."

"Wait a minute, I was born and raised a Catholic," Bethany said. "I attended Catholic school. My parents were religious people. How come I've never heard of this...of him, Padre Pio, before? More importantly, why should I care? Why don't they talk about him in church? In school?"

Bethany didn't know what to make of this whole thing.

"Let me ask you somethin'," Jimmy said. "Is there someone in your life who's sick?"

A chill went down Bethany's spine. For some reason she believed that Jimmy already knew the answer to that question. She said, "Yes. My father."

"Padre Pio cures the sick,"

Bethany stared at him. "I assumed he was dead."

"He is. Died in 1968. He still performs miracles, though."

"What? I don't understand this. He's dead...he can cure people...like Jesus Christ?"

With that, Jimmy opened up his leather jacket and put his hand inside the interior pocket. He pulled out what looked to be a small prayer card. "Take this," he said, sliding it across the table. "Keep it with you and pray to Padre Pio. Pray to him to help both you and your father."

"I've given up praying," Bethany said. "Why me? Why are you telling *me* this? You don't know me."

Jimmy tucked his chin in and said to her, "Pray to him." He stood up and zipped his jacket. "I'll see you around," he said.

Bethany sat silently holding the card in complete confusion and disbelief as Jimmy left the bakery. Not knowing what else to do, she rose from the table and headed back toward the kitchen, all the while going over and over again what had just happened. As she walked by the cash register, something caught her eye. There lay a piece of paper with her handwriting on it. She picked it up and, oddly enough, it was the missing wedding cake order.

Ten

The rest of the week was a blur. Bethany could not comprehend her strange encounter with Jimmy. It simply made no sense. She kept his card by her nightstand, but she wasn't quite sure why. After all, she had given up praying, and some crazy stranger certainly wasn't going to change that.

The one good thing was that her father was improving both physically and mentally. By Saturday he was ready to come home. Although Bethany didn't know how things would be once he was back, she was relieved that she didn't have to go running back and forth anymore. Things would hopefully return to normal, whatever normal was these days.

It was agreed that Rob would pick John up so Bethany could work. Saturdays were always busy at the bakery, and the week before she had taken too much time away. Bethany was finally able to finish up work by around four-thirty, so she headed home. "You're here early, Bethany," Cherie said smiling as Bethany walked into the kitchen. "I'm sure your daddy will be happy to see you." Cherie continued to clean up some dishes that were in the sink, while Bethany hung up her keys, removed her coat, and unraveled her scarf.

"What's all the racket?" Bethany asked, hearing loud music coming from the parlor down the hall.

"Your daddy's so happy to be home he insisted on playing Tommy Dorsey."

He hasn't played that in years. She took it as a good sign.

"You go on in and see him," Cherie said, as she began drying the dishes. "Rob is upstairs taking a shower, and I'm almost ready to leave. Everything is done. I would have made dinner for you for tonight..."

"Don't be silly, Cherie," Bethany said. "You've done enough. I promised my dad that I would make him something special tonight, so we could celebrate his being home."

"That's right. That's what he told me," said Cherie, taking off her apron. "Rob went to the butcher like you asked him."

"Are you sure you can't stay for dinner?" Bethany asked.

"I appreciate the offer, but I'm seeing one of my girlfriends tonight. We're seeing that new chick flick," she said and laughed. "And we're getting a bite to eat afterwards, but thank you anyway. You know it's hard for me to refuse your cooking." Cherie gave Bethany a wide smile.

"Well you go and have a great time. You've been a tremendous help, Cherie."

"No problem, no problem." She laughed and her eyes sparkled. "That's the Jamaican way. I'm always here to help."

"It means a lot though," Bethany said as she gave Cherie a big hug.

"You go and tell that daddy of yours to turn down that music now before he goes deaf."

"I'll tell him you said that." Bethany smiled and left the room.

The music got louder as she approached the parlor doorway.

"You mind if I turn this down a bit?" Bethany yelled to her father as she walked over to the stereo. "Cherie thinks you're going to go deaf."

"Oh, Bethany!" he said with a big smile, "Of course. Please...go ahead." The dogs, who had been lying by his feet, woke at the sound of Bethany's voice. Both dogs slowly made their way over to greet her.

"And how are you two doing?" Bethany asked after turning down the stereo. "What good dogs." She bent over to pet them as they wagged their tails. "I'm sure they're glad you're back, Daddy." Bethany stood and went over to him, kissed him on the cheek and sat down at the sofa next to him. "So...how are you doing?"

"Couldn't be better," he announced. "I'm back home in my favorite chair and I feel pretty good."

"I'm glad," replied Bethany. "I've been worried about you, you know."

"Yes, I do know, Bethany," he began, "which reminds me...I wanted to apologize for my less than acceptable behavior. I didn't mean to take it out on you. I hadn't felt that miserable since your mother died. I don't know what got into me," he said, "but something was different this time. I don't know if it was the medicine, the environment. I just wasn't myself in a lot of ways. I hope that you will forgive me."

"There's nothing to forgive, Daddy. I just hated seeing you that way. That's all. I didn't know how to help you. You had to go to rehab before you came home. There was no other choice," Bethany explained.

"And that's why I'm sorry, Bethany. I didn't mean to cause you more stress and grief."

Bethany looked at her father, whose face had aged, and studied him for a moment. She was happy he was home with her now. How long would he stay this way? She didn't know, but she was going to accept this time as one of those good moments. She was grateful for the little things.

"I'm surprised you haven't asked what's for dinner," Bethany said, smiling.

"I didn't forget," he said. "I was just about to ask."

"You can definitely use some protein, so I had Rob pick up some beautiful rib-eye steaks from the butcher. I made an herbed butter last night to top it off with, since you can't have any salt right now," Bethany said. "I'm going to make some homemade creamed spinach and potatoes with onions and peppers. An official steakhouse!"

"It sounds wonderful, honey. I can't wait."

"I'm glad you have an appetite finally."

"And dessert?" he asked.

"Well, we'll have to see about that. I'm sure I can find something to whip up," Bethany said. "Can I get you anything in the meantime? Some water?"

"No, I don't think so, but you can turn my music up again if you don't mind."

"I still think you're too young to be such a huge Tommy Dorsey fan," Bethany said.

"Ahh, there's nothing like the classics though."

Bethany had to admit that she happened to like Dorsey's music. Maybe the thought of going back to some other period in time intrigued her. Whatever it was, it did help her to forget about her problems temporarily.

As she made her way over to the stereo to turn it back up, she paused and turned to her father. "Can I ask you a question?" she asked.

"Of course," he replied.

"Have you ever heard of a Franciscan friar named Padre Pio? He was from Italy."

Her father paused a moment. "Vaguely," he said. "Wasn't he the stigmatic?"

Bethany was surprised Daddy had heard of him. "Yes, I believe that's him. How do you know about him?"

"I was waiting to talk to Father Michael after Mass a few years ago, when I overheard a conversation he was having with a parishioner, a woman who wanted him to put up a statue of Padre Pio. To my knowledge the statue was never put up. Could be there now, I wouldn't know."

"Hmmm," Bethany said.

"Why do you ask?

"Someone mentioned him to me last week. I had never heard about him. I...I was thinking about praying to him...praying to him to help you," Bethany said, surprising herself.

"Prayer never hurts, that's for sure."

"Anyway, I'm so glad that you're home. Let's try to keep you healthy and out of the hospital," she said, putting a hand on her father's shoulder. "I'm going to go get dinner started."

Bethany turned up Tommy Dorsey and glanced at her father before leaving the room. He was smiling.

"I love you, Daddy."

"I love you, too, Bethany."

"Your cannoli-eating friend is back and he wants to speak to you," Alison said as she poked her head into the bakery's kitchen. "He's right on time too. Eleven o'clock."

It was Tuesday morning and Bethany had just put a few loaves of bread in the oven. She looked at Alison, but wasn't as surprised this time. She knew he would be back.

"Okay," she said. "I'll be right out."

Alison walked away without further questions, while Bethany cleaned her hands on a nearby towel. She set the timer for the bread and made her way out of the kitchen. When she did so, she found Jimmy sitting in the same spot, eating a cannoli and drinking a cappuccino. He did not look up when Bethany walked over in her chef's coat and checkered pants and sat down across from him. She said nothing and waited for him to speak.

"These are delicious," he said with a mouthful of cannoli. "I've been meanin' to tell you that."

Bethany did not reply. She still didn't know what to make of Jimmy, nor did she feel at ease in his presence. Part of her even wondered why she was sitting here with him now.

"How's your father?" Jimmy asked after taking a sip of his cappuccino.

Bethany studied his face as he looked directly at her; his pale blue eyes pierced through her.

"He's okay at the moment," she answered.

"He has a disease?"

"Yes…multiple sclerosis."

"There's this woman I know…she had a lump. She went to the doctor and found out she had breast cancer," Jimmy said. He paused to take another bite of his cannoli. "I told her about Padre Pio. I told her to pray to him every day. When it came time to do the surgery, the doctors went to go in and nothin'...the lump was gone...completely gone."

"I don't understand. How could it just disappear?"

"I told you...he's very powerful."

"I'm just not getting this. Why doesn't everyone know about him? Why doesn't everyone get cured?" Bethany asked.

"A lotta people are cured. Those who aren't are here to serve some other purpose...a purpose and a plan they chose before they came here, you know what I'm sayin'?"

"Before they came here?"

"Yeah, you know, everyone decides what their plight in life is going to be before they're born. It's all to advance spiritually."

"I hardly think I would have picked the road I've been on."

"You'd be surprised. Anyways, Padre Pio performs miracles. He cures the sick."

"So you've told me," Bethany said, still a bit skeptical.

"It's all about faith. Padre Pio had a lot of faith and a huge love for Jesus Christ. He wants us to do the same. Ask and it will be given to you, seek and you will find, knock and it will be opened to you, you hear what I'm sayin'?"

"Are you saying that if I ask Padre Pio to cure my father, he will?"

"If he is supposed to cure your father...if God wants your father to be cured, he will."

"And what if I do what you say and I pray to Padre Pio. What if my father doesn't get better? What if he doesn't cure him?"

"There are reasons for everything. It will be revealed to you at some time." Jimmy wiped his mouth with his napkin and leaned back into the chair, waiting for Bethany to respond.

She stared directly at him, and he met her gaze. Finally she folded her arms, and asked, "How do you know these things?"

"I just know."

Bethany shook her head and let out a sarcastic laugh. "This is ludicrous."

Jimmy reached inside his jacket pocket, never taking his eyes off Bethany. He tossed what appeared to be another prayer card in front of her.

"You see that on the bottom there?" Jimmy said, pointing to the card.

Bethany picked it up and studied it.

"That's a relic. It's a piece of the fabric worn by Padre Pio. This card is from Italy."

Above the tiny relic was a photograph of Padre Pio holding the Eucharist. Bethany opened the small booklet and saw a prayer on the left side, and the words Jimmy had just recited about "seek and you will find," was written on the other side. The back contained information on Padre Pio's life, and the address of San Giovanni Rotondo. Bethany looked it over, placed it back on the table, and folded her arms again.

"See that there, where it says San Giovanni Rotondo?" Jimmy pointed to the prayer card. "It's in Italy. He gave masses there. Hundreds, thousands of people flocked and took pilgrimages to attend his Mass or to go to his confessional. You have to understand. This was a very poor part of Italy. People made their way through the mountains, across all sorts of rough terrain, to see him and to be cured."

"Really?" Bethany said a bit sarcastically.

"Pray to him," Jimmy ordered. "I have other things for you too. I'll give them to you when the time is right."

Bethany scrunched her eyebrows and tried to stare the man down. He simply stared right back at her. He stood and zipped up his jacket.

"When you go home tonight, go on your computer," Jimmy said. "Do an Internet search on Padre Pio. You'll get your answer about how many people know and pray to Padre Pio. Faith is believin' even when you can't see, Beth. Believe. I'll see you around."

Jimmy collected his garbage, tossed it in the trash, and left Giovanni's Bakery. Bethany remained seated, her arms still crossed.

Eleven

W hat was that about?" Alison had asked shortly after Bethany returned to the kitchen.

"I don't know," Bethany said. "I never told you that he managed to find his way in here last Monday when the bakery was closed. He nearly scared me half to death."

"How did he get in?" asked Alison.

"I don't know. He claimed the door was unlocked. I may be losing it these days, but I know without a doubt I locked that door the night before."

"That's kind of creepy," Alison replied, leaning against the counter.

"Tell me about it. Anyway, he started talking to me about miracles and about some man, a Franciscan friar named Padre Pio. It was really weird because I was having an extremely bad day up to that point, and I was really at my wits' end. I thought maybe I was losing my mind," Bethany said.

"That's bizarre. Did he know about your father? Did he know he was sick or something? Padre Pio cures people, doesn't he?"

"You've heard of him?" Bethany asked.

"Yeah, I'm half Italian remember? People swear by him."

"Well, this is great. Am I the only person in the world who's never heard of Padre Pio?"

"Maybe you were never looking," Alison replied.

Bethany stared at Alison and contemplated this.

"God works in crazy ways, Beth. What did he give you anyway?" asked Alison.

"He gave me this," Bethany said, handing her the prayer booklet. "It's from Italy. It contains a relic." She watched Alison look it over.

"And what did he tell you?"

"He told me to pray to him."

"Are you going to?"

Bethany shrugged.

"How could you not, Beth? This man comes out of nowhere, he knows your father is sick, and he gives you this?"

"Let me ask you this...how did he know that I had someone in my life who was sick? I told him about my father *after* he started talking to me about miracles."

"I don't know what to tell you," said Alison, "but I think it's a sign."

"Of course you do. You believe in everything, and you're superstitious too," said Bethany.

"I think you're crazy if you don't try this. Pray to Padre Pio."

Alison handed Bethany back the prayer booklet and Bethany studied it.

"You have nothing to lose," said Alison. "Look, I know you well enough to understand when you want to talk about things, and when you don't. Lately you've really shut down. I know you're hurting, Beth, even if you don't tell me. Maybe this was all meant to be. What if this Jimmy guy was supposed to enter your life...to help you?"

"It just seems crazy, though. Absurd."

"Why is that? Is it any crazier than what happened to me? When I found out I was pregnant and Jeff wasn't sticking around, I didn't know what to do. I was devastated...ashamed. I felt used, and my self-esteem was in the toilet. Life was so difficult...living with my parents, not having a job...Then a year or two goes by, and I meet you. You didn't judge me, you gave me a job. You understood the hard times I was going through. No one would help me...but you did. You took a chance on me. Maybe now the tables are turned and you need to take a chance on Jimmy. Let him help you, Beth."

"Are you trying to make me cry or something?" Beth made her best attempt to smile. "I really didn't know that I'd made such an impact on your life."

"Well, you did. Why do you think I work so damn hard around here?" Alison laughed. "I owe you one."

"You don't owe me anything, Al. I'm sorry I've been so grouchy and that I've shut you out. Thanks for being a friend."

"Grouchy is an understatement! I think you're worse than my dad."

"No! Never!" Bethany laughed. "Okay, all joking aside, you've convinced me. I'll try to be better and I'll listen to what Jimmy has to say."

"Good. Now let me get back to work. I have a bakery to manage." Alison smiled.

Things were relatively quiet when Bethany arrived home. The last several days had been uneventful and pleasant since her father's return. Bethany didn't want to get too used to things being good, because she was always ready for the next shoe to drop. She knew this was a negative way to look at life, but she had based it on past experience.

Bethany prepared a pasta dinner, and after they ate and she cleaned up the dishes, she spent some time talking with her father in the parlor. He seemed to be doing great, and he was very talkative. He asked Bethany about what was going on at the bakery. She purposely left out anything having to do with Jimmy. She still had to get a handle on that somehow.

When her father started getting tired, she buzzed Rob so he could come down and take him to bed. When he did, Bethany took the dogs for a walk down by the beach so she could think about the things Jimmy had told her. She tried desperately to make sense of it all, but couldn't. When she arrived back at the house, she brought the dogs inside, gave them a treat, and closed up for the night. John was already asleep and Rob was in his room. The house was quiet.

Bethany headed upstairs to the office above the kitchen. Once her mother's space, over the years Bethany began to take it over and make it her own. She turned on the computer and waited for it to boot up. She took the little Padre Pio booklet out of her pocket and looked at it again. Padre Pio was a very simple-looking man with a light gray receding hairline. His dark, bushy eyebrows were the color of clouds before a thunderstorm, and he had a salt and pepper-colored full beard, and a dark, almost black, mustache. His face seemed kind and holy.

When the computer was up and running, she decided to do a search on Padre Pio. Bethany was completely shocked at what popped up.

There were over 1.7 million references to Padre Pio. Bethany's mouth nearly dropped at the number. She scrolled down and read: "Padre Pio: the Stigmatic;" "Padre Pio Shrine;" "Signs, wonders, miracles;" "supernatural gifts from God;" "Padre Pio articles, posts, blogs;" "mystic;" "blessed;" "answered prayers."

Bethany scanned page after page. "Padre Pio, the stigmatic, lived in the modern world but was no ordinary man." "Doctors claim no natural cause for the wounds could be found." "The church had no explanation, other than it was a miracle."

These references and accounts were overwhelming. About an hour later, Bethany shut down the computer and looked at the prayer booklet. She rubbed her finger over the small relic and wondered about the man who once wore the garment from which this tiny piece of cloth was taken. She went back to her room and got ready for bed. On her nightstand, Bethany picked up the prayer card Jimmy had given her during her first encounter with him. She read it again. *Padre Pio of Pietrelcina. Pray, hope, and don't worry. Trust in the infinite goodness of almighty God.* Bethany carefully placed it back on the nightstand and climbed into bed. In her hand she held the prayer booklet. She looked at the face of Padre Pio and ran her finger over the relic again. She opened it and began to pray.

When morning arrived, Bethany, although tired, got ready fast and headed off to work once she knew that everything was set for the day with her father. She was anxious to get to work and back to some sense of normalcy.

Bethany drove the two minute drive to Giovanni's, parked her car in its usual spot, and walked toward the back door, which by now had a fresh coat of paint. As she was unlocking the door, she had the sudden feeling that someone was standing behind her. She turned around quickly and jumped.

"You've got to stop doing that!" Bethany yelled as she turned to see Jimmy standing ten feet away. There he was with his slicked back hair and leather jacket. He looked as if he just jumped out of an Italian mobster movie. "You scared me half to death." She clutched her keys over her chest and tried to slow her breathing.

"I apologize," Jimmy said. "What are you doin' after work today?"

"What?" Bethany asked.

"I need to tell you some things I think you should know about Padre Pio. Did you look him up on the Internet like I told ya?"

"Yes...yes...I did," Bethany said, feeling very rattled. "I looked at it quickly. I didn't have time to read much."

"What time do you finish up?"

Bethany scrunched her eyes and considered him for a moment. She did not want to be with this man she barely knew after hours, but something inside her was pulling her toward meeting with him. For what reason, she had no idea. She still didn't know if he was crazy, if he was some kind of a religious fanatic or if he was a stalker. What then compelled her to answer him?

"Six," she said.

"Good," said Jimmy.

Coming to her senses, Bethany added, "Actually, I have to take care of my father. I have to get home."

"I'll wait."

He said nothing else. Instead he stood there with his hands in his pockets and stared at her.

Bethany stared right back at him. "Fine," she finally said. "I can meet you at eight tonight. Where do you want to meet?"

"How 'bout here?"

She contemplated this, again wondering if this was a safe move. "Okay," she said, against her better judgment, "but wait for me out front. I'll open the door for you."

"No problem. See you then." Without taking his hands out of his pockets, Jimmy turned and slowly walked away.

Bethany stood motionless. What was she doing? She quickly changed her mind and ran after him. She would tell him she had made plans with a friend. In the second it took to turn the corner of the building, Jimmy was gone. Bethany looked left and right. There was no one around. There were no cars, no people, nothing. He had simply disappeared. *This is absolutely insane.*

Twelve

At seven forty-five Bethany drove back to the bakery. She came in through the back and turned on the kitchen lights. She hung her jacket, scarf, and bag on the hook and made her way into the bakery. She turned on the main overhead lights and looked around. Not knowing what else to do, she went toward the front door and peered out. Her heart was racing. Within seconds she saw Jimmy walking toward the entrance. She undid the locks, took a deep breath, and opened the door. He was dressed the same as he had been that morning: jeans, a black mock turtleneck, and his brown leather jacket.

"Hello," he said, walking through the door.

Bethany remained quiet. Jimmy made his way toward the counter and peered into the darkened cases. He looked up at Bethany and asked, "Do you have any cannolis?"

Beth raised her eyebrows. *Does this man eat anything besides cannolis?*

"I should," Bethany said as she walked behind the counter. She flipped a switch and the inside lights went on in the case.

"Ahhh, that one right over there," Jimmy said, still hunched over.

Bethany took a piece of bakery tissue and pulled out the one he had pointed to near the front of the case. She grabbed a small paper plate and napkin off the counter.

"I don't have the cappuccino machine on, but I can make some coffee if you like."

"Nah. It don't matter. This is fine." Jimmy reached into his jeans pocket and pulled out some money.

"Please. It's on me," Bethany said.

"Thanks," said Jimmy as he took a bite of the cannoli while standing.

Bethany raised her eyebrows and let out a small sigh. "Would you like to sit?"

"Yeah, sure."

Jimmy sat down without bothering to take off his jacket. He sat silently eating the cannoli as if Bethany wasn't even there. Bethany folded her hands on the table, stared at him, and waited.

"These are really good, you know?" he finally said.

"So you've told me."

Jimmy finished his last bite, wiped his mouth with his napkin, and then crumpled it up and threw it on the plate.

"So," he said loudly, leaning back in his chair. "About Padre Pio." Jimmy let out a huge sigh and began. "You know, we all go through stuff and sometimes we think God is punishing us."

Bethany straightened in her chair feeling a bit uncomfortable.

"Things happen in life. We feel like we got the raw deal and we blame God." Jimmy paused and his blue eyes shot right through Bethany. It was almost as if he was reading her inner most thoughts and feelings. *How could that be?*

"Padre Pio was no exception, you know. You think you got problems? It's nothin' compared to what that man went through, and why? He went through everything so he could help us...so he could serve Jesus Christ and make a difference in the world."

Bethany sat in complete silence with nothing more to do than to listen to him.

"Padre Pio was very ill most of his life," Jimmy continued. "He had all sorts of health problems, even as a child. He'd get these crazy fevers most people wouldn't live through. Doctors couldn't explain it. In 1915 he was drafted into the army, but thirty days later he was sent home because of his health. He was back and forth with the army, but he never seemed to stay long. Finally he was diagnosed with pulmonary tuberculosis and he was sent back on permanent leave. He had some kind of hernia, a cyst in his neck, all kinds of crazy stuff." Jimmy paused and leaned back in his chair.

"Anyhow, not long after he became a friar, along with his physical illnesses, all sorts of strange phenomena began to happen to him. There were all kinds of stories. Some of the other friars reported hearing screams and banging noises coming from Padre Pio's room at night. Many say he was tormented by the devil because he was such a holy man and the devil tried to win him over. In his diaries Padre Pio wrote about being physically attacked by an unknown source who he believed to be the devil himself. He said he was terrorized because he refused to give up God's grace. Sometimes when the friars heard all this racket goin' on in the middle of the night, they'd rush to his room where they'd find him soakin' wet from sweat. Sometimes he was even bleedin', and he was always quite shaken up. No one could explain this. Padre Pio claimed to have seen all sorts of horrible, ugly images…works of the devil. No matta what happened to him, he would not give in. He would not abandon God." Jimmy let that sink in a moment while he studied Bethany intently.

Bethany wanted to know more. She could not fathom such a story.

Jimmy continued. "So this spiritual director is called in to check him out, you followin' me? Some people didn't believe what was happenin' to him. They thought he'd gone nuts. But, speaking to Padre Pio, the spiritual director determined that he was in fact, sufferin' from a form of diabolical harassment. Now Padre Pio stood firm in his convictions to follow God despite what was happenin' to him. At the same time, he also said he'd received help and guidance from his guardian angel as well as from Madonnina, which was his term of endearment for the Blessed Mother. On one occasion when the friars entered his room, they found him lyin' on the floor with a gash across his face. He was helpless and couldn't get up, you know what I'm sayin'? Strangely enough, there was a pillow under his head.

When the friars asked Padre Pio how it got there, he told them Madonnina put it there."

"I don't understand," Bethany said. "If he was so holy and God knew this, why did God allow for such terrible things to happen to him?"

"We're all faced with challenges in life, and at times it's good versus evil. It's up to us to choose. Just as God is powerful, the devil is powerful as well."

"So he was really being put to the test," Bethany said.

"Yeah, you could definitely say that," Jimmy said. "All of these tests would prepare him for the gifts he would soon receive. He had to be worthy of them first, you know? As horrible as his experiences were, he also had wonderful visions from heaven in which he was in pure ecstasy. One of the friars saw him during one of these moments and said Padre Pio was levitating above the ground."

"Levitating?" Bethany said.

"I'm tellin' you the truth. And this was just the beginning." Jimmy looked down at his watch. "Listen, I've gotta go," he said suddenly and stood up.

"But you said there's more," Bethany said.

Jimmy chuckled. "There's a lot more. But enough for one night. You go home and think about what I told ya. Take care of your father and pray to Padre Pio, I'm tellin' you."

"Thank you," Bethany said quietly as she rose from her chair.

"Thanks for what?"

"For telling me these things…for helping me."

He looked at her momentarily before he answered. "It's what I do." He turned and walked toward the door.

It's what I do? Who is this man? What is it exactly that he does? She didn't ask another question, instead she unlocked the door and let him out. As he made his way through the doorway he turned around in the darkness. His pale face seemed to illuminate in the moonlight.

"I'll see you around," he said.

Bethany knew she would indeed.

Thirteen

Y ou're father's doing pretty well," Rob said to Bethany early the next morning.

"I noticed that too," Bethany said as she stirred cream into her morning coffee.

"You seem better also, Beth. I know you've been through a lot. It hasn't been easy, and with juggling a business..."

Bethany smiled. "No, it hasn't been easy, but you're right. I am feeling a bit better."

"Why the change of heart?"

"I don't know." Bethany shrugged, although an image of Jimmy and Padre Pio flashed in her head. "I'm trying."

"Well you're doing a great job," said Rob, patting Bethany on her back as he passed by to get a cup of coffee. "How did work go last night?"

"Hmmm?" Bethany asked.

"You said you had to go back to the bakery to do more work. You have a lot of orders coming in or something?"

"Oh, that," Bethany said. "Just things to catch up on. Paperwork, that kind of thing. I'm going to go say hello to Daddy before I have to leave. He's up?"

"Yeah. Not dressed for the day yet, but he's up. He's still in bed."

"Okay. You have everything covered for today?"

"Yes, and Cherie will be by too."

"When's his next doctor's appointment?"

"Friday. And don't worry about coming. I've got it under control. We'll fill you in when we get home."

"Are you sure? It would help me out actually. I have orders I have to start filling for Saturday."

"Positive. I figured as much."

"I appreciate it." Bethany left the kitchen holding her cup of coffee. She knocked lightly on the half open door of her father's bedroom. "Good morning," she said, peering inside the room.

"Hello, love," he answered. "Come in."

Bethany entered the room and sat at the foot of the bed. Her father was sitting up and he looked bright and well.

"You look good today," she remarked.

"I feel pretty good," he answered. "You know I walked around a bit yesterday?"

"So I've heard. Thanks for not attempting anything without Rob being around. I don't want you to get hurt. Then we'll have to start all over again."

"I know, I know, but I think it helps. It's good for me to move. It helps keep the edema away."

"I think you've adjusted to the medication okay."

"Yeah, I guess so. I don't feel so heavy now. It was an awful feeling. It was like having tree trunks for legs."

"I can only imagine." Bethany lifted up part of the blanket and examined her father's legs. "Wow. Pretty good. What a difference."

"I hope things stay this way so maybe in a few weeks when it starts to get warm out I can finally go outside and sit."

"That would be nice. I feel like it will never be warm. I'm so tired of wearing coats and scarves."

John chuckled. "Busy day today?"

"It shouldn't be too bad. It's only Wednesday. Not much happening. Just the usual stuff."

"Would you mind bringing me home a cannoli tonight? I don't know why, but I've really been in the mood for one lately. You still make them, don't you?"

Bethany laughed out loud. "Of course I do. In fact, I've been going through a lot of cannolis these days, oddly enough. I'll be sure to bring you home one. I promise."

"Wonderful. I'll be looking forward to it."

The two dogs pushed their way through the door panting and wagging their tails.

"Well, hello you two," Daddy said happily as he pet them on their heads.

"I'm gonna run," Bethany announced as she stood up. "Alison is opening up for me today, but I still need to get in soon."

"No problem. You go. Have a wonderful day."

Bethany kissed her father on the cheek. "You too, Daddy, and take care of yourself. Listen to Rob."

"I will, I will," he said. "And don't forget my cannoli."

"Believe me...I won't."

Within fifteen minutes, Bethany was already making her way around the bakery's kitchen. In her usual routine she did feel somewhat better, although she didn't quite know why. Maybe it had something to do with the night before. At eleven o'clock she poked her head out of the kitchen and looked around at the tables in the main area of the bakery.

"Is everything okay?" asked Alison. "Do you need something?"

"Oh no. Nothing," Bethany said. "Just wanted to see how things were going out here," she lied. She went back into the kitchen, folded her arms and leaned up against the counter. *What's happening to me? Why am I looking for him?* She wanted to know more about Padre Pio, and she wanted to hear it from Jimmy. Somehow it had made her feel better. The mystery surrounding the stigmata intrigued her. Bethany wished that the church would talk more about these kinds of things. Bethany continued to look out into the bakery throughout the day hoping Jimmy would return. She knew he would definitely be back, but when?

"You sure you're alright?" Alison asked around four. "You just seem like you've been looking for something all day."

"No. I'm fine. Really. Just looking around," Bethany said.

"Okay, if you say so. Do you mind if I leave a little bit early today? My mom has somewhere to be and I need to get home for Justin."

"Not a problem at all. Thanks for opening up this morning, by the way. It's slow now. Miranda will be fine working the counter by herself for the next hour or so."

"Thanks, I really appreciate it," Alison said as she untied the back of her apron and hung it up. "I'll see you tomorrow then." She smiled.

"See you tomorrow."

Miranda, a high school senior who worked three afternoons after school, went around the main area of the bakery wiping the tables and pushing in the chairs while Bethany spent time cleaning up things around the kitchen. No other customers had come in. By five-thirty Bethany told Miranda, who was now clearly bored, that she could go home. Less than five minutes later Bethany heard the jingle of the front door opening. She assumed it was Miranda coming back for something she'd forgotten. When Bethany walked out of the kitchen to check, she saw Jimmy walking toward her instead.

"I brought you somethin'," was all he said.

"You did?" asked Bethany, trying not to seem too excited.

"Yeah. I wanted to come in earlier. I know you're gettin' ready to close soon. I had some things I needed to take care of."

Bethany wondered what things he had to take care of. She really knew nothing about this man at all, but she felt funny asking him anything personal.

"Anyhow..." Jimmy reached into his jacket pocket and pulled out a small, round object. It was a little bigger than a dime. "I want you to have this. Give it to your father. Make sure he wears it. Get him a nice chain."

Bethany held out her palm as Jimmy gently placed the item in it. It was a silver medal which looked considerably old. On it was a raised image of Padre Pio from the chest up; his hand held up in a blessing. Above him were the words. "Padre Pio of Pietrelcina Capp."

"Turn it over," Jimmy said, after Bethany examined the front.

She did as she was told.

"It's a relic," Jimmy said. "It's an actual piece of Padre Pio's cloth."

Bethany brought it closer to her face to get a better look. A diamond-shaped fragment of dark brown cloth was encased in a small piece of raised glass. Underneath it was the word "RELIC." She was amazed.

"This is the real deal," Jimmy said. "It's from Italy. This particular medal is very old. It's very special. Give it to your father and tell him to wear it. Pray to Padre Pio."

Bethany looked up, and Jimmy's eyes were once again piercing through her.

"You understand me?" he asked.

Bethany nodded. "Thank you. I don't know what to say. How did you get it?"

"Don't worry about it," Jimmy said as he waved his hand and dismissed her. "Just tell him to wear it. Get a chain."

"I will." Bethany turned it over and ran her finger across the image of Padre Pio.

"Here's a prayer card for your father too." Jimmy reached into his pants pocket and pulled out a different card than the one he had given to Bethany.

"Thanks," she said.

"You have a minute?" Jimmy asked.

"Sure," Bethany replied.

"Let me tell you a little story."

Bethany pulled over a stool and sat down.

"There was this girl," Jimmy began, "Gemma di Giorgi of Sicily. She was blind. Born without pupils. In 1947 she was seven years old. Her grandmother, a woman of great faith, heard about Padre Pio and his miracles. She decided to take the girl on a pilgrimage to see him. She went all the way to San Giovanni Rotondo, praying for a miracle the whole time. They were about halfway to Foggia from their journey from Sicily, when the little girl started telling the grandmother that she could see the sea and a steamboat. The others who were with them thought this might be a miracle, you know? But the grandmother's exhausted from the trip, right? So she thinks the girl must be dreamin' instead. Anyhow, they continued their journey. The grandmother was determined to reach Padre Pio because she believed he could cure her granddaughter. Even though the girl told the grandmother she could see, the old woman didn't believe the girl because she still had no pupils. You can't see without pupils. You understand what I'm sayin'?"

Bethany nodded and waited for Jimmy to continue.

"So they finally get to San Giovanni Rotondo, and the grandmother goes to confession with Padre Pio. Immediately after her confession, now listen to this, she asks Padre Pio to give sight to her granddaughter. Padre Pio asked the woman if she had faith and he told her she must not weep because the girl can already see. You believin' this? He told her about the girl seein' the ship on the journey. The woman didn't know what to say. After that, Padre Pio gave the little girl, Gemma, her first Holy Communion in front of all the church. Then he took his fingers, the ones that had just held the Eucharist, and he made the sign of the cross over each of Gemma's eyes. After the long trip back, the grandmother brought Gemma to an eye specialist to get checked out. As soon as the doctor saw her, he said, 'She's blind. She can't possibly see without pupils.' The girl insisted she could see, so the doctor held up some objects. She named every one. She could name them because she could see. You know what I'm sayin'?" Jimmy said as he pointed at Bethany. He paused and stared at her. He was so close that Bethany wanted to take a step back, but she felt as if she couldn't move.

"So the doctor yells out, 'This is impossible! This girl does not have pupils. One cannot see without pupils! It must be a miracle!'" Jimmy shouted. "All kinds of eye doctors heard about it and came from all over Italy to examine Gemma's eyes. They all said the same thing: it's *absolutely* impossible to see without pupils, so it must be a miracle." Jimmy paused. "The little girl...well, she's an older woman now. She's still alive and she can see."

"It's pretty remarkable," Bethany said. "These stories...they're all true?"

"Of course they're true. I ain't lyin' to you, kid, and there's more. Plenty more stories," Jimmy added. "I've gotta get out of here though. Hey listen, can I get a cannoli to go?"

"Yes, of course." Bethany slipped the medal into her pants pocket and went behind the counter. *How could these things really have happened?*

"Do you have a preference?" she asked him.

Bending over, Jimmy said, "Give me that beauty over there."

Bethany chuckled to herself as she handed him the cannoli and again refused to take money from him.

"I'll give my father the medal as soon as I get a chain for it."

"Do it soon," Jimmy said.

Jimmy walked toward the front door and opened it. With his hand on the doorknob he stopped and turned back around. "Hey, Beth. Don't forget to bring home a cannoli for your father. He really likes them."

Fourteen

L ate that same evening Bethany sat at her computer, the silver medal next to her, searching for anything she could find on Padre Pio. The amount of information which was out there was astounding. Padre Pio had been thirty-one-years-old when he received the visible stigmata. Word spread not only in Italy but throughout the world, and before long people from all over were making pilgrimages to see him. For fifty years the stigmata stayed with Padre Pio. Bethany read that over time, Padre Pio said the wounds, although painful, invigorated and sustained him throughout his life. Doctors could not make sense of it. Just like Jimmy had told her, Bethany read how Padre Pio received very little nourishment. He ate hardly any food. How could a man, let alone a sickly man, live without food and nourishment and lose approximately a cup of blood per day? Only through divine intervention could this be possible.

The other interesting point she discovered was that Padre Pio's five open wounds never became infected. In fact, the effusion of blood was often accompanied by a wonderful, sweet fragrance which was thought to be another miracle. There have been many people who have claimed to experience the smell, as well as the smell of roses and tobacco. In these incidences, the faithful knew that Padre Pio was near and would answer their prayer.

Bethany's mind was spinning on overload. She rubbed her tired eyes and shut down the computer. "Enough for one night," she said. She picked up the medal and examined it again. While she did so she thought of Jimmy. *How on earth did he know my father asked me to bring him home a cannoli?* Was she reading into this? Maybe he had just said it because he happened to be bringing home a cannoli, and it was a coincidence. *That's all it must be.* But somehow she really believed that Jimmy just knew that her father had asked her. That was impossible of course, but lately everything seemed crazy and nothing seemed to make complete sense to her.

Bethany turned the lights off and headed to her bedroom with the silver medal in hand. She did as Jimmy told her; she prayed to Padre Pio and asked him to help her father as well as herself. She didn't know if she believed, but she had nothing to lose. She asked for guidance and for more faith, and she promised to try harder and to have hope.

When the next morning arrived, she didn't want to give her father the medal just yet. She would surprise him once she bought the chain. There was a small jewelry store called Lorenzo's Jewelry, and it was located just down the street from her bakery. She would find a few minutes during the day to run over there and pick something out.

By one o'clock everything at the bakery was running smoothly, and Bethany decided now was her chance to head out. Before doing so, she decided she wanted to talk to Alison.

"Can I talk to you for a minute?" she asked Alison, pulling her aside.

"Sure. Is everything okay?"

"Yes, I mean, I guess so," Bethany said. "I wanted to share something with you. I don't want you to think I've gone crazy or anything, and I debated not telling you at all." Bethany stumbled around with her words while Alison waited patiently. Bethany then went on to explain about her encounters with Jimmy, the things he had told her, and then finally she showed Alison the medal.

"This is amazing, Beth," Alison said as she turned the silver medal over in her hand. "Something's going on here for sure."

"What do you mean?" Bethany asked.

"I don't know. I think you're getting a sign or something. It's just too...odd. The whole thing is odd. This guy Jimmy comes to you when you're at your wits' end, the stories, the medal, and him knowing that you were supposed to bring home a cannoli for your father! I don't think that was a coincidence, I really don't." Alison paused and looked at the medal again. "Come on, Beth. Something divine is going on here. I'd stick with it and see what happens. What have you got to lose?" She handed the medal back to Bethany.

"I don't want anybody else knowing right now though, okay? I'm not telling my friends. Rob will of course see the medal on my father, but I don't want people to think I've lost it, that I'm clutching on to anything I can find. Am I doing that?" Bethany asked.

"No, not at all. You're having hope again, Beth. You're getting your faith back."

"Yeah, but what am I supposed to believe? That if I pray to Padre Pio, if my father wears this necklace, he'll be cured? What if he doesn't get cured? Is he supposed to?"

"Wait and see what happens. Maybe he will get better or maybe there's some other reason for all of this, but I'm telling you, something is going on here."

"Oh, and one more thing. If, I mean when Jimmy comes in again, just act normal. Don't act like anything strange is going on, okay?"

Alison laughed. "I'll be good. I promise. Now go. I've got things covered here. Go and get your father the chain."

Bethany thanked her for listening and then she made her way down the street and around the corner to the jeweler. She couldn't remember the last time she was in there. Because of her profession and her lack of a social life, Bethany really didn't wear much jewelry at all. She rang the outside buzzer, and someone behind the counter let her in.

"I'll be right with you," a pleasant woman said as Bethany entered the store. The woman went back to helping the customer she was with, while Bethany wandered around the small but elegant store.

She looked in the cases at the dazzling diamonds that she could not even imagine owning, let alone wearing. She worked her way toward the back of the store where two other people were looking at jewelry. Bethany bent over the counter to take a closer look at a beautiful sapphire and diamond bracelet. For a split second she felt sorry for herself and wondered what it would be like to get jewelry from a man. Sarah was constantly getting beautiful gifts of jewelry from her husband, sometimes for no reason at all.

Bethany started to feel those familiar, painful feelings return. Before she had too much time to focus on them, however, something in her peripheral vision caught her eye. She slowly lifted her head away from the counter and looked upward. When she stood to see what had caught her attention, her jaw almost dropped. On a shelf against the wall, directly across from the counter was a two-foot-tall statue of Padre Pio. He was holding a pair of rosary beads and he appeared to be looking down at her. She took a quick step back in complete surprise.

"Okay, what it is that you're looking for?" the pleasant woman said, interrupting Bethany's shock. The woman, like Jimmy, had eyes the color of the sky on a sunny day. She had black, curly hair, a bit on the wild side, which fell to her shoulders. Her face was made up with a lot of makeup, more than Bethany thought she needed, and the woman wore large, sparkling diamond earrings which caught Bethany's attention immediately.

"Umm…I need a silver chain…for a man," Bethany said.

"We have several," the woman said. "I'll bring them over."

As the saleswoman walked away, Bethany could hear the sound of the woman's silver bangle bracelets as she walked. Bethany looked at the statue again. The statue's eyes, like Jimmy's eyes, seemed to pierce right through her. All she could do was stare.

"I have several different lengths as well," the woman said when she came back with a group of chains displayed over a velvet box.

"Can I see this one?" Bethany said pointing to a chain.

"Sure." The woman took the chain off the display and handed it to Bethany.

"I think this one will do. I have something I'd like to put on it. May I take a look and see how they go together?"

"Of course. I'd be happy to put it on for you," the clerk said, as she held out her hand.

Bethany reached into her bag and pulled out a folded tissue. She carefully opened it, took out the medal and handed it to the woman. The woman was about to put it on the chain when she paused, and lifted it toward her eyes for a closer look.

"Padre Pio," she said.

"Yes," Bethany replied. "It was given to me...for my father."

"Jimmy?"

"You know him?" Bethany asked in surprise.

The woman nodded, smiled, and then looked upward as if to the heavens. Her reaction caused Bethany's eyes to well up, and she fought to hold back tears.

The woman placed her hand caringly over Bethany's. "My name is Francine. Francine Lorenzo. I'm the owner of the store."

Bethany shook her hand but was so embarrassed that she began to cry. She didn't even quite know why. Bethany wanted to ask her questions about Jimmy, but she just couldn't get the words out. She didn't know where to begin.

"You know that God has a plan for each of us," Francine said, "It's your father who's sick?"

Bethany nodded yes.

"Pray to Padre Pio to help your father, but don't become angry if he's not cured. It may not be a part of God's plan, or the plan your father worked out with God before he came to Earth. Padre Pio will help and guide both you and your father; that I am sure of. If a miracle is to take place, that will ultimately be up to God. Don't give up faith. There's a reason for everything. This is a gift," she said, turning the medal over in her hand. "Make sure your father wears it. It's a very old medal. I haven't seen one like this in some time."

"And Jimmy? I don't even know his last name."

Francine smiled at her with compassionate eyes and put her hand over Bethany's again. "Listen to him," she said softly, as more tears rolled down Bethany's face. She put her head down in embarrassment and wiped away her tears.

Francine carefully put the medal on the silver chain and held it up. "This is very powerful. May he wear it well." She placed it in a box and took it in the back to wrap.

Bethany looked up at the statue of Padre Pio. Maybe Alison was right. Maybe something divine was happening to her, but why? A minute later Francine came back with a beautifully wrapped box. They finalized the purchase and said their goodbyes.

"I'm sure I'll see you again," said Francine as she shook Bethany's hand.

Bethany nodded in agreement. "Thank you," she said.

"My pleasure."

As Bethany left the store and headed back to the bakery, for the first time in a very, very long time she actually believed that maybe, just maybe, God had finally heard her.

Fifteen

"Daddy, do you have a minute?" Bethany asked her father later that evening.

"Oh, I think I can manage a minute or two for you," he said happily as he turned off the TV. He had been sitting in the larger living room off his bedroom. "Nothing good in the news anyway. Is there ever?"

Bethany smiled and sat down in a comfortable chair next to her father. In her hand she held the wrapped box containing the medal. "I have something for you," she said. "But first I need to tell you a few things."

Her father seemed surprised. "For me? It's not even my birthday."

"I've had some strange things happening lately, things I can't really make much sense of," she began. "Remember when I asked you about Padre Pio?"

"Yes," he said and nodded.

"Well, it has to do with that."

"Okay," he said patiently.

Bethany started from the very beginning when she first saw Jimmy eating alone in the restaurant. She went on to tell her father how difficult it has been for her to see him this way, so sick, and how she was really struggling with her faith. She omitted the part about trashing the bakery's kitchen, but she made it clear that she was really having a rough time. Her father listened intently at everything she had to say.

Bethany told him all the stories about Padre Pio—his life, the miracles, and anything else she could remember.

"As you know, I knew of him," her father said. "But what you're telling me I really wasn't aware of. It truly is remarkable. Who is this man Jimmy though? Where did he come from?"

"I honestly don't even know, and I can't ask him. It's like I can't get the words out. I'm simply too mesmerized by what he's telling me. He's also very...how should I say it? Intimidating, I guess? He's so matter-of-fact and he's a bit abrupt when he talks to me. Not in a bad way, but just...different."

"It sounds to me like he may not be of this world." Her father smiled.

"What?" Bethany asked. "What are you talking about?"

"God works in mysterious ways. He sends to us those who can help us, and oftentimes they are the ones we least expect."

"You're still not explaining this, Daddy. You said, 'not of this world.'"

"Because maybe he's not."

"Well what would he be then?"

"An angel, perhaps."

"An angel!" Bethany laughed. "You're kidding, right? That's ridiculous! He's this big Italian guy who eats cannolis like they're going out of style. There is no way he's an angel. It's impossible."

"Why would it be impossible?"

"Because it's crazy, that's why."

"Well what do you think an angel is? What should it look like? Should it fly and have wings?"

"Well, no, of course not, but an angel is some invisible being that we can't see or hear. Some sort of childlike cherub."

"Really?" Her father laughed. "And when we die we will all be sitting on a cloud with our wings playing the harp?"

"Daddy, you know what I mean, don't you? Jimmy's intimidating, he's big, he's Italian, a little rough around the edges maybe. He should be in the movies or something. He doesn't seem like the 'angel' type, and besides, other people have seen him. Alison has seen him. If he was an angel wouldn't he just appear to me?"

"I will tell you again, Bethany," he said softly. "God works in very strange and very mysterious ways. You just never know."

Bethany sat back in her chair and was speechless. Finally she said, "I don't know what to make of this. Like my head wasn't spinning enough with Padre Pio. This is all nuts, you know."

"Why is that?"

"Because it is! God hasn't listened to me. I even denounced him at one point out of sheer frustration. Why would God send *me* an angel?"

"Because you needed help."

Bethany sat silently taking this in for a moment. *It can't be true.*

"I suggest you pay attention to your friend the next time he comes in. Listen to him, watch him. Maybe you'll get better insight," her father suggested.

"He gave me something to give to you. I went out today and bought a chain for it." Bethany handed her father the box.

Slowly and with some difficulty, he opened it. He carefully took the silver medal and chain out of the velvet box. He reached alongside the table and picked up his glasses and put them on. "It's wonderful," he replied, once he had a good look at it. "This is a beautiful gift."

"He wants you to wear it always," Bethany said. "I don't know what to believe though, Daddy. Do you actually think you can be cured by wearing this? I don't want to get my hopes up." Bethany then went on to explain what Francine from the jewelry store had told her.

"She's right, Bethany," her father added. "It's up to God whether I'm cured or not. Just like Padre Pio had his cross to bear in life, this very well could be mine."

"But why? You're such a wonderful person. You do so much good."

"And so was Padre Pio, wasn't he? Why did he have to go through all he had to?"

Bethany thought about that for a moment. "But Padre Pio went on to do amazing things. What would God have you do?"

"Maybe teach people...teach my daughter to have faith; that God does exist."

Bethany didn't know how to reply, and then images of her mother came through. "And what about Mom then? Why did she die? What was her purpose?"

"Maybe you and I are living her purpose now."

Trying to take it all in, Bethany rubbed her temples as if her head was aching.

"This is a lot," she finally replied.

"Yes, it is," was all her father said. "Well, while you're pondering these little things like the meaning of life, why don't you put this necklace on for me?" He smiled at her.

"Of course," Bethany said, standing up to help her father. "I almost forgot. Here's a prayer card for you too." She took the card out of her pocket. "From Jimmy, of course. I have one also."

"I'd like to meet this Jimmy sometime."

Bethany placed the silver medal around her father's neck. The length of the chain was just right.

"I feel good that you have it on," Bethany said.

"I feel good wearing it. Something tells me that this medal is something we both need."

Friday arrived and Rob got John ready for his doctor's appointment. Rob promised Bethany he would call her as soon as they got home. Bethany, in the meantime, kept herself positive and focused on her work. The hours seemed to go by quickly.

At one in the afternoon, Alison entered the kitchen.

"He's back, and he wants to see you."

"Jimmy?" Bethany asked, removing a cake from the oven.

"Yep."

"Tell him I'll be right there. What's he doing?"

"What do you think he's doing? Eating."

"Stupid question. I'll be right out."

Bethany wiped her hands on a towel and left the kitchen. Jimmy was sitting at his usual table eating his cannoli and cappuccino.

"Hi," Bethany said as she reached the table.

"Did you give your father the medal? Sit." He motioned toward an empty chair.

"Yes, I did. He was taken aback. I got him a nice chain for it."

"Good. And the prayer card?"

"I gave him that too."

Jimmy finished off the last bite of cannoli and then looked at her. "Go back to church," he said.

"Excuse me?"

"Go back to church. It's been quite some time since you've gone, hasn't it?"

"Well, yes...I guess," Bethany said, wondering how he knew. Thoughts of her discussion with her father came flooding into her mind. *I still don't believe it.*

"Whatever Mass you go to, stick around afterwards. Walk around the church. You may find somethin'."

"Find something?" she asked.

"Yeah, you never know." Jimmy wiped his mouth, crumpled the napkin, and threw it down.

"And how will I know if I've found something?" Bethany asked cautiously.

"You'll know."

Just then Alison appeared at the table. "Hey, Bethany, I'm really sorry to interrupt but Rob's on the phone for you. Your dad's back from his doctor's appointment and I know you've been waiting to find out how it went."

"Yes, of course. Tell him I'll be right there." She turned back and looked at Jimmy who was already staring at her.

"Go. Take your phone call," he said.

"Okay, I'll be right back." Bethany stood and made her way to the kitchen.

"Hi, Rob. How did it go?" Bethany said when she reached the phone.

"Unbelievably well," Rob said on the other end. "In fact, the doctor was amazed at how well he's doing after all he went through. He has no edema at all now, his numbers are good; heart rate is good. Even his blood pressure is good, and it's been pretty spiked the last couple of weeks. It's actually completely normal. Your dad is also getting around better today. I'm astonished; he's been getting around with the walker. He insisted he use it to walk into the doctor's office."

"What? He's only used his walker to get to the bathroom these days. He's barely been able to get into the parlor. He didn't use the wheelchair?"

"No, he insisted. I had the wheelchair with me in the car, but we got a parking spot right up front, I helped him out of the car, and he made it right into the building," Rob explained.

"I just can't believe this."

"Well, like I said, the edema is completely gone. This is what was holding him back, I think. His legs were too heavy with fluid to move."

"He's been confined to the wheelchair for weeks."

"I know, Beth, I know. I'm as amazed as you are. You're father's really happy. Do you want to speak with him?"

"I'd love to," Bethany replied, "but I actually have someone waiting for me. Tell him how happy I am and that we'll catch up on everything tonight. Thanks so much for calling, Rob. I really appreciate it."

"No problem. I'll see you later."

"Sounds good. Take care."

"Unbelievable," Bethany said. She couldn't wait to tell Jimmy. She quickly left the kitchen and went out into the bakery. Jimmy was gone.

Sixteen

Saturday came around and Bethany asked Alison if she could close up for her at the end of the day. She decided she would listen to Jimmy's advice and go to five o'clock Mass. When she arrived, she found out that Father Michael was serving the Mass. The theme of the Gospel was about having faith. She took both as good signs.

Bethany did not feel angry like she had at church in the past, instead she felt sorry. She was sorry for her actions and for her thoughts of anger and despair, and she prayed for continued guidance, whatever that may be.

When the Mass was over she went to say hello to Father Michael. He was in the church's foyer speaking with several parishioners. While she waited, Bethany decided to take a walk around the church, in search of what, she didn't know. All she knew was that Jimmy told her to go to Mass and look for something. Once again, she listened to him. She felt somewhat stupid, like she was trying to solve some puzzle and was in search of the missing piece.

She headed up the church's main aisle. St. Francis had been built like a cross. There were pews on either side of the main aisle which faced the altar. Then there were rows of pews located on either side of the altar with an aisle that separated them. Small alcoves containing statues and votive candles appeared in these sections. Bethany turned left first and passed by a statue of St. Francis and then one of the Blessed Mother. She paused and reflected for a moment. She then made her way around, past the altar, blessed herself, and then went to the right side of the church. As soon as she made her way to the first alcove in that section, she knew she had found what she was looking for. There in the right corner was a statue of Padre Pio close to four feet tall. Like the smaller statue she saw in Lorenzo's Jewelry, this one also seemed to be staring down at her. One of Padre Pio's gloved hands was raised.

This must be it. She knew without a doubt that this statue had never been there before. In the center of that same alcove was a painting of the Divine Mercy of Christ. In the painting, the resurrected Jesus was pointing to his pierced heart, from which powerful rays of red poured out from one side, while pale white rays poured out from the other side. The red represented the blood of Christ which was shed for mankind, the life of souls, while the white symbolized water, which made souls righteous. Underneath the image, the words "Jesus I Trust in You" appeared. The painting, Bethany knew, symbolized Christ's mercy, forgiveness, and love. She felt it was appropriate that the painting was located next to a statue of Padre Pio, who also symbolized those virtues.

Bethany knelt down on the kneeler in front of the painting where she also had a good view of the Padre Pio statue. Flickering votive candles surrounded her. She started to pray, but when she did, she began to cry.

"I don't know what's happening," she said softly. "Please give me the strength and courage to go on. Please help my father. I don't want to lose him. Please help me understand why Padre Pio or Jimmy has come into my life."

She read the words, "Jesus I Trust in You" to herself. "I will do my best," she said aloud. Bethany wiped her eyes and blessed herself. She stood, reached into her pocketbook, and took out two dollars. She placed the money in the tiny receptacle and lit a candle for her father beneath the statue of Padre Pio.

Bethany zipped up her jacket and was headed toward the side entrance of the church when she ran into Father Michael.

"Well, hello, Bethany. How are you?" he said giving her a hug.

"I'm okay."

"And John? I went to see him a day or two after he arrived home from the rehab. He looked good and his spirits were up," Father Michael said.

"Yes, I meant to call you to thank you for coming by. It really meant a lot to him."

"Now that he's a little better, I told him I'd have a Eucharistic minister swing by tomorrow to give him Communion. Maybe in a few weeks when spring is finally here he'll be able to attend Mass...if he's feeling up to it."

"He'd love to come back. He really misses it here. Even on good days though, we've been afraid to send him out because it's winter and so many people are sick. Since his immune system is compromised he's susceptible to everything. We just don't want to take a chance on him getting sick."

"I understand, and I don't blame you. We just miss him." He smiled. "It's wonderful to see you, Beth, it really is. How are *you* holding up?"

"I'm getting by a little better, I think," Bethany said. "I've been reading up on Padre Pio actually, and I started praying to him. I wanted to ask you, when did the statue of him get here? I don't remember seeing it before."

"Funny you should mention it. A gentleman, a new parishioner, came to speak to me at the rectory a few days ago. He said he wanted to make a donation of not only the statue but the base as well. It was quite a gift," Father Michael remarked. "I've had a few other people ask for us to get a statue of Padre Pio. We just didn't have the funds, so when this man offered I couldn't refuse. It's a beautiful one, isn't it?"

"Yes, it is," Bethany replied, as she turned her head around and glanced back at the statue. "Would you happen to remember the name of the man who donated it, if you don't mind my asking?"

"Oh gosh," he said, putting his fingers to his head. "I honestly can't remember. Isn't that terrible? I know I have it on file in my office. I asked him if he wanted his name as the donor on a small, gold plaque but he said no. Nice guy. He was a big Italian fellow."

Bethany's eyes grew wide. "Jimmy?" she asked.

"Yes…yes, I do believe that was his name. Do you know him?" Father Michael asked.

"He's been coming into my bakery. He has a thing for my cannolis." She smiled. "He was the one who told me about Padre Pio."

"Really? Well, what a coincidence."

"Yes, it is," Bethany said, knowing there had been one too many coincidences lately. "Can I ask you a question?"

"Of course," Father Michael replied.

"Why is this the first time I've ever heard of Padre Pio? Why is he never talked about at Mass?"

Father Michael paused and put a finger to his chin. "He's thought of as a mystic. There are some in the church who have been skeptical toward him. I believe the church would rather focus on the good things he's done and his love of Jesus rather than on the mystical powers he seemed to possess."

"Hmmm. Interesting," Bethany said. Putting her hand on Father Michael's arm, she said, "Well, it was good to see you, Father. I don't want to take up any more of your time. I'll tell my father you said hello."

"Please do. It's always a pleasure, Bethany." Father Michael hugged her. "God bless."

Bethany watched as Father Michael left behind the sacristy. The church was now empty and quiet. She turned around and headed toward the exit. When she stopped to bless herself with the holy water, a now familiar voice began to speak, sending shivers up her spine.

"He's not given the credit he deserves."

Bethany turned abruptly to see Jimmy sitting in the darkness in the last pew by the confessionals.

"What are you doing here? How long have you been sitting there?" she asked.

As usual Jimmy did not answer her question. Instead, he said, "I'm tellin' you the church is afraid of him."

"Padre Pio?" Bethany asked.

Jimmy nodded. She did not make a move toward Jimmy. Instead, she stood and stared from a distance as Jimmy remained seated in the pew. Had he been there the whole time? Had he overheard her conversation?

"You put the statue there," she said.

"I did."

"Who are you?" Bethany asked.

"I'm an advocate for Padre Pio."

It was not exactly what Bethany wanted to hear, but she felt like she could not question him further.

"It's good you came to Mass tonight. I told you you'd find somethin'. Keep lighting candles for your father each week, you understand?"

"He seems to be doing better," Bethany said. "I was going to tell you yesterday but you had already left."

Jimmy said nothing.

"I appreciate what you're doing for me. I was having a difficult time before you came around," Bethany said.

"I know."

Bethany knew that Jimmy was telling the truth. She didn't know how it was possible, but she was beginning to believe that he was sent to her, whoever or whatever he was.

"I'll see you around?" Bethany asked, not knowing what else to say.

Still seated in the darkened pew, Jimmy replied, "Yeah...I'll see you around."

Seventeen

There was a small religious store located fifteen minutes from Northport in downtown Huntington Village. On Monday, Bethany's day off, she decided to take a ride over there. She didn't know exactly what she was looking for, but something in her head told her to go. Bethany had only been in the store once that she could remember. She had gone there to find a First Holy Communion gift for one of Sarah's children. She had forgotten how beautiful and peaceful the store was. The lighting and dark walls and wood were reminiscent of a miniature church. Soft, religious music played quietly in the background.

"Welcome," said a kind-faced woman in her late fifties. "Are you looking for something in particular?"

"I'm not really sure," Bethany said. "I think I'll just walk around a bit first if you don't mind."

"Certainly. Take your time. There's lots to see." The woman smiled.

Bethany started making her way around the store. There were rosary beads, statues, prayer cards, CDs, books, Bibles; anything you could think of. Bethany found that being in the store felt comforting. She walked towards the books which were located against the back wall. As she got closer she began to peruse the titles. A book on angels caught her attention first. She slowly pulled the book off the shelf and examined the cover. On it was a typical image of an angel. White wings, golden halo. She smiled when she saw the angel's classic, round cherubic face. *There's just no way. There is just no way Jimmy could be an angel. It's impossible.* She flipped through the book. There were chapters on the history of angels throughout religion, chapters on guardian angels, connecting with the angels; archangels. As Bethany turned the pages her eyes grew wide when she read, "Angels on Earth." Nearby was a chair with a big red cushion on it, and next to it was a lamp. She quickly took a seat and began to read. The book explained that the word "angel" comes from the Greek word *angelos* which means "messenger." The book stated that since bringing messages was one of an angel's primary duties, oftentimes they appear in human form. *What?* She continued to read. "Angels represent God and are chosen by God to give divine messages or hope to those in need. They appear mysteriously during a time of crisis, and their kindness and firmness draws in the person they were sent to help. They appear to already know and understand the crisis the person is going through without ever being told. They offer help and solutions, guiding people back to God. When the crisis or problem is over, the angel disappears as quickly as it came."

Bethany closed the book. "Oh, my God," she said softly. She put her hand to her mouth in utter disbelief. The description sounded exactly like her experience with Jimmy. She replayed over and over in her head everything that had taken place since she first saw him. Despite all of it, she still could not fathom the thought. "An angel?" she asked.

"Is everything alright?" the salesclerk asked as she made her way over to Bethany.

Embarrassed, Bethany said, "Oh, yes...I'm sorry, I was just thinking out loud."

"Can I help you find another book?" she asked, smiling again.

Bethany stood up. "Actually, do you have anything on Padre Pio?"

"Yes, several," the woman said as she walked toward the bookcase. She pulled out a few books and showed them to Bethany.

"Thank you," Bethany said, taking them from her. She handed the woman the angel book. "I'll definitely take this one."

"Very good. I'll bring it up front for you."

The woman headed back toward the counter while Bethany looked at the titles. She decided to buy two books. One book was about Padre Pio's life, and the other one was a daily book of blessings which was written by Padre Pio himself. She put the remaining two back on the shelf. With books in hand, she looked at the statues on the other side of the store. They were beautifully made, and many of them were from Italy. On the second to last shelf from the bottom she found a wonderful statue of Padre Pio. It was about three inches tall. She picked it up and studied the details, especially on his face. She decided to buy it. When she looked down she saw another identical statue. Checking the price on the bottom of the one she had in her hand, she decided to buy the second one and give it to her father. She brought all of the items up to the counter and decided to take one last look around. It was so peaceful that she didn't want to leave just yet. While she roamed, the woman behind the counter carefully wrapped the statues and wrote the prices down on a receipt pad.

About ten minutes later Bethany was ready to get going and she approached the counter. Everything was all ready for her in a beautiful bag with tissue paper.

"How nice," Bethany said upon seeing it.

Bethany paid for her purchases and the woman handed the bag to her and said, "Have a wonderful day, and God bless."

"You have a good day too," said Bethany, "and thank you."

Instead of going straight home, Bethany swung by the bakery to write out a few bills she knew she wouldn't get to when she came in on Tuesday. She brought the bag from the religious store in with her so she could take a look at the books she'd purchased. She took off her jacket, sat down on her stool, and told herself that the bills could wait a few minutes. When she reached into her bag she noticed there was a folded piece of paper in with the items. She removed it from the bag and opened it up. Bethany was surprised by what she found. The paper was a flyer from St. Michael's Church in Oyster Bay, the next county over. The church's prayer group was inviting the general public to a special prayer meeting and presentation. The presentation was to be given by a woman named Antoinette Filetti and it was entitled "My Time with Padre Pio." The flyer went on to explain how the woman had a miraculous encounter with Padre Pio years after his death. An experience of divine intervention had saved the woman's life, and she was coming to St. Michael's to tell her amazing story.

Bethany wondered if she was getting her own divine intervention. "This just can't all be coincidence," she said.

She looked at the date on the flyer. The event was to take place at the end of April, a few weeks away. It was at night so she'd have no problem fitting it into her schedule. It was about a thirty-five minute drive for her. Bethany definitely wanted to attend.

Bethany then took out the two books about Padre Pio and the book on angels. Looking at the covers she said, "Are you trying to tell me something?" She looked at the kind face of Padre Pio on the cover and she wished that he could answer her. "I desperately want to know what's going on. All of it."

Bethany opened up the angel book. She read that there were different forms of angels, and how there have been reports of angels throughout the whole world, in every culture and religion. She learned that most were higher, celestial beings, but that others served as messengers who sometimes took on human form. They often would come to those who had lost faith and they helped to heal that person. Bethany put the book down in her lap and stared across the kitchen while she wondered if she actually believed what she was reading. If she did, was this what Jimmy was? She rubbed her head trying to make sense of it all. She wondered when she'd see Jimmy again, and if knowing this information would change anything for her. She thought, too, how strange it was that her father's condition had been improving ever since Jimmy came into the picture. It was another thing that could not be explained.

Putting the book down on the counter, Bethany hopped off the stool and walked around the kitchen with her hands on her hips. She cleared her throat and began.

"So let me get this straight, God. I said some terrible things to you. I was angry. I had nothing left to give. Then this guy appears...a guy who could be an angel. It's not too often a person encounters an angel, let alone in human form, yet you pick *me* to have the encounter. But it's not with some beautiful, fair-haired being who showers me with kindness and love; instead you send me some big, tough Italian guy who eats cannolis. Do you see how I would be a little confused, God?" Bethany continued to pace the floor. "And then there's Padre Pio. I do believe the stories, but why am I getting this information, and why now? And why from Jimmy? Will my father be cured? Will he just get better for a little while? I'm praying, too, God...praying to you and to Padre Pio. What else do you want me to do with all of this?" She stopped pacing and stood silently as if waiting for an answer. She heard only silence so she sat back down on her stool with a sigh. "Maybe I'm thinking too much. Maybe I should just let it go and see what happens."

Bethany repacked the bag, wrote out her bills, and headed back home. When she arrived and entered the kitchen, she found her father standing there with his walker. He looked wonderful.

"Look at you!" Bethany said.

"I've been walking around all day," her father said, a smile lighting up his face.

"He's right," Rob added as he entered from the hall. "He was out on the porch and then he got himself down the steps and to the Adirondack chairs."

"What? Are you kidding me?" Bethany asked.

"I'm not kidding you! We finally got a mild day. I wanted to get some fresh air. Spring is around the corner," her father said.

"But I don't understand. You haven't done the porch stairs in a year at least. How do you know you're not overdoing it?"

"Because I feel great," he explained.

"I was with him the whole time, Beth. I swear," said Rob. "It's completely amazing."

Bethany could not stop smiling and neither could her father.

"This is wonderful," Bethany said. "Let me get some dinner on. After that I have another present for you." She held up the bag.

"I don't know why I'm so deserving of all these presents lately," her father stated.

Bethany went over and gently hugged him. "Because you're deserving of them. That's all," she said as she pulled away and looked into her father's eyes.

A couple of hours later, dinner was finished and the kitchen was clean. While Rob got John ready for bed, Bethany took the dogs out for a walk. She planned to give her father the Padre Pio statue as soon as she returned.

Bethany hooked the dogs up with their leashes and headed out the door. She was pleased that the night air was just a touch warmer than it had been. Spring was definitely on its way, and with it came a feeling of rebirth. She knew it wasn't just the weather that made her feel this way. Her father was physically, mentally, and emotionally better. Not cured, but better. She felt like she was getting help from God even if she still questioned it at times. She met Jimmy, and maybe she had Padre Pio on her side. How would it all turn out? She had no idea, but the simple act of walking her dogs on a still and starlit evening filled her with joy and hope. She felt better than she had in a long time, and she wanted to hang on to the moment. Was she in denial, believing that her father would never again go through difficult times? She walked along the quiet streets and contemplated this. Ultimately she knew in her heart that hard times would come venturing back at some point, but as for now was her father in some sort of remission, or was it really Padre Pio helping him? Was it an intervention, a plan that came from God? She had spent so many of her days feeling worried and upset that she didn't want anything to change her present feelings of happiness and content, even if it would be short-lived. She wondered what the purpose was of everything that had happened to her recently. Had she been given a second chance?

Bethany hoped that she'd see Jimmy tomorrow. There was something about him that still scared her, but she wanted to know more, and she really believed that Jimmy knew her inner feelings and thoughts even though she revealed nothing to him. She felt that somehow this stranger understood her better than her best friends. That didn't make sense, but it was how she felt.

As she continued along her walk, Bethany wondered what her mother would have thought about all of these things. Would she too think it was God at work? Then she thought of her brother Steven. What would he think? Should she tell him?

As she neared the house Bethany looked up at the stars and wondered about who was up there in the universe, helping her and guiding her. "Is it you, God?" she asked quietly as she looked into the vast sky. "If it is…thank you, and please continue to give me the strength to go on."

Eighteen

John had been thrilled with the Padre Pio statue when Bethany had given it to him. He placed it on his night table, just as Bethany had done with hers. Both father and daughter continued their prayers, and everyday going forward, her father seemed to be improving.

Later that week while at the bakery, Bethany had taken some sourdough bread out of the oven and was getting ready to make a fruit and custard tart. It was another beautiful day, and a mild one, so Bethany had the back door open so she could get some fresh air through the screen door. The wonderful scent of baked bread wafted out the kitchen and into the streets of Northport.

As she turned off the processor, which contained the dough for the fruit tart, she saw someone peering in from the screen door. Jimmy. When he knew she'd seen him, he opened the door and came inside.

"I didn't want to scare you again," he said, smiling.

Bethany smiled back. She was glad to see him. "So what brings you through the back door?"

"I hate botherin' the girls behind the counter, you know? They work hard," Jimmy said. "I figured I'd go around back so they don't have to get you out of the kitchen and everything."

Bethany let out a small laugh. "Okay, that's fine. What's up?" She folded her arms and leaned up against the counter.

"I know you're busy and all here," Jimmy said. "But I have more stories for you."

"I was hoping you would. I've come to enjoy your stories. It's a peaceful break in my hectic day. I look forward to them."

"Good. How's your father?"

"I have to say, he's doing unbelievably well."

"See? I told ya. He's wearing the medal I gave you?"

"Yes. And I went down to the religious store in Huntington and got us each a Padre Pio statue. I picked up some books while I was there too."

"That's good. That's real good. Keep it up. I told you," he said, pointing at her.

Bethany studied him for a moment, his pale skin, his blue eyes, his slicked back hair, his rough-around-the-edges personality. She couldn't help but think about the angel book. She waited for him to continue.

"Smells good in here," he said as he walked over to the bread on the cooling rack. "What kinda bread is this?"

"Sourdough," Bethany replied.

"You're pretty talented, you know?"

"Thanks, I try. Would you like a cannoli?" she asked.

"Nah. I'll have one later. I just had some breakfast and I'm tryin' to be good," Jimmy said, tapping his belly. "I've been gaining some weight since I've been comin' here, you know?"

"Do you live in Northport?" Bethany asked. "Did you just move here?"

"Around."

"Around?"

"Yeah, I live around here," Jimmy said as he continued to walk through the kitchen and look.

"Oh," Bethany replied to his vague answer. She decided to challenge him again. "Do you work? Are you retired?"

"Yeah, I work," Jimmy said.

"What do you do?" Bethany asked, still leaning against the counter with her arms folded.

"I guess you could say I'm in social work, you know? Helpin' people."

Bethany nodded. "Oh. Sounds interesting."

"It's good work. I have a good boss."

Bethany couldn't help but smile. "Well, that's good. Having a good boss always helps. I'm glad you enjoy what you do."

"Yeah." Jimmy smiled back. He stopped pacing. "Listen, you wanna meet here tonight for those stories? I'll tell you some more about the miracles."

"I'd love to hear them. Do you mind if it's a little later again, like around eight? This way I can give my father dinner."

"Sure. That's okay. I'll take you up on that cannoli then." He laughed. "So don't give 'em all away." He headed for the door. "I'll see ya."

"See ya." Bethany waved. She folded her arms again and shook her head as she watched the door slam behind him. "Unbelievable," she said.

Just then Alison came in. "Who were you talking to?" she asked.

Bethany turned and said, "Jimmy."

"You're kidding! I didn't see him come in."

"That's because he came through the back."

"Oh my gosh! Did he scare you?"

"No. I've been half-expecting him. I'm starting to get used to him just 'appearing,'" Bethany said.

"What did he say?" Alison asked.

Bethany went back to working with the tart dough as she spoke. "He wants to meet with me, tonight, to tell me some more stories about Padre Pio's miracles."

"And what did you tell him?"

"I said, sure."

"Wow. This is really amazing stuff," Alison said. "Did you tell him how great your dad is doing?"

"Of course. He said to keep praying."

"Keep going girl," Alison replied.

"So he's coming back here at eight. He wants me to make sure I put aside a cannoli for him. Apparently he's watching his figure. He can only have them once a day." Bethany grinned.

Alison laughed. "If I see we're getting low I'll put one aside, just in case we have a run on cannolis."

"Thanks. I appreciate that." Bethany laughed.

At exactly eight o'clock that night, Jimmy was standing at the front entrance of the bakery. Bethany unlocked the door and let him in. He was surprised to see a cannoli and a cup of cappuccino already waiting for him at his table.

"You made cappuccino for me?" Jimmy asked in surprise.

"It's the least I can do for all the time you've spent with me, telling me about Padre Pio and everything."

"Thanks." Jimmy sat down and immediately took a sip. "Delicious."

"I'm glad you like it," Bethany said. She waited for Jimmy to begin.

"There's so many stories, you know?" Jimmy said in between bites of cannoli. "There's this woman I know. She had these cancerous tumors and stuff. She prayed to Padre Pio. She even went to Italy, to the Rotondo, that's how much she believes. She's been fightin' cancer for ten years. All of the tumors shrunk. She's okay. It's amazin', right?"

Bethany nodded.

"Another one...a little boy, born premature. He wasn't expected to live. A medal like yours was placed in the incubator," Jimmy continued. "The kid was fine. He lived. He's runnin' around today. Then there was a twenty-two-year-old girl...cancer. She prayed to Padre Pio. She's completely cured and she's gettin' married. There's so many of them. You know what I'm sayin'?"

Bethany nodded and waited for him to continue. Jimmy took the last bite of his cannoli and wiped his mouth.

"A little girl. She was like three years old. She was gettin' open heart surgery. They didn't figure her to live, you know? She had the medal and she was fine. Three days after the operation she was runnin' around."

Bethany asked, "What do the doctors say?"

"The doctors don't say anything really. I mean, they don't know. But the people know. The people prayed and knew it was Padre Pio helpin' them. There were a couple of people with breast cancer too. They were given medals and afterwards they were perfect."

"Where do they get the medals from?" Bethany asked.

Jimmy stared at Bethany and said, "From me."

Bethany raised her eyebrow. "From you?"

"Yeah. I give medals out. I like to help people."

"Because you're in social work, right?"

"Yeah, yeah, that's why."

"Hmmm. I see. Go on."

"I've given out a lot of medals, and every single one of them helped. Like the one I gave your father."

"Have you ever heard of anyone not getting better after you gave them a medal?"

"Let me put it this way. Every single one of them has helped in some way or another. People got better, some got their faith back, some people got more time to live, and many were cured. You know what I'm sayin'? It helped in one way or another. We're all gonna die one day, Beth. But some people ain't finished with what they have to do here and they get a second chance. For others, it's their time to go. God has some other plan for them, you know?"

"I just don't know what to make of this in terms of my father. He has a disease with no cure. Because he has the medal, because we pray, should I expect him one day to just get up and walk and be perfectly fine?" Bethany asked.

"Let me ask you this…has your father been better since he's had the medal?

"Yes. Even the doctors can't believe how well he's doing. They say he could be in remission though, even though they thought remission at this stage was out of the question."

"You see," Jimmy said as he leaned back in his chair and pointed a finger at her. "It's workin'. I think you're doin' better too, no?"

"I am actually…since I met you," she said.

"Good. That's what it's all about. Padre Pio will always be there for your father. You remember that. If you think, if you believe he's gonna help you, Padre Pio will help you," Jimmy said. "There's no doubt about it. You might not win, but he's gonna make you win. Do you know what I'm sayin'?"

"I think so," said Bethany.

"Let me tell you some more."

Jimmy continued to tell her story after story until at least an hour had passed. Bethany was spellbound.

Bethany took a long breath. "I don't know what to say. It's amazing. It's unbelievable."

"All true. On that note, I gotta run. It's ten already," he said, looking at his watch. "I have more for you though. Lots more. We'll get together next week." Jimmy stood and zipped up his jacket.

"Everything's gonna be fine, Beth...I'm tellin' you."

Bethany felt like she was going to cry, but she was able to stay in control. There was just something about the way he spoke to her and understood her. She stood up and looked Jimmy in the eye. "I know I've told you before...but thank you. Thank you for helping me."

"You're alright, kid. Just keep prayin'." Jimmy gave her a smile and headed out the door.

Nineteen

John Fitzpatrick continued to gain strength and get better, while Jimmy continued to check on Bethany and tell her stories of Padre Pio. Because her father was doing so well, Bethany had a little more flexibility and freedom. She decided to try and set up a date to see Sarah and Cassandra. They were able to coordinate their schedules and decided to meet at a Japanese restaurant in Huntington the following Friday.

Bethany couldn't believe how much better she was feeling than the last time they had all gotten together. She debated whether or not to tell them about Jimmy. A part of her wanted to share the experience with her friends, but she decided to wait and see how the evening was going.

Bethany arrived at the restaurant first. She was greeted by a very friendly, Japanese hostess dressed in black. "Right this way," the woman said in broken English, leading Bethany to a booth. Bethany sat down and began to peruse the menu. Everything looked wonderful, and it had been some time since she had eaten Japanese food. She had her eye on a tuna sashimi dish when she saw Cassandra walk in and wave.

"Hi!" Cassandra said with her usual happy smile. "You look great!" She took a step back and admired Bethany. For the first time in quite a while Bethany had spent some time fixing herself up. She was so accustomed to always having her hair up in a ponytail at the bakery, she had forgotten how nice it was to wear it down and styled. She had even taken her time applying makeup.

"I feel good," Bethany said.

"I'm so glad," Cassandra said, giving her a hug before she sat down. She opened her menu.

"So where's Sarah?" Bethany asked. "The queen hasn't left the castle yet?" She grinned.

"You're so bad." Cassandra laughed.

As if on cue, Sarah bolted through the door, overdressed in her fur coat.

"Hello, hello," she said. "Sorry I'm late. Brian hadn't come home yet and I had to wait for my mom to come over to watch the kids. Oh, where can I put this?" Sarah asked, wondering what to do with her gigantic fur coat.

"Isn't it starting to get a little warm for that?" Bethany asked with a smile. Cassandra tried not to laugh.

"Oh, I just threw on the first thing I saw and out the door I went," she explained, carefully folding her napkin on her lap.

"To be you..." Bethany said.

"I'm serious," Sarah said. "It was like a madhouse just trying to get out the door."

Bethany smiled.

"So what are you girls ordering? How is everyone?" Sarah asked.

It only took them a moment to decide what to order. Once they had placed their orders and started to sip their wine, Sarah finally seemed to relax. She spoke first, which was usually the custom. She always seemed to have the most to say.

"Disney was fabulous," said Sarah. "It wasn't too crowded, the weather was great...The kids were just on cloud nine. I managed to get in some spa time which I *so* needed. Disney's a big place. Do you realize how much walking we did?"

Bethany and Cassandra raised their eyebrows and smiled.

"Anyway, so all was good until it came time to go to the airport. Christopher threw up his breakfast on the shuttle! Can you imagine? What a disaster!"

"Were there other people on the shuttle with you?" asked Cassandra.

"Of course! Please..." Sarah waved her hand around. "I wanted to throw up myself."

"This is lovely dinner conversation," said Bethany.

"I apologize, but I just *had* to tell you. I'll spare you the details of what we had to do to get him cleaned up. Then, the day after we got home, my interior designer wanted to swing by and talk about my latest project. Ugh, I just didn't feel like dealing with her. She can be so difficult sometimes. It's her way or no way."

"Didn't you hire her though?" Bethany asked.

"Well, yes, she's the best there is. The problem is she knows it. It's her attitude that gets to me... "

"It's not easy being you." Cassandra smiled.

"I'm telling you...it's just craziness! It doesn't stop."

When Sarah had exhausted herself, Bethany asked Cassandra what she'd been up to lately.

"Well, nothing quite as interesting as Sarah," she said. "While you were enjoying Disney, Sarah, I was busy cleaning up a flood in the basement. You missed all the rain. I spent the day with the Shop-vac."

"Where was Mark?" Sarah asked.

"Working of course." Cassandra laughed. "These things never happen when he's home. That would be too convenient. If that's not bad enough, we just found out we need a new roof. I was hoping we'd get another year out of it, but it's not looking good. We just don't have the money for it right now. We'll have to somehow come up with it. But...on the positive side, everything else is good. The kids are doing well...everyone is fine. Work is good. I can't complain." Cassandra smiled again.

Bethany couldn't believe how different all of their lives seemed to be. It was amazing they got along as well as they did. By the time Bethany had gotten a chance to speak they had finished their appetizers and were almost through with their entrees.

"So tell us, Beth, how are things at the bakery? And what wonderful news that your father is doing so well!" Sarah said.

Bethany filled them in on the bakery, which took all of about two minutes, and then she moved on to talking about her father. She began by telling them about the hospital stay and the rehab, which they both had already heard a little about during a prior phone conversation, and then Bethany began telling them how much he had improved since coming home.

"That's unbelievable. He was doing so terribly, and now...well, it's amazing," Cassandra said.

"What do his doctors make of it?" Sarah asked. "I guess he's in remission."

"That's what a lot of people say," Bethany said. "However, in his case a remission to this degree wasn't too likely. Even the doctors can't explain it."

"Well, there's nothing else it could be though, right?" asked Sarah.

Bethany looked at her friends who were waiting patiently for her to continue. She wondered if she should tell them. She looked from one to the other.

"What is it?" Cassandra asked. "Is everything okay?"

Bethany took a deep breath and let out a sigh. She placed her chopsticks down on the side of the bowl and began to speak.

"Everything is definitely okay, but I just don't know where to begin. A lot of strange things have been happening to me lately."

"You found a boyfriend!" Sarah interrupted excitedly.

"What? No. No, that's not it at all. What does that have to do with anything anyway?" Bethany asked.

"I'm sorry, I'm sorry. You just look so good...go on."

"Boy, I must have looked like a real wreck when I saw you two last."

"I said I'm sorry."

"Okay, well, you knew how upset I was about everything that was going on with my father."

"Of course we did," said Cassandra. "We always felt so helpless. We wish we could take the pain away for you." Sarah nodded in agreement.

"I appreciate that," Bethany said, "but no one really knows what it's like to go through this unless you've actually gone through it.

However, there has been someone who's been helping me. One of my customers from the bakery."

"Really?" asked Sarah.

"Yeah, it's really weird. He just started showing up one day and telling me things. In fact, remember when we went to Villa La Marco? He was there that night. He was eating alone. I recognized him when he came into the bakery."

Sarah gave a quick glance to Cassandra. "So there *is* a guy then. He's interested in you."

"Oh, God, no," Bethany quickly said. "It's not like that at all. He's older. Late fifties, early sixties. A big Italian guy from Brooklyn. At least I think he's from Brooklyn. He sounds like he is, but then again..." Bethany looked at her friends who seemed confused. "It's all kind of strange, actually. Have either of you heard of a man named Padre Pio? He was a friar in Italy."

"No. I can't say I've ever heard of him," said Cassandra.

"Me neither," Sarah said.

"He had the stigmata...the five wounds of Christ," Bethany said.

"Is he still alive?" Sarah asked.

"He died in 1968." said Bethany. "Anyway, it's possible he may become a saint one day. He performed miracles. He still does."

"How is that possible if he's dead?" asked Sarah.

"Well that's just it," said Bethany, "he still performs miracles. He cures people; he helps the sick. He has so many other gifts too. The gift of perfume, reading hearts...he knows if someone is lying; he's appeared in two places at the same time. People have even seen him since his death."

Bethany waited for her friends to say something, but they simply stared at her. "What?" Bethany asked, frustrated that they didn't seem to be following her.

"We're all Catholic here, Beth. Why haven't we heard of this guy?" asked Sarah.

"He's very well known in Italy, but he's getting really popular here in the United States as well," Bethany said. "Jimmy told me that the church is scared of him. They don't know what to make of him."

"This guy Jimmy…he's the one who's been coming into Giovanni's?" asked Sarah.

"Yes," said Bethany.

"How does he know about Padre Pio and why was he telling you?" asked Cassandra.

"He came to me at a really bad time. I was at the end of my rope. He started telling me about Padre Pio. I've enjoyed his stories and his company, frankly. He's made me feel like I'm not in this whole thing alone. Anyway, he told me I should pray to Padre Pio to help my father. He gave me a silver medal from Italy which has a relic on the back. He told me to give it to my dad. Ever since, he's been doing well," Bethany stated.

"Are you sure this guy Jimmy isn't some crazy fanatic?" asked Sarah.

"He's not. I know he's not. You'd have to meet him to understand," said Bethany.

"How much do you know about him?" Cassandra asked.

"About who? Jimmy?"

Cassandra nodded.

"I know a little," Bethany said. "He lives around Northport somewhere and he's some kind of social worker. He likes my cannolis."

Sarah glanced at Cassandra, which made Bethany somewhat uncomfortable. "What is it?" Bethany asked. "What's wrong?"

"You really don't know who he is, do you?" asked Sarah.

"Actually I think I do know who he is, but you'll probably never believe me." Bethany took a deep breath. "I don't know if he's of this world."

"What?" exclaimed Cassandra.

Bethany regretted saying it as soon as it came out of her mouth. She must have sounded nuts. She had to give some explanation now.

"What is that supposed to mean, Beth?" asked Sarah.

"I've been reading up about angels…there is a possibility he is one."

Sarah and Cassandra both leaned back in their chairs. They exchanged glances again.

"What is going on with you two?" Bethany said. "Why don't you believe me? You said yourself I'm better, and my father is better. How do you think that's possible?"

"Honey, listen…" Sarah said softly. "You've been through so much. We can't even comprehend what it must be like for you."

You have no idea, Bethany thought.

"It's just when you're in a state like that, you become vulnerable," Sarah continued. "Someone comes around and you start falling for things. Did this guy say your father would be cured, Beth? If so, he's taking advantage of you. Why? I have no idea, but he's playing with your head."

"We're worried about you," Cassandra added. "That's all."

"He's taking advantage of me? Are you kidding?" Bethany could feel her blood pressure rising along with her voice. "He's helped me through this whole thing. So what do you think; that I've gone nuts or something? You don't believe me?"

"Beth, look at yourself. Listen to what you're saying. It sounds preposterous. It sounds scary and creepy, if you ask me. This is not reality here. We're looking out for your well-being," Sarah said, leaning in closer to Bethany.

"I'm really shocked by the two of you. I really am…and hurt also. You wouldn't even let me finish what I had to say before you started jumping to conclusions and lecturing me. I can't believe that you actually don't believe me! Jimmy is the only person who understands what I go through. He is the only person who has given me hope and strength and something to live for, and you want to try to convince me that he's some kind of a nut job? A stalker? What exactly do you think?"

Bethany paused and stared at them for a moment. They didn't respond. "I'm a big girl," Bethany continued. "You forget how old I was when I lost my mother…you forget how old I was when I had to give up everything, all of my dreams to take care of my father. I had to grow up real fast. So I'd like to remind you that I can take care of myself, and neither one of you have the right to tell me who I can and cannot be friends with. I've spoken to my father about Jimmy and he believes me. He thinks the same thing. So is he crazy also?

Oh, but that's right, I forgot that people get crazy when they're sick and old, don't they?"

Bethany turned and looked at Cassandra who was crying. Sarah remained stone-faced. With neither of them saying anything in return, Bethany picked up her pocketbook, pulled out some twenties from her wallet, and threw them on the table. She stood up and looked down at them. "Thanks for a great evening."

She saw the looks on the other customers' faces and she didn't care what they thought. Bethany stormed out of the restaurant, and it wasn't until she was safely in her car that she burst into tears.

Twenty

Bethany arrived at the bakery earlier than usual on Saturday morning. She'd had a terrible night's sleep. Rather than tossing and turning in the early morning hours, she got herself up, showered, and left Rob and her father a note stating that she was heading out early. She arrived at the bakery just as the sun was beginning to rise. She wasn't as emotional as when she left the restaurant the night before, but she was still quite upset and hurt.

What bothered her most about everything that had happened was that she had begun to question herself. What if it *was* a coincidence that her father was getting better? What if Jimmy wasn't an angel? Who was he then, and what was she getting involved in? Prior to last night she had been feeling so much better. She felt like she had been given a second chance with God, that she had found a friend who understood her, as odd as her relationship with Jimmy was. Bethany didn't like having doubts now.

She busied herself in the kitchen so her mind would stop thinking further on the matter. Cooking was the one thing that always offered her an escape. She prepared bread dough; she made muffins, scones, a cheesecake. By the time Alison arrived, the cases were fully stocked.

"Wow, you've been busy!" Alison said when she came in at seven. "How'd you get all this done so fast?"

"I came in early," Bethany said.

Alison did not ask any more questions. She put on her apron and headed out front to put on pots of coffee.

Bethany started making the mix for a chocolate mousse cake. By eight it was already set to go into the oven and she started making Italian pastries. Two hours later Bethany looked up at the clock. She was surprised by all she had accomplished.

"I'm taking a break," Bethany said to Alison as she grabbed herself a cup of coffee. "I'll be out back." When Bethany first took over the bakery, she had placed a small garden bench in a grassy area next to the back parking lot. This was where she went when she needed solitude. The patio tables outside the front of the store offered much better views, but Saturday mornings were typically busy, with customers coming in and out. It was a beautiful, sunny day, and Bethany knew that people would want to sit around the tables. She just wasn't in the mood to talk to anyone, so her bench provided her the seclusion she longed for.

Bethany, in her chef's coat and black and white checkered pants, left the kitchen and headed to the bench and sat down. For the first time in a long time the bench was warm beneath her. It made her feel better somehow. She sat sipping her long awaited cup of coffee, and then she looked up to the sun and enjoyed the rays on her face. She pulled her hair out of its ponytail and tucked the loose strands behind her ears. She took a sip of coffee and sat silently, trying desperately not to keep going over last night's chain of events.

She closed her eyes and tried to image herself elsewhere, on the beach maybe, having nothing to do but relax. She began to think what if must feel like to truly relax, to take a vacation, to not have a care in the world. Her thoughts were quickly interrupted.

"What's up?"

Bethany opened her eyes and saw Jimmy walking toward her.

"Hi," she said sadly.

"What's goin' on?"

"Nothing really. Taking a break."

Bethany stared down at her almost empty cup of coffee.

Jimmy said, "Mind if I sit down?"

She moved over on the bench. He sat down and said nothing. Bethany turned her head and looked over at him. He was staring out in the distance. She put her head back down, not having anything to say.

"Tell me what's goin' on," Jimmy said. "I know it's not your father this time."

"It's nothing, really," Bethany said. There was silence again.

Jimmy seemed to be thinking. "Don't listen to them," he said suddenly.

Bethany turned abruptly. "What are you talking about?"

"I said, don't listen to them. They don't know what they're talkin' about. They can't understand."

"Who?"

"Your friends," Jimmy said. He turned and looked at her and their eyes locked.

Bethany just stared at him for a moment. "How do you know this?" Bethany asked.

"Because I know stuff."

Bethany bent forward, put her elbows on her knees, and propped her head up. She began rubbing her forehead as if to wake up her brain. She didn't know what to make of this. She sat up and looked at him again. She had so many more questions, but what could she possibly say to him?

"Your life is kinda runnin' parallel to Jesus Christ and Padre Pio right now; you understand what I'm sayin'?"

"What do you mean?"

"Jesus knew stuff. He experienced stuff. Padre Pio knew stuff and he experienced stuff. When they tried to tell people, no one believed them." He turned and looked at Bethany. "They knew people would come around eventually, but it was a lonely world for them, you know? People didn't believe them. People thought they were crazy. The people wanted proof. And you know why they wanted proof?" Jimmy asked. "Because they didn't have any faith. They would only believe if they saw."

Bethany thought about that for a moment.

"Go with what's in your heart…what feels right," Jimmy said, tapping his chest. "It's all in here. All the answers."

"I doubt things sometimes," Bethany revealed. "They put doubt in my head."

"Don't listen to them. You've come too far, Beth. Don't let it get the best of you. You know what I'm sayin' here? You've got your faith back. God is on your side, helpin' you through these tough times…and so is Padre Pio. I'm tellin' you. You'll see." They sat together quietly for a few minutes. "Can I ask you somethin'?"

Bethany nodded. "Sure."

"What happened? How'd you come to take care of your dad. Where's your mother? If you don't mind my askin'."

Bethany sat up, took a deep breath and sighed. It wasn't a topic she talked about much anymore, but since he asked, she felt compelled to tell him. "It was March...my senior year at the Culinary Institute. It was two months until graduation. I was fortunate because I had this really good job lined up in New York City. I was going to work and train with this renowned pastry chef on the Upper East Side. My mom and I had begun looking for an apartment." She smiled sadly. "Late one night I received a phone call from my father. He sounded frantic. I thought something had happened to him, but it didn't make sense. If something did happen my mother would have been the one to call, not him. My father proceeded to tell me that my mother had been in a terrible accident…a car accident. Then he started crying over the phone. I couldn't register what was going on. I can remember it so clearly, like it happened yesterday. My heart was beating so fast. I was screaming, 'Daddy, what happened?' He then told me that my mother was gone...dead. The details at the time were a blur. Apparently, my mom had been driving home from her best friend Laney's house. She lived in Cold Spring Harbor. Laney was a breast cancer survivor, and she'd just come home from the hospital after having a small procedure. My mom, as always, was there to help and had brought her over a home cooked meal. She stayed with Laney until eight that evening. By the time she left it had started raining. Mom was a cautious driver. I'm sure she was taking her time. She was less than a mile from home when it happened."

Bethany took another deep breath. It was painful for her to talk about it. "As she drove around that sharp bend on Route 25A, an SUV headed westbound took the turn too fast. The SUV lost control, and slammed into my mom's car. The impact sent my mom's car into a tailspin. Her Nissan flipped over and hit a tree...she died upon impact. The three teenage boys in the SUV walked away without even a scratch." Bethany turned her head and looked at Jimmy.

"I'm sorry," Jimmy said. "I can't tell you why these things happen. I'm guessin' your father was already sick at the time?"

"Yes, he was. He had been diagnosed with MS during my junior year of high school. Those were awful days too. It had taken the doctor a solid year to figure out what was wrong with him. His early symptoms seemed minor, but they were definitely noticeable. He'd drop his fork while eating...when resting with his feet up, his right leg would start to shake and his knee would pop up. His walking became different, stiff, and he would trip over the littlest of things. He would blame it on being tired. It wasn't until one Christmas Eve when everything came to a head. In the busy rush between masses at church, my Dad tripped and fell. Do you have any idea, Jimmy, what it was like to watch my tall, proud father come crashing to the ground like a tree that was just cut down?"

Bethany didn't wait for him to answer. "It was so horrible. It came out of nowhere. His reaction was slow. He never even put his hands out in an attempt to stop the fall. I remember my mother yelled out when she saw my Dad on the ground in his suit and tie. He rolled to one side, and there was blood on his left hand and left cheek from cuts sustained from hitting the graveled pavement. My brother, Steven, immediately rushed to his side, and with the help of another parishioner, they lifted him to his feet. I just stood there frozen and in shock as I watched the scene unfold. I honestly don't know what upset me more, the physical act of my father falling and the threat of him getting hurt, or the humiliation I knew my dad was feeling. My father was a strong, powerful, and generous man. I've looked up to him my entire life. I still do. I knew then something was terribly wrong. It was awful because he was only forty-eight when he was diagnosed. They tested him for everything known to man...a brain tumor, Parkinson's disease, Lou Gehrig's disease, to name a few. After months of studies, observations, and tests, it was finally determined that he had MS. None of us knew anything about the disease at the time. It was slow to progress, but he began to have difficulty walking. He felt defeated when he had no choice but to start using a cane. My mom did everything for him. She took him to his doctors' appointments, laid out all his medications, helped him get dressed on his bad days, helped him when he had difficulty walking..."

Bethany paused a moment before continuing. "He was a lawyer, and he began to work less and less because he would become extremely fatigued. He had trouble typing and holding a pen; even reading strained his eyes, which were also affected by the disease. Because his reflexes were slowing down, my Dad could no longer drive a car either. It was really upsetting to watch." Bethany lowered her head as she remembered those early days.

"You mentioned a brother. What happened to him?" Jimmy asked. "He's not around to help you?"

Bethany paused as she collected her thoughts. "My brother Steven had a really difficult time of it. Instead of becoming more involved and trying to help, he distanced himself. He couldn't mentally deal with what was happening. My father had always been a tower of strength to Steven...to us all, but it was hard for him. Eventually he met a woman from Colorado. He found a job out there and they got married. Her family lives there. I didn't fault him, but there was a part of me that begrudged him. When my mother died he came in for several weeks, but ultimately it was me who was going to have to take care of my father. Knowing this, I gave up the job and moved back home."

"That musta been hard for you."

"It was. It wasn't just that though. I always thought I'd get married too."

"You still have time for that, you know? You're young. You got a lotta years ahead of you."

Bethany shrugged. "As long as my father is this way and I'm the one taking care of him, it's not going to happen. I don't even have time to date. I don't know why I'm telling you all of this." She looked back at Jimmy wondering if he somehow already knew about all the things she said.

"Things change. They always do, Beth."

"I know, and please don't think I wish anything bad on my father. I don't. I love him so much. It's difficult at times, but I don't regret my decisions. His siblings wanted to put him in a nursing home. They said I was too young to take care of him...that it would be too much of a burden. How could I put the man who raised me, a man so young, in a nursing home? I couldn't, Jimmy."

"I understand where you're comin' from. You're a lot stronger than you think. You know?"

Bethany smiled. "I don't think so...but thanks."

"And how'd you get this place?"

"The bakery? By luck, I guess you could say. I worked as a sous chef at some local restaurants for a while until I landed a job as a pastry chef in a restaurant in Roslyn. I had a live-in aide by then, which helped. His name is Rob. He's still with us. He's been my life support. And then there's Cherie. She's an aide too, but works part-time. She helps with a lot of the cleaning. Anyway, even with all the help, the forty-five minute commute to Roslyn and back was too much. I felt like I was too far away if something happened. After three years I found out the Olde Towne Bakery was up for sale. The Thomsons, the bakery's original owners, decided they were ready to retire. They were looking for someone to buy them out and take over the bakery. They knew my family for years, so they offered the business to me first. I knew I was young, but I had a lot of experience. I wanted something that was mine. The fact that it was less than a mile away was perfect. I could get home if I needed to. I had saved quite a bit of money over the years from not having had to pay rent or expenses. That was one benefit to the situation, I suppose. My father offered me money so I wouldn't have to take out a loan for the rest, but I felt I needed to do this on my own, so I did. Renovations began almost immediately. The bakery had been here for forty years and looked the same as it did when it first opened. There was a part of me that felt bad for having changed it, but like I said, I needed something of my own. Something a little more modern and upscale."

"You've done good. You know that? It couldn't have been easy takin' on somethin' like that, especially under the circumstances."

"I worried about it a little, but things seemed to work out. It was a good decision."

"How'd you come up with the name?" asked Jimmy.

"That was the easy part. Giovanni was my mother's maiden name. She was the first person who taught me how to cook and bake. It was only fitting."

"That was definitely a good choice."

"I think so." Bethany looked at Jimmy and smiled. "Well...that's my story."

Jimmy studied her for a moment. "And you don't believe, after everything you've told me...that you're a strong person? Look at what you've been capable of doin'. Look at what you've achieved. You gotta apply that strength to what your goin' through now. You understand me? Things get rough sometimes. Know that you *are* strong...that you *can* make it through. No matta what anybody tells you...no matta what anyone believes."

Bethany listened to him intently. "It just hurts when my own friends question me...doubt me. They don't understand."

"That's right they don't understand. They may try, but they're not in your shoes. Don't doubt yourself because they don't understand. You hear me?"

Bethany nodded.

"Let me tell you somethin'," said Jimmy. "It's amazin' what Padre Pio went through. I think I may have told you that the church was scared of him. They were scared of Padre Pio because he had the stigmata, and he had special powers and stuff. Just like Jesus Christ. They didn't believe him, just like your friends ain't believin' you now. You know somethin' else? If Christ came back today, you think the church would believe it was him? Look what the Pharisees did to Christ way back when. They didn't believe him." Jimmy paused. "Same goes with Padre Pio. They put him in seclusion, you know? He couldn't do nothin' for years. The church said he was a fraud, that he cut his hands, this and that. They tested him, just like they tested Jesus. They really tortured Padre Pio. They put him through all kinds of medical tests. He suffered a lotta years...a lotta years." Jimmy paused "After eight years, eight years, Bethany, if you can believe it, they stopped the tests and investigations. I think it was 1933. He was finally released of all the accusations. Lies...that's all it was. They were scared of him...I'm tellin' you. The point I'm tryin' to make here is that what you're goin' through is kinda like what Padre Pio went through, the pain, the sufferin', nobody believin' him. Think about it. If you need Padre Pio, he's there for you, so don't listen to whatever anybody else tells you. What do they know? Don't doubt, Bethany...believe."

Everything Jimmy said made sense to her. If Padre Pio could get through those terrible times, she could surely get through this.

"It's gonna be alright. I've told you. You'll see," said Jimmy. He patted her on the knee. "You feel better?"

Bethany smiled. "I do actually. And I'll think about what you said."

"You do that...and keep prayin'." Jimmy stood up and looked down at Bethany. "I'll see ya around?"

"Yeah, Jimmy. I'll see you around."

She watched as he walked away. "Jimmy!" He stopped and turned around. "Thank you...again."

"Believe, Beth...just believe."

Twenty-One

In the days that followed, Bethany began to feel more like herself again. She apologized to her friends for overreacting. In turn, Sarah and Cassandra admitted they could have been a little bit more understanding and heard Bethany out. She was sure that they still thought she was nuts though. Going forward, Bethany decided it would be best if she didn't bring Jimmy up to them.

Jimmy had stopped by Giovanni's at least twice that week to check on Bethany and to make sure that she was back on track. At the same time, Bethany's father continued to do exceptionally well.

Easter came and went, and Bethany was extremely busy at the bakery filling orders for cakes and pastries. The spring was always her craziest time, between Easter, communions, confirmations, weddings, proms, and graduations. At night, she tried to take some time for herself and took the dogs for long walks once daylight savings had arrived. Afterwards she would join her father in the parlor where they'd talk about everything under the sun.

When Bethany looked at him she felt happy. She could not imagine his condition getting worse again, and she sometimes wondered if he was on borrowed time. She did her best to push those thoughts out of her mind. He was doing fine and that's all that mattered. She hoped that when the time came, everything she had been through and learned would give her strength. For now, she just wanted to spend as much time with her father as possible.

The night of the presentation by Antoinette Filetti at the church in Oyster Bay was quickly approaching. Bethany was looking forward to going and listening to the woman's story.

She made it to St. Michael's church in plenty of time. There were already a good amount of people sitting in the pews. Bethany looked around the small church, which was quite old and enriched in beautiful stonework and stained glass windows. In one corner she saw rows of votive candles on display, and she decided to make her way over to light a candle for her father. After she did so, she placed two dollars in the receptacle and then she knelt down to pray. When she looked up, there was a picture of Padre Pio's face looking down upon her. It appeared in a simple frame and stood upright on a large marble slab. Next to it was a giant statue of St. Francis. Bethany recalled reading that St. Francis, like Padre Pio, had the stigmata. He had been a friar as well. Padre Pio had a vision of St. Francis when he was five years old and then again when he went into the military. According to what Bethany had read, Padre Pio was quite upset to be away from the Capuchin Friars during his time in the military. For some reason he believed his order would dismiss him. It was St. Francis who came to him in a vision in order to console him. From that point on, Padre Pio had a deep love and devotion to the saint and he imitated his life.

Bethany stared at the statue of St. Francis and of the picture of Padre Pio. She knew for some reason that she was supposed to be here in St. Michael's Church. She bowed her head and blessed herself, and then said a prayer. Bethany rose and walked around to the left side of the church, and was led by an usher to a pew in the middle section. She was handed a booklet. She thanked the man and sat down. When she looked through the booklet she discovered that immediately following the presentation, a special healing ceremony would take place. Bethany had heard of healing masses before, but had never attended one. She really had no idea what to expect.

Within a few moments a woman came out onto the altar and announced that the presentation would begin. Another woman sat down at a nearby piano while three other women dressed in long, burgundy robes stood behind her. When the woman began to play the piano, the women behind her started to sing. Almost instantly the majority of the people in the pews stood and began waving their arms back and forth, high in the air, while singing along loudly.

Oh my God, Bethany thought as she looked around. She had not expected this to be a charismatic event at all, and she felt quite uncomfortable and out of place. She didn't know what to do. Bethany was very reserved when it came to her religion and prayer. She was very private about the whole thing and seeing this spectacle confused her. *The holy rollers.* She was glad when the song ended and everyone sat down. A priest went over to the altar, bowed, and gave a blessing. He then walked over to the pulpit where he did the sign of the cross and thanked everyone for coming.

"Tonight we are going to hear the most remarkable story of divine intervention," the priest began. "Antoinette Filetti will share with you her difficult journey through illness, and her renewed faith and joy because of her encounter with a Capuchin Friar from Italy named Padre Pio."

The crowd instantly began to cheer and shout out Padre Pio's name. Bethany could not believe it. She had never seen people cheering for someone in a church before. When the crowd quieted the priest continued.

"It was through Padre Pio that Mrs. Filetti became glorified with God; that she believed and had faith that God would stand by her. Through his powerful intercession he sent Padre Pio to cure her, and the experience has changed her life forever. At this time, I would like you to please welcome Antoinette Filetti."

Everyone began to clap and Bethany watched as a tall, middle-aged woman with cropped blond hair made her way to the pulpit. After thanking the audience for coming, Antoinette started to reveal her story. She spoke of being diagnosed with a very aggressive form of breast cancer which would require a complete mastectomy of both breasts. If she didn't have the surgery she would be dead within six months. She told the audience how devastated she'd been, how it affected her family, how she'd thought God had given up on her.

Bethany listened intently and was able to relate to so many of the woman's feelings of hopelessness. Two weeks before Antoinette's scheduled surgery, she'd decided to go down to a nearby beach and take a peaceful walk. She explained that as she walked the secluded beach she spoke to God and begged him to help her, to give her a sign, to somehow rid her of this terrible disease. She walked for about an hour and then headed back to her car. As she began driving out of the parking lot, she sensed that something was very wrong with the car. To her dismay, her left front tire had gone flat. When she went to place a call from her cell phone to get help, she realized she wasn't getting a signal. She tried not to panic. There was not a soul around, and it wasn't a location where traffic would be passing. She got out of the car and checked the trunk for the spare. It was flat. She closed the trunk, leaned up against her car, and began to cry.

A tear rolled down Bethany's cheek as she listened.

"After about ten minutes I got back in my car and just sat there, completely clueless as to what to do," Antoinette said. "I happened to look in my rearview mirror. In it, I saw a man walking towards my car. He was about a hundred or so feet away. I didn't know whether to feel relieved or scared. Where had this man come from? I felt very unnerved and vulnerable. I really didn't know if I was safe. I rolled my window up more than halfway and locked the doors." Antoinette paused for a few moments, her eyes closed, seemingly reliving the day. She then looked out at her rapt audience, smiled, and continued.

"As he approached, I could see that he was an older man, late sixties maybe. He had grayish white hair and a beard. He was dressed all in black. I sat in my car nervously as he approached. He immediately saw the flat tire. He asked me through my window if I had a spare. I explained that it was flat. He must have known that I was upset. He told me he'd wait with me until someone came around. He told me not to be afraid. Cautiously I got out of the car. There was something very pleasant and comforting about his face, and I felt somewhat reassured that I wasn't in the presence of a rapist or murderer. I leaned up against the car and started telling him what had happened, and that I couldn't get service on my cell phone. He reassured me that everything would be okay, and that he wouldn't leave me until help arrived. I insisted he didn't have to do that. It never even dawned on me to ask him where his own car was or where he had come from. I began to relax. He seemed very, very kind.

"While we waited, he began to ask me questions. 'Is everything all right with you?' he asked. 'It seems like there is more troubling you than the flat tire.' I looked at him and felt compelled to tell him of my cancer. I told him how afraid I felt.

"At one point I started to cry." Antoinette cleared her throat and looked out at the crowd. "The man put his hand on my shoulder. I could not believe how comforting this stranger was. 'God will help you,' he said to me. Then he asked if I would mind if he prayed over me. I was surprised at his gesture but I didn't refuse. He stood and faced me. He then lowered his head and raised his hand over me. When he began to speak, it wasn't in English. It was in Italian, which surprised me, because he had no accent when he spoke to me in English. 'You will be cured,' he said to me. I honestly didn't know what to make of that. No sooner did he say that, than I felt electricity fill up inside me. Something was happening but I didn't know what. Something was telling me that it was going to be okay. The feelings lasted a few minutes. I felt overwhelmed by the experience. As soon as the sensation stopped, a tow truck just happened to come around the bend. I couldn't have been happier. The driver saw my situation and pulled over. I walked over to talk to him. He said he'd tow the car to town and then he'd blow up the spare tire and put it on for me. I was overjoyed. When I turned around to go back to my car, the man with the beard was gone...completely gone. 'Where is the man who was with me?' I asked the tow truck driver. 'Did you see him leave?' He looked at me, confused, and told me he hadn't seen a man when he pulled up. I thought maybe I was going crazy. I looked around again, but the man was clearly gone. He had simply vanished."

Bethany was mesmerized by her every word. Her story was just like the ones Jimmy had told her. Maybe all of Jimmy's stories really were true. Antoinette continued to tell the chain of events which led up to the day before her surgery. She was told to go to the hospital for some pre-op procedures. When the doctors took one last set of films they were completely shocked by what they saw. The tumors in her breasts were completely gone. They were nonexistent, and for the life of them, they couldn't figure out how. More blood was drawn to determine the white blood count, and a rush was placed on the lab to get the results as soon as possible. Her tests came out clean and her white blood count levels were normal.

"I knew immediately that it had been the man who came to me. I cannot begin to tell you how elated I was. A miracle had taken place," Antoinette announced to the crowd, who began to cheer.

Several weeks later Antoinette Filetti was visiting her daughter at college and was completely cancer free. At a church near the school, Antoinette had stumbled upon a photograph and a statue of Padre Pio. She started excitedly telling her daughter that this was the man who had cured her. Her daughter took a closer look at the photo. She explained to her mother that it was impossible. The man's birth and death dates appeared below the photograph. It was from that point on that Antoinette Filetti began her journey to learn more about Padre Pio.

Bethany eyes welled up and more tears began to fall. Antoinette left the pulpit and headed back to her seat while the audience applauded loudly. Bethany took a tissue out of her pocketbook and wiped her eyes. Shortly thereafter, a gentleman came up to the altar and stated that the healing part of the evening was going to begin. People quickly began leaving their pews and started to line up in the center aisle. Bethany remained seated. She wanted to see what this was all about. The man who had just spoken, along with two other women and the priest, stood in a semicircle at the altar. Two other men stood alongside them. When they were ready, they called the people up one at a time. A woman about the same age as Bethany was first. The woman walked up to the group and they raised their hands over her and began saying prayers. Meanwhile, the two men who had been standing by went and stood behind the woman. Within seconds the woman looked as if she had passed out. The men behind her caught her and then placed her gently down on the floor of the altar. Bethany rose slightly out of her seat, scared by what she had just witnessed. *What was happening to this woman?*

The priest and the other people who were praying seemed unfazed by the incident. Bethany could not figure out what was going on. She had only read about such things. A minute or so later, the woman sat up and seemed a little stunned. The men helped her up and she simply walked away. Bethany watched as person after person made their way up to the altar. There were people of all ages. Some of them were people who were physically ill, while others came for spiritual healing. Whatever their reasons, practically every single person fainted. Bethany could not understand this. She blamed it on the fact that they were the holy rollers, the ones who wanted to make spectacles of themselves in the name of religion. While Bethany was contemplating this she was tapped on the shoulder.

"Would you like to go up, ma'am?" a woman said to her.

Bethany felt instantly sick. She didn't know what to do. Something had led her to all of this, so a part of her thought she needed to continue. The other part of her was terrified...terrified of the unknown; of what would happen, of what she was getting involved in. Despite these feelings, her legs seemed to have a mind of their own. Before she could think further, her decision was made. Bethany was headed up to the altar. She felt her heart pounding in her chest. She wanted to run but she couldn't. She kept saying to herself that she would stay standing. She would not faint and find herself lying in this church at the altar. She didn't know what the people on the line were trying to prove or what they were doing.

Her heart beat even faster when she witnessed the person in front of her collapsing. Bethany's eyes were wide with fright. She hesitated when it was her turn. One of the men on the altar encouraged her. She slowly walked up and faced the small group. All of them were smiling. The two men took their places behind her. Bethany stood stiff as a board, clutching the pocketbook on her shoulder. The priest asked her to close her eyes and to listen to the word of God. When she did so, she sensed their hands rise above her, and then she heard them begin to pray and chant. All of a sudden Bethany felt a pulling sensation, an energy between their hands and her head. At the same time, she began to see a white light...the brightest light she had ever seen in her life. She wanted to see more of it. She fought hard to open her eyes, which were fluttering wildly, but she couldn't. The voices of the people praying over her began to change. She heard something she had only read about. She started to hear the gift of tongues. Each person was speaking an unknown language which made no sense to Bethany. There seemed to be voices coming from everywhere, all while the extreme white light was shining through her. As quickly as the unknown languages had come, the experience was over, and the light was gone. Bethany felt as if she had been through a whirlwind, spinning around and around.

She opened her eyes and looked up at the ceiling of the church. She quickly glanced left and then right only to be at eye level with the feet of those who had prayed over her. In a state of shock, she felt the hands of the men behind her push her gently forward. Once she was sitting up, directly in front of her were the priest's knees. Her facial expression must have said a thousand words as she realized she had been lying on the floor at the altar, her pocketbook strewn to the side of her. The men carefully helped her up and the women asked her if she was alright.

"I think so," Bethany said groggily while still in a state of shock.

"You've been touched by the Holy Spirit," the priest said and smiled.

Bethany looked at him, puzzled.

"Your eyes were fluttering more than we've seen in anyone. You fought so hard to open them. It was not your time to fully see the light of God," the priest said. "Take up your cross and give thanks to God." He blessed her by giving the sign of the cross.

Bethany picked up her pocketbook and headed out the side entrance of the church. She had absolutely no idea how she was going to manage to drive home.

Twenty-Two

When Bethany arrived home her father was already asleep, and Rob had retired to his room. She had no one to talk to about her experience at the church. She went into the parlor with the dogs following behind and sat with a cup of coffee while she pondered all that had transpired that evening. It was obvious that everything she was experiencing—Jimmy, the information on Padre Pio, her father's illness, the presentation by Antoinette Filetti, and the healing ceremony—was all somehow connected. What she didn't understand was why, with the amount of people suffering in the world, it was her who was getting help. The doubts she started to have after the night out with her friends had disappeared completely.

The story of Antoinette Filetti had a profound impact on Bethany, nor could she forget her own experience on the altar during the healing ceremony. Bethany was still in shock at how powerful it all was. She wished to see the bright, white light again; to take it in and to absorb what was happening. She was mystified by the praying in tongues. Although she had heard of the gift, it was something she never quite believed could exist in modern day. What exactly was happening to her? Bethany thought and thought until she drifted off to sleep.

"Beth, wake up…wake up," Rob said as he gently pushed her shoulders.

Bethany sat up immediately, confused and dazed.

"It's six-thirty. Don't you have to be at the bakery this morning?" Rob asked.

"Six-thirty? Oh, my God, I've got to get out of here!" Bethany jumped to her feet.

"What happened? You fell asleep here last night?" asked Rob.

"Yes…I must have." She looked around for her shoes. "Can you make Daddy something for breakfast? I told him I was going to make him something today."

"No problem. Just go. Take care of yourself," Rob said as he took the coffee cup which had been left on the end table.

"What a way to start the day," Bethany said racing out of the room. From the staircase she yelled "And tell Daddy I'll talk to him tonight."

She quickly showered and pulled her wet hair into a sleek ponytail, and within minutes she was out the door. When she arrived at Giovanni's, she found Alison waiting outside.

"I was just about to call you," Alison said. "Was I supposed to open up today? I didn't bring the key."

"No, not at all," Bethany said, rushing to unlock the back door. "It's my fault. I fell asleep in the parlor last night. Rob found me there this morning and woke me."

"Jeez, that's not like you," Alison said. "Here, I'll help."

The two women worked quickly to get the bakery open and running. Bethany found some muffin batter in the refrigerator and poured it into muffin tins while Alison went around turning on the ovens. Within forty minutes, things had calmed down and customers began arriving. Scones, bread, and muffins were coming out of the ovens. Bethany felt somewhat out of sync, having started the day in such a hectic manner. Her neck also ached from the way she must have slept in the chair. Despite all of it, she worked through everything and around ten-thirty, she decided to head out the back door with a bottle of water for a much needed break. To her surprise, as she headed toward her bench, Jimmy was already sitting there with his hands folded.

"How you doin'?" he asked in his usual fashion.

"I was hoping you'd come," Bethany said and sat down next to him. "I wanted to tell you about last night."

"Yeah?"

Bethany took a sip from the water bottle. Putting the cap back on she continued, "Remember I told you about the Padre Pio presentation at St. Michael's Church in Oyster Bay?"

Jimmy nodded.

"Well, it was last night. I heard the most amazing story and I had the most incredible experience."

"Tell me about it."

As Bethany began to tell him everything, there was a part of her that believed he already knew what she was going to say. He listened intently, though, and Bethany was excited to talk about it.

"I keep tellin' you…Padre Pio is a powerful man, and he's still around," Jimmy said when Bethany finished talking.

"I did have some questions for you that I hope you'd be able to answer," Bethany said. "It's about the healing part of the evening."

"Okay, I'll see what I can do."

"First, I've heard of tongues, mainly from the Bible, but I didn't really believe, or know for that matter, that people today can speak in tongues. What is it exactly?"

"Speakin' in tongues has been around for a long time," Jimmy said. "You got no idea what they're sayin', but I've heard it." He laughed. "From what I understand, all types of cultures and religions have been able to speak in tongues. For Christians though, speaking in tongues started during Pentecost, you know? Fifty days after Christ's crucifixion. You know about Pentecost, don't you?" Jimmy asked.

"I think I need a bit of a refresher course, I'm embarrassed to say," Bethany said.

"I'll tell you about it." Jimmy turned and looked at her. "The apostles and some of Jesus's followers were makin' their way to Jerusalem. They were comin' to celebrate the Jewish harvest festival. You understand?"

Bethany nodded.

"They were in some building, some house or a temple or somethin' when all of a sudden this huge sound of wind comes through, you know? Right through the house." Jimmy raised his hands up and demonstrated. "They're all sittin' there sayin', 'What the hell was that?'" Jimmy smiled and turned his head around and around as if he were experiencing it.

Bethany smiled at his reenactment.

"Anyways, there were these tongues, these fiery tongues that came through. It was the Holy Spirit. Each of these tongues reached out and touched all the people there, you know? No sooner did that happen than the people began speakin' all kinds of languages they didn't know and didn't understand neither. Can you imagine this? So here are all these people and they're told by the Holy Spirit to go out and preach the Gospel. So they go out. Now there were a lot of people in Jerusalem at the time, and they were from all over. They didn't speak the language that was spoken there. Well, the apostles, they come out in the streets, you know, and they start speaking, tellin' the Gospel. Now here's where it gets really amazin'." Jimmy smiled.

"Each person there could hear his language in his native tongue. Every single person, I'm tellin' you. This way all the people could understand. You know there were three thousand people converted that day. It was a miracle." Jimmy paused.

"It all comes back to the miracles again, doesn't it?" Bethany asked.

"That's right. So you got to experience two miracles last night. You *heard* the Holy Spirit comin' through, and you *saw* the Holy Spirit comin' through. Pretty amazin' stuff. Powerful."

"Sometimes I just can't believe all that's happened to me the last few months. Why I'm experiencing all this," Bethany said.

"You were losin' your faith."

Bethany nodded.

"You know in Italy they celebrate Pentecost by scattering red rose petals from the ceiling of the church. It represents the fiery tongues comin' down." Jimmy smiled.

They sat in silence for a moment.

"So the reason for all of this?" Bethany asked. "To help me with my faith? To help me be stronger?"

"You got it, kid. You think God's left you but he hasn't. He hasn't left your father neither. You gotta believe, I'm tellin' you. He sends Padre Pio to remind people of this; to help them. You heard the stories last night. And you also experienced a miracle. What more proof do you want?"

"I know it sounds selfish, Jimmy, but why can't my father be cured completely, like that woman I listened to?"

"What I'm gonna tell you the church don't buy into. There's a plan. Before we come down here, before we're born, we pick who we're gonna be and who we're gonna be with. There's a path we follow. It's to get us to the next level spiritually. It's how to get closer to God. Now, listen to me here," Jimmy said. "God gave us free will. We pick which way we want to go. It all works out in the end, as long as we don't screw it up along the way. If your father doesn't get cured, Beth, it don't mean God ain't there. It don't mean Padre Pio ain't there. They are. Your father's a religious man, am I correct?"

Bethany nodded.

"Well, he may have chosen this path for himself in order to move up spiritually. Sort of gettin' to the next level, if you know what I'm sayin'. Climbin' the spiritual ladder."

"So it's possible he *chose* to get MS and suffer?"

"I'm sayin' yeah, it's possible. How he lives his life, how he handles the illness, the sufferin'. It's all part of it. It also might have to do with the way you handle things as well. To make sure you stay focused and keep your faith."

"And that could be why this is all happening to me?"

"Exactly. Everyone's gonna' die, Beth. I've told you this before. And nothin's gonna change that. Even the people Padre Pio cured are gonna die. You know what I'm sayin'? But it all depends on the plan. If you mess it up, you keep comin' back until you get it right, you understand?"

"Reincarnation?" Bethany asked. "Is that what you're talking about? It definitely doesn't sound like something the church would teach."

"No, they don't teach it. The church, Beth is like a box. They teach you what's in the box. That's all they're supposed to do. You know what I'm sayin'? Some people stick to what's safe, what's in the box. Some people go deeper and go outside the box to learn more. That's okay. It's a good thing. Padre Pio went outside the box." Jimmy paused. "For now, your father's doin' good. Am I right? Padre Pio's helpin' him. That's all that matters right now, okay? When the day comes when somethin' happens that's not so good, you'll have the strength, Beth. I'm tellin' you. I ain't lyin', you know. And your father will be in a better place."

"How come you know so much?" asked Bethany.

Jimmy gave her a wide smile. "I told you...I just know stuff."

Bethany studied his face. "You want to come in for a cannoli?"

"Now you're talkin'," said Jimmy. "You just made me an offer I can't refuse."

Twenty-Three

That evening Bethany left work early so she could spend some extra time with her father. Alison was happy to close up the bakery for her. When Bethany arrived home she was pleased to see her father sitting outside in the Adirondack chair. This in itself was a miracle. She never thought her father would make it outside to his favorite spot and not be in the wheelchair.

"Mind if I join you?" Bethany asked as she sat down in the chair next to her father. He had been working on a large print crossword puzzle. He peered above his reading glasses and smiled.

"Why, of course not. I was hoping you'd be home soon. I wanted to find out about last night."

"I'm sorry about this morning," Bethany said. "Would you believe that I was so exhausted that I fell asleep in the parlor? I couldn't believe it. I was there all night." Bethany put her legs up on the ottoman and crossed her feet at the ankles while she unbuttoned her chef's coat.

"Rob told me he had to wake you."

"I'm sorry I couldn't make you a nice breakfast like I said I would."

"It was no problem at all. Cherie actually made me breakfast, and lunch too. She brought over some of her homemade Jamaican patties for lunch. They were delicious." Bethany's father removed his glasses and put them down on top of the crossword puzzle.

"Would you like me to take those for you?" Bethany asked.

"That would be great. Thanks."

Bethany placed them carefully on the small white table which was between them.

"It was quite an evening, I have to say," said Bethany. "There were two parts to the evening. One was the presentation by Antoinette Filetti, the most amazing story which I'll tell you about, and the other was the healing part of the evening which I didn't even know they were going to have. I wish you could have been there."

"Too bad the presentation wasn't during the day. I think I could have gone. It was just too late for me. I still get kind of weak at night."

"Well, look at how much you've been getting around," Bethany said. "I think it's okay to get tired at night." Bethany went on telling John all the details of Antoinette's story as he listened intently. Then Bethany told him all about her own experience with the healing ceremony, as well as what Jimmy had told her.

"You're angel friend is right," John said when she had finished. "Your mother and I went to a healing mass once and we had a similar experience."

"I don't remember you mentioning that!" Bethany said.

"Oh, it was a long time ago, way before you were born. Just remembered now, as a matter of fact. How is your angel friend anyway?" he asked.

"I think it's funny that you refer to him that way. You're the only one who believes me, or even considers the possibility. It's crazy."

"But not *im*possible."

"I suppose not. It's so weird how he just appears, and always when I seem to be down or have questions or doubts. It's really strange. I still don't actually understand how it could be. I'd never ask him, of course. I could make a fool out of myself. 'By the way, are you an angel?' I'm not taking that kind of chance. Can you imagine if he said no? He'd think I was nuts. I think just believing he's an angel is fine with me. What do you think?"

"I've told you before. God works in mysterious ways. Ways that make no sense to us. He may send us the most unlikely people to throw us off guard so we won't think that person was an angel. Maybe he likes to keep us guessing."

"Well, if you heard what Jimmy sounds like and what he looks like—not that there is anything wrong with that of course, but…I don't know. He's not the angel type, if that makes sense."

Her father laughed. "You haven't told your brother anything about this, have you?"

"Oh, God no. He would think I was out of my mind. He'd think we were *both* out of our minds." Bethany paused for a minute. "I do miss him though…Steven, I mean. He's so far away. We see him what, once a year, twice maybe?

"I know." He sighed. "I miss him too. At least he's good about calling all the time. And you're probably right. All this stuff that's been going on…he'd think we were off our rockers."

Bethany laughed. "Yes. I definitely think so. He's convinced you're in remission. He thinks more practically, and after Mom died he wasn't much into religion either."

"I feel badly about that. How we raised you both and how involved we were in the church. It makes me sad sometimes."

"I know, but with everything that's happened in our lives, it's easy to abandon religion. I almost did…if it weren't for Jimmy. Even through everything, it seems like *your* faith never wavered. Why?" Bethany asked.

Her father sat quietly, looking out over the trees to the calm water below. "Losing your mother was the most difficult thing that ever happened to me. Worse than this." He waved his hand at his walker. "Don't think I didn't question God, Bethany. I did. I'm only human. I spent a lot of time talking to Father Michael, as you know. I came to realize that God has a plan for all of us, and I think your friend Jimmy is right. We choose our plan with God ahead of time, and we have to work it through."

"So Mom *planned* to die that way? Isn't that a bit extreme?"

"We don't have all the answers, Bethany, do we? Maybe God needed her for some other purpose. Maybe it happened to make us stronger. Who knows? I'm sure we'll all find out one day. I do rest in the comfort that when my body finally does give out, I will see her again. It will make me so happy."

"Well, I hope you're not rushing your time here," Bethany said.

"Of course not. I'm enjoying every moment with you," her father said, patting Bethany's knee. "You take such good care of me. I just want you to know how much I appreciate it."

"I know," Bethany answered. "But we do have help. I don't think either of us could manage without Rob or Cherie."

"I agree. Maybe God sent them to us too. Everyone is part of the plan."

Bethany thought about that for a moment. "It kinda makes sense though, I guess. So you agree with Jimmy's thoughts then? That it's a way for all of us to advance spiritually while on Earth? I hope that means we'll have it easier on the other side."

"I think we will, Bethany. We're good people just doing the best we can. That's why I've accepted my illness. I could be miserable and make myself miserable and everyone around me miserable. What is that going to do? I've had my moments of frustration. You saw that a few times this year, but I prayed about it; prayed for God to give me strength, just like you prayed for the same thing. I think God is listening. Don't you?"

Bethany nodded in agreement. "I still get scared though. What's going to happen in the future? I can't help but think of it and worry sometimes. I don't want you to be so sick again, hurting and struggling. I don't want to see you in hospitals. I'm scared, Daddy. And I don't want to lose you." Bethany reached out and touched her father's hand. He gave it a gentle squeeze.

"It will be what it will be, Bethany. You have to accept that."

"But aren't you scared?"

"Sometimes. I try not to dwell on it though. There's not a whole lot I can do about it, is there? I believe God will take care of me, and I know your mother is still taking care of me too."

"Mom?"

"I can sense when she's around. I believe if heaven is a perfect place, then those we love can come and be with us at any time...to help us on our own life's journey. I find it very comforting."

"I've never looked at it like that before," said Bethany.

"If you open yourself up to the idea and you become more aware, I think you would sense your mother as well. You may have already and not even known it."

The night she had sat in her father's office came to mind. Part of her felt as if her mother was there trying to console her, but she blew it off thinking she had simply wished it.

"Remember, Bethany. You're running around all day busy as can be. You may not be aware. I was married to your mother a long time. I'm here with not a whole lot to do. I simply notice things more."

"If that's true, I hope that you'll stay with me someday too, Daddy. I promise to listen and become more aware. Promise me you'll be with me and help me to get through." Bethany's voice began to crack as she tried to hold back her tears.

"I will always be with you. And so will your mother. I promise. When you weren't in the hospital with me and when I was alone, I knew your mother was beside me."

"How did you know?"

"I just knew. I can't really explain it. And I'm not making this up. I knew without a doubt she was there comforting me. It was a feeling...a sense."

"I believe you, Daddy. I wish I felt something strong like that."

"Be open, Bethany. You'll be surprised what you discover. There are signs everywhere. And that, my dear daughter, is also how I get through."

"Just don't leave me."

"I will never leave you, Bethany. Trust me. I will always be there."

Twenty-Four

Before Bethany knew it, summer had arrived, and the days were hot and long. Bethany worried about how the heat would affect her father, but so far he was holding his own. He only ventured out in the early evening when the sea breeze came up over the hill, but John was fine with that. Bethany began to think her father was right. He looked so peaceful when he sat outside, and she often wondered if her mother was beside him. It started to bring her some comfort as well.

The spring rush had come and gone at the bakery. Bethany had finished the last of her graduation cake orders and she was looking forward to a lighter schedule. She even began going to the beach some Mondays when she was off, and for once she didn't feel guilty about it. Her only concern was that it had been at least three weeks since she had last seen Jimmy. She hoped that everything was alright.

Her concerns were alleviated one afternoon when he came strolling in through the bakery's kitchen door, unexpected as usual.

"Jimmy! How are you?" Bethany asked. She went over to him and, for the first time, gave him a kiss on the cheek. "Where have you been?" She was glad to see him.

"I've been around," he said. "I had some people who needed me."

"Oh, for your social work?" Bethany asked.

"Yeah, you could say that. How've you been? Good?"

"Yes. Everything has been fine. My dad is doing great. I had a productive spring at the bakery. I can't complain."

"Good. That's what I like to hear." Jimmy wandered around the kitchen as if he were looking for something. Bethany wasn't used to seeing him without his jacket. He wore a more casual short sleeve, buttoned down shirt, which was untucked. The pattern was a bit busy, as if he had just come back from Florida or some other tropical place. His hair was neatly slicked back as always, and Bethany watched as he checked out everything in her kitchen. She couldn't help but smile.

"What's this?" he asked finally. He was pointing to some empty cannoli shells.

"Look what you found," Bethany teased as she walked over to him. "You found the pot of gold!"

"These are cannoli shells, am I right?"

"You are correct. I just made them a little while ago. I must have known you were coming in."

Jimmy picked one up and examined it. "How do you get the stuff in here?"

"I'll show you." Bethany went into the refrigerator and pulled out a bowl of fresh cannoli cream. "I just have to add the mini chocolate chips." She opened up a bag and carefully folded them in. Jimmy stood close by and peered over her shoulder.

"I like your cannolis because they have chocolate chips in them. I hate those green and red things some bakeries use. What is that crap anyway?"

Bethany ignored his question and just laughed. "Okay, now I'll put it in the pastry bag like this." She held it up and then demonstrated how to get all the filling in really tight.

"You're good," Jimmy said. "Now you're gonna fill the shells?"

"Yep. I'll show you how I do it."

"I've never before seen this done, you know? It's interestin'. I can see a lot of work goes in."

"Yes, it's a bit of a fiddle, but once you get the hang of it, it's pretty easy. Watch." Bethany held up a cannoli shell in her left hand

and the tightly wrapped pastry bag in her right hand. With incredible ease, she pushed the cream through the bag and filled up one side of the shell. She then turned the shell around and did the other side.

"You know what I like too?" Jimmy asked. "You fill up the whole shell. You ever get a cannoli and there's nothin' in the center? It's kinda like an empty hole. There's no cream. That ain't right. Those people must be cuttin' corners or somethin'. I don't like it."

"I agree. That's why I always make sure I fill them completely so my customers get their money's worth."

"That's right."

Bethany tried not to laugh. He couldn't take his eyes off what she was doing. He seemed so intrigued and so child-like, especially for such a big guy.

"Would you like to try?" she asked him after she had done three.

"Me?" he asked, raising his eyes in disbelief.

"Sure, why not? Give it a try," Bethany said, holding out the pastry bag.

"I couldn't. I don't know," Jimmy said.

"You can do it." Bethany smiled trying to encourage him. She could tell he was debating what to do. She knew he wanted to try it, so she waited patiently.

"Maybe I'll give it a go. You won't be sellin' this to no customers though?"

"No. You can have whatever you make," Bethany said.

Jimmy slowly held out his large hands. He took the pastry bag from Bethany and held it awkwardly. Bethany placed her hands over his and turned the bag slightly.

"You want to have a firm grip on it like this," she said, moving the bag in his hand. "Got it?"

"Okay. Now what?"

"Pick up one of the shells with your left hand."

"I'm not gonna break it or nothin', am I?"

"Hopefully not. They're not as fragile as they look. Just be careful. Hold it like this," Bethany suggested, demonstrating with her own hand.

"Like this?" Jimmy asked as he picked up one of the shells.

"That's right. Perfect. Now bring the bag toward the shell, place the tip of the bag into the shell, and squeeze gently."

Jimmy squeezed too hard and the cannoli cream went in and out of the other side of the shell.

"Oh, shit!"

"It's okay, it's okay," Bethany said and chuckled. "It takes a little bit to get used to it. You just pressed too hard, that's all." She placed her hand on his and gently squeezed. "See, like this. That's better."

Jimmy turned it around and filled the other side. "It's kinda messy," he said, examining his work.

"That's okay. It's your first one. You didn't do badly at all. Try another one."

"You sure?" he asked, looking over at Bethany. She nodded yes.

He took a deep breath and picked up another shell. Carefully he applied pressure. "Nothin's comin' out now. What's goin' on here?"

"Now you're not applying enough pressure. Squeeze a little more."

"This is hard work. You know what I'm sayin?"

Bethany bit the side of her lip so she wouldn't laugh. She couldn't believe how serious he was about this.

"It's comin' now. Ahhh, look at that, hey!"

"Very good. Now do the other side."

Jimmy filled the rest of the pastry. "Look at that beauty," he said, holding it up. "You mind if I try one more? I think I'm gettin' the hang of this now, you know?"

"I know," Bethany said. "Go ahead, sure. Do another one. You're on a roll."

Jimmy repeated the procedure with a fresh shell and it came out perfectly. "Look at that one," he said, holding it up high. "I got it! I got the hang of this thing." He smiled proudly.

Alison stepped into the kitchen and hesitated when she saw what was going on. She put her hand over her mouth and Bethany knew she was laughing. Behind Jimmy's back Bethany waved Alison away. Jimmy was so happy with his creation that he never noticed the exchange.

"Now you get to take all of these home with you," Bethany said as she grabbed a box. She carefully picked up Jimmy's cannolis with tissue and placed them in the box. She closed up the box and taped the sides. "And here you go. You're all set." She handed Jimmy the box.

"Wow. Thank you. I didn't think I could do it, you know? I don't have those fine motor skills or somethin'. You know what I'm sayin'?"

"Well, I think you did just fine."

"Mind if I stick around a bit? Am I holdin' you up? I have some more stories for you if you want to hear them."

"You're not holding me up. I'll finish the rest of the cannolis if you don't mind me working while you're talking to me."

"Not at all. I have some good ones to tell you."

"New ones?"

"Well, they happened a while back but I just found out now."

"Who told you?"

"Some people."

"Oh. Okay. Go ahead. Tell me."

"You know Padre Pio could tell when people were lyin', right?"

Bethany nodded as she stuffed another shell. "I remember reading about that in the book I bought. He knew if people were lying to him in the confessional."

"That's right," Jimmy said. "Well, listen to this. When Padre Pio was alive he was giving this woman confession. She waited for hours to see him. After a few minutes Padre Pio says, 'Get out of this confessional...you're not tellin' the truth.' Then he says, 'Go back...go back to the water where you drowned your baby.'"

Bethany instantly stopped what she was doing and turned toward Jimmy.

"What?" she asked.

"I'm tellin' you. He says, 'Go back to the water where you drowned your baby.'"

"That's horrible! She drowned her baby?"

"Yeah, and he knew it."

"Oh my gosh."

"Anyhow, he knew it before she said it. So she went back to the water, and then she went back to the confessional and she confessed her sins. Ain't that amazin'?"

"Yes. Unbelievable."

"Then there's another story…a girl got in an accident in Italy; bones broken. Everything. Can't live. She's on life support. The whole nine yards. She's in there, the hospital, a week maybe, and she's gonna die. Everybody left, you know, the family, everybody. Then all of a sudden the next day she's sittin' in a chair ready to go home. Nothin' wrong with her."

"Really?"

"And she seen Padre Pio. After he was dead. I'm tellin' you. So many stories. So many people. There's old ladies who have seen him; a guy with prostate cancer who seen him. He's helped so many people. You know what I'm sayin'? Getta load of this one. You know how they say that Padre Pio had bilocation? He could be in two places at the same time?"

"Sure. You've mentioned it and I read up on it," Bethany said.

Jimmy continued. "Well, listen to this. Padre Pio was in Italy, right? While the war was goin' on in Germany. Well, while he was in Italy, his body was in Germany helpin' the troops. He was shakin' because it was so cold there in Germany, yet he really was in Italy. His body actually left him and went to Germany to help the troops."

"I can't believe how many stories you have, Jimmy," Bethany said. "It truly is amazing."

"I'm tellin' you. It's the truth."

"I believe you."

"On that note, I've gotta get outta here."

"Don't forget your cannolis."

"I can't forget that," he said with a wink.

Jimmy headed toward the kitchen door with his box in hand. As he opened the door to leave, Bethany said, "Jimmy…I'm glad you came today."

"Me too," he replied. "*Ci Vediamo.*"

Part II

Twenty-Five

The days grew longer and everything in Bethany's life seemed brighter and easier as the summer wore on. John's condition remained stable, and Jimmy continued to visit Bethany and tell her stories about Padre Pio and his miracles. It was a month before Thanksgiving, when Bethany came home and walked into a disaster.

"John, try to grab my arm," Bethany heard Rob say loudly when she entered the house from the kitchen.

"Oh, my God, his head is bleeding!" Cherie cried.

Bethany threw down her keys and purse and ran down the hall, her heart racing. She followed the voices to the parlor. Once she reached the open doorway, she stopped dead in her tracks and put her hand over her mouth. "Oh, my God," she said.

Cherie and Rob both turned quickly at the sound of her voice. Her father was lying down on the floor next to his comfortable chair. The wheelchair was strewn to one side of the room. Her father's eyes were closed and blood was coming from a small gash on his head. Blood was on the chair, the rug, and on her father's shirt. She raced toward her father to see how she could help.

"We've got to get him up and back in the wheelchair," Rob said. "He's not doing well."

Bethany could hear in Rob's voice that he was concerned. It was not like him to appear nervous even in the worst situations.

"What happened?" Bethany asked, trying to assist both Rob and Cherie.

"He was fine," Rob said. "He'd been in the therapeutic lift chair in the parlor for about three hours. I came in about ten minutes ago to get him in the wheelchair and take him to the bathroom, and when I helped him up, his leg spasmed terribly and just gave out. Something's going on. He was like a tree coming down. Dead weight. He threw my balance off and I couldn't support him. Down he went."

"He must have hit his head on the end table," said Cherie. "It happened so fast. I come running in when I heard the commotion."

John's body was completely inflexible. He couldn't move. After a few minutes, the three of them were able to get him in the wheelchair. His eyes remained closed and his head hung strangely to one side.

"What's happening?" Bethany asked, her voice cracking.

"We need to call an ambulance," Rob said. "We've got to get him to a hospital. He has a fever and he shut down."

"It's going to be okay, Daddy. Can you hear me?" Bethany asked while tears ran down her face.

Her father didn't answer. His head still hung to one side and he tried to open his eyes but couldn't. Rob went into action and called for an ambulance while he shouted out orders to Cherie to put together some cold compresses. Bethany knelt helplessly on the ground, holding her father's limp hand.

Cherie returned with the compresses and held them on John's forehead. Handing a smaller one to Bethany she said, "Here, put this on his wrist at the pressure point. It will help to cool him."

As Bethany looked down and did what she was told, she suddenly noticed the size of her father's legs. They were huge. Edema had settled in again. Within seconds Rob was back in the parlor.

"They're on their way," he said. "John, the ambulance is coming for you. We're going to take you to the hospital. It's going to be okay."

Bethany stood up. "I don't understand what happened. He wasn't like this when I left this morning."

"You saw him in bed. When I went to get him dressed he seemed really weak. I told him I thought it was a good idea if he spent the day in bed. He wouldn't hear of it. I took his temperature because he just didn't seem right. It was normal. He insisted I get him ready for the day and that he wanted to go into the parlor. He was talking; he was alert. His legs were a little more swollen than they have been but he had just gotten up. They were nothing like this," Rob said, pointing to John's legs. "I've never seen anything come on this quickly. He was fine once I got him in his chair. He seemed comfortable and I gave him lunch in here but he didn't eat much. Said he wasn't hungry. I checked his temperature again about two hours ago. Still no fever. He definitely has one now. They'll take it at the hospital." Rob paused. "I was in and out of here all day. I just don't know what happened all of a sudden."

"It's not your fault this happened, Rob. Please know that," Bethany said, gently placing her hand on Rob's arm. Rob looked away, clearly upset. He quietly nodded. Bethany rubbed his arm.

"I just hate seeing him like this," Rob finally said. "It happened so fast, Beth. He just came down. I couldn't support him."

"It's okay," Bethany whispered. "It's okay."

Cherie had changed the compresses and bandaged the cut on John's head. Within minutes the ambulance arrived and two EMTs entered with a stretcher.

"We're going to lift you and get you up on the stretcher," one of them said to John. The two young men lifted him with limited trouble, and Bethany wondered just how many times they must encounter situations like this.

"You go," Cherie said to Bethany and Rob as they wheeled John down the hallway. "I will clean everything here and lock up when I'm through. Leave me a message later when you know something, honey, okay?"

"I will," said Bethany. "Thank you, and oh, could you take care of the dogs too? They'll need to be walked, fed..."

"You go. It's no problem. I take care of everything." Cherie waved.

Rob and Bethany hopped in Bethany's SUV and followed behind the ambulance. Neither of them spoke. A million thoughts entered Bethany's mind while she tried to focus on the road. Thankfully the traffic was easy and they made it to the hospital emergency in no time. Rob went with John while Bethany sat at admissions and dealt with the paperwork. By the time it was taken care of, Bethany made her way around the emergency department and found her father and Rob behind a curtain.

"Has anyone been in to see him yet?" Bethany asked.

"A nurse," Rob said. "His fever is 103. They're coming back to put him on an IV so they can administer fluids and medication. He has an infection of some kind."

Her father was so out of it that Bethany had no idea whether he even knew what was happening. She sat gently on the bed next to him and held his hand. It seemed an eternity until someone came in to help him. Blood was drawn, and then the IV was hooked up. Bethany watched as fluid rushed into her father's arm.

Hours went by with very little information or change in John's condition. Doctors came in and did tests and asked Rob questions. Besides making one call to Alison to tell her she wouldn't be back and to close up at the end of the day, Bethany never left her father's side. She quietly prayed to Padre Pio. By now her father had been put into a hospital gown. The silver Padre Pio medal hung from John's neck, and Bethany watched it gently rise and fall on her father's chest in sync with his breathing. Although she was frightened, the sight of the medal brought her comfort. One of the nurses tried to take it off, but Bethany was adamant that her father keep it on no matter what.

When her mind drifted to worst case scenarios she would think of Jimmy and the stories he would tell her about the miracles and about Padre Pio. She began to consider that Padre Pio himself may even be in the room with them. What a difference she felt. Somehow she knew she would get through this.

By eight that evening, a young, rather short Asian doctor with a clipboard came in through the curtain. "I'm Dr. Wang," he said. "We're going to admit him to ICU," he said. "The fever, the blood work, and the tests all point to an infection that seems to be taking over his body right now. It's what's causing the edema as well." He paused and then continued. "As you know, the immune system is greatly weakened in a patient with MS. He probably picked up something as simple as a cold from someone, and it materialized into this."

"But he hasn't been anywhere," Bethany said. "He's only been with us, and we haven't been sick. We're fine."

"You're fine because you have a healthy immune system," the doctor said. "You could have been a carrier of something that you picked up from someone you came in contact with. Your immune system fought it off without you even being aware that anything was going on. But in John's condition the immune system is compromised. His body simply can't fight it."

Bethany nodded.

"Whatever the case may be, it is our job to get rid of his infection. He will continue to receive fluids throughout the night and will be monitored carefully. That's why we're putting him in ICU. I'll feel better when we get his fever down. Do you have any other questions?"

"No. Thank you, Doctor," Bethany said.

As the doctor went to leave he turned back to them and said, "They'll be in shortly to move him over. Stay as long as you like. Once he's settled you may want to go home and get some rest. He'll be in good hands." He turned and left, pulling the curtain closed behind him.

"He's probably right," Rob said to Bethany. "Once John's settled in we should get home. Tomorrow may be another long day."

Bethany nodded and sat back down on the edge of the bed. She stared at her father and the medal.

Twenty-Six

Thankfully Bethany did not receive any phone calls from the hospital during the night so she assumed everything was status quo. She had difficulty sleeping and rose at four-thirty. If she wanted to get to the hospital in the morning, she knew she had to be up and at the bakery by five-thirty at the latest. Bethany headed to the store and baked what she needed for the day, and by eight-thirty Alison had the bakery running in full swing. Instead of going home to change, Bethany decided to go straight to the hospital. She was anxious to see her father.

She arrived at the hospital by nine and ran into Rob in the hall of ICU.

"How is he?" she asked.

"Well, his fever broke, which is good…"

"Is he awake? Can he talk?"

"He's awake but he's not too lucid, Beth," Rob said.

"What do you mean?"

"He's having some side effects to the medication they put him on. I just want you to be prepared."

"How bad is it? What is he saying?"

"I think you should see for yourself." Rob led Bethany into the room.

"Hi, Daddy," she said, taking a seat next to his bed. Bethany looked at her father's face. It seemed drawn and tense and washed out. "How are you feeling?"

"I didn't do it. I'm telling you I didn't do it," he said frantically.

"What didn't you do, Daddy?" Bethany asked.

"I didn't take the clothes…the man's clothes next to me. They said I took his clothes."

There was no man in the bed next to him. Bethany glanced at Rob.

"What would I do with his clothes? That nurse…that nurse out there told me she was going to kill me because I took his clothes."

"No one is going to kill you, Daddy. You're in the hospital. They are trying to help you and make you better."

"No, no, no." Her father shook his head. "It's a conspiracy. They are trying to kill me. It's true! You have to believe me. The nurse tried to give me poison. See?" He pointed to a small cup on the mayo stand which contained three pills.

Bethany looked in the cup and then at Rob.

"One is a water pill for the edema, the other is an antibiotic now that he's off the drip, and the other is a mild sedative because apparently he was really nuts earlier," Rob whispered.

"What's causing this? What kind of dosage did he receive in the drip?" Bethany whispered back.

"Some patients just have a reaction," said Rob.

Bethany turned back and looked at her father. He was staring at her strangely and then he began pointing a finger angrily at her. "So you're in on it too! I should have known. You don't care about me. You want them to poison me. You want them to kill me!"

Bethany's heart began to pound wildly and her eyes instantly welled up with tears. "No Daddy, no! That's not true. No one's trying to kill you. You must believe me."

"You're one of them. You're trying to kill me," he repeated loudly. "You think I took his clothes too!"

The tears began to fall. This was too much for Bethany to bear. As bad as his illness ever was, John always had his mind. This couldn't be happening. Even if it was the medication and this state was temporary, the pain his words caused was just incredible. It was as if a knife was being jammed into Bethany's heart.

"You're one of them! You're one of them!" her father began to shout.

Rob quickly pulled Bethany up by her arm and whisked her out of the room.

"I need a bathroom right away," Bethany said to Rob.

He quickly looked around, and then dragged her into the first bathroom he found in the nearest room. Bethany vomited violently. When she was done, she washed up and splashed water on her face. Rob looked out into the hall to make sure no one was coming. As Bethany left the bathroom she saw the room's resident lying in a bed. The man looked well over a hundred years old. The sight of him scared her. His body was like that of a wraith. His eyes were closed and his mouth was open. To her, he already looked dead. Her stomach churned again, but there was nothing left in her.

"I don't think I can do this, Rob," Bethany said, leaning up against a wall. "I don't think I can deal with this."

Rob rubbed her arms. "John is going to be okay, Beth. He's not your father right now. It's the medicine. He'll come out of this and won't remember anything."

"But I will," Bethany said, looking up at him.

Rob studied her face. "This will pass and you'll put it behind you."

Bethany looked down and nodded.

"Here comes the doctor," Rob said.

Bethany stood straight and stopped Dr. Wang in the hall. "Excuse me, I'm Bethany Fitzpatrick. You've been treating my father, John?"

"Yes," the doctor said as he put a pen inside the front pocket of his white coat. He lowered his clipboard. He looked at her patiently through large, dark rimmed glasses.

"My father's condition...what's going on? He's hallucinating or something."

"Yes, I know. I spent some time with him earlier and he wasn't making sense. We were aggressive last night in treating the infection. Twenty to thirty percent of patients can have a reaction to the medication in the drip, which would cause this type of hallucinating. It usually takes twenty-four hours to get out of the system. He won't remember a thing. His fever broke around five this morning. It had been up and down throughout the night. His vitals are all good now. His blood pressure was quite high when he arrived, probably because he was in a stressful situation. We'll continue to monitor it. The edema has also come down substantially. We're hoping that maybe by tonight we can transfer him out of the ICU and put him in a room to recover. His neurologist called around eight this morning to check on him."

"Yes, I put a call into his service last night," said Bethany.

"I updated him on John's condition. I'm not an expert when it comes to patients with MS, but because of the high fever it's likely that more damage has been done to the nervous system, almost as if it shorted out. Once the damage is done, it's irreversible, as you know. We won't know for a few days just how it's affected him," the doctor said.

Bethany's heart sank. She took a deep breath.

"If you don't have any other questions, I have to be on my way. I have more rounds to make."

"I think that's all. Thank you, Doctor," Bethany said softly as he walked away.

"You okay?" Rob asked her when he was gone.

Bethany shrugged.

"Look, there's not much you can do here today. Let's not get your dad excited. We should let him be. There's no point in you staying here. Go back to the bakery. Do what you have to do. I'll stay here and call you if anything changes. You can come back tonight. Sound good?"

Bethany folded her arms and contemplated it for a moment. She tried to be rational about the whole thing. "As much as I want to stay, you're probably right. What good will it do? Clearly it will get my father more upset, as long as he's in this condition, and honestly I just don't know if I can go through it."

"You shouldn't have to. If he were lucid and you were keeping him company, that's one thing. But this isn't your father. You know that, Beth, don't you?"

"I know, Rob. But it's still hard. Should I say goodbye to him?"

"He's quiet now. Let him be. If he asks, I'll tell him you had to get back to the bakery. You'll be back here in a few hours."

Bethany nodded. "It's hard to leave," she said as a tear rolled down her face.

"Keep the faith," Rob said.

Bethany headed back to Northport, but was completely drained. She tried her best to put aside the terrible things her father had said to her. Even though she knew he didn't mean them, nor did he understand what he was saying, it was very hurtful and disturbing.

Bethany walked around the back to the kitchen. When she opened the door she found Jimmy leaning against the counter with his arms folded.

"How's he doin'?" he asked.

Bethany studied Jimmy for a moment. "How's he doing? He's doing terribly, Jimmy. God's not listening to *me* and neither is Padre Pio."

"Don't say that, kid. It takes time,"

"I'm all out of time, Jimmy! I've had enough!" Bethany began to pace the kitchen and started recklessly tossing pots and pans around. "I've had enough of my father's illness, enough of having hope, enough of praying..." She whirled around and faced him. "And I've had enough of you and your stupid stories. What have they done for me? Where has it gotten my father? Nowhere! It's gotten us nowhere, Jimmy."

Jimmy had a dumfounded look on his face. He stood up straight and stared into Bethany's eyes. "Beth, you gotta believe."

"I don't *gotta* believe anything! My friends were right. You're crazy! What have I gotten myself into? You've taken advantage of me. You got me when I was down and vulnerable. I put my trust in you," Bethany said, shaking an empty saucepan in his direction. "Why? Why did I listen to you? You want me to believe in things that will never be. My father will never be well!" She began to cry, and Jimmy walked over to her and cautiously touched her arm. Bethany quickly pulled away.

"Get away from me. Just go! Get out of my life! Get out of my bakery!" She sobbed and sat down on a stool.

Jimmy stood before her. His shoulders slumped. "As you wish."

As Jimmy left through the back door, Alison came rushing in from the front.

"Bethany, my God! What happened?"

Bethany couldn't speak. She sat slouched over on the stool and cried even harder as Alison held her.

Twenty-Seven

Bethany eventually calmed down and her work kept her preoccupied until it was time to go back to the hospital. Bethany was dreading the visit, because a phone call to Rob revealed that her father was still talking crazy.

On the ride over Bethany concentrated on her breathing, taking deep, slow breaths to relax herself. She wouldn't stay at the hospital long, but she felt that she had really no choice but to go despite the situation.

When she had arrived her father was no longer talking about taking another patient's clothes. This time he believed he was in a mental hospital and that the doctors and nurses were giving him medications to further his insanity. Once again he blamed Bethany, and even Rob, for being "in" on the ridiculous claim. Bethany wondered where her father was, lost somewhere inside a limiting body. Would he come back to her? She focused on the silver medal around her father's neck, and thought about what had happened with Jimmy just hours earlier. She didn't know what to make of the medal anymore. She shivered, suddenly becoming quite cold, and rubbed her arms. She had an odd sensation that someone was standing next to her. Instinctively she looked around, but found no one there. At the same time, her father began to quiet down and became silent. For a moment, her father's eyes seemed to be fixated on something next to Bethany before they became heavy as he finally drifted off to sleep. Bethany watched him for a while lying peacefully.

Bethany tried her best to sleep that night. After opening the bakery at the regular time, she drove over to the hospital.

"He's doing great," said Rob as soon as he saw Bethany in the hallway.

"Is he back?" she asked.

"He's back," Rob said, smiling. "He's calm and he's been asking for you."

Bethany sighed.

"Since you're here now I'm just going to go downstairs and get something to eat. You want anything?" asked Rob.

"No, I'm good. I'm anxious to see how he's doing. Take your time. I have an hour or so before I have to get back," Bethany said.

"I think you'll be pleased," Rob said before he continued down the hallway.

Bethany walked into her father's room and he began to smile.

"How's my girl?" he said, which almost brought Bethany to tears.

"I'm good, I'm good," Bethany said as she sat in the chair next to the bed. "But how are you?"

"Well, I feel very weak," he began, "but I do feel more like myself. I didn't feel quite right yesterday." Her father squinted and was quiet for a moment. "I don't remember much, actually. Isn't that strange?"

"As long as you feel like yourself today, that's all that matters," Bethany said. "Has the doctor been in?"

"Yes, the short, Asian fellow. The one with the big, black glasses. Have you met him?"

"I did yesterday."

"Well, he didn't say much. Just looked over my charts; asked a few questions. You know these doctors don't tell you much," her father said.

"I'll try to find him later and see what's going on. My feeling is that you're probably going to have to go back into rehab, Daddy," Bethany said.

"I was afraid of that." He frowned. "I want to be home for Thanksgiving."

"We'll make that our goal," Bethany said. "You know I can't make any promises though. It's not up to me to decide."

He nodded.

"Did anyone tell you when you were getting out of ICU? I was under the impression it was supposed to happen last night."

"I asked the nurse this morning. She said I was causing a racket so they decided to keep me here overnight. I wasn't quite sure what she was referring to." Her father chuckled.

Bethany looked at him sympathetically. "I'm sure whatever it was doesn't matter now. What about the doctor? Did you ask him when he came in about going to a room?"

"Yeah. He said it would be sometime before noon. What time is it?"

Bethany pulled up the sleeve of her coat and looked at her watch. "It's eleven-thirty," she said.

A nurse and orderly entered the room, seemingly ready for action.

"Okay, Mr. Fitzpatrick, we're moving you upstairs," said the rather large, dark-skinned nurse in an accent Bethany didn't recognize. "We have a room with a bed by the window." The nurse unhooked the monitors attached to her father. "Paul here is going to take you up. He's all yours," the nurse said to the muscular orderly. She raised the bars on either side of John's bed, took one last look at his chart, wrote something on it, and then sent him on his way. "Feel better, Mr. Fitzpatrick," she said and shuffled out of the room.

"How are you today, sir?" Paul, the young orderly, asked before John could say anything.

"I'm good, I guess," Bethany's father said. "I'd feel better if I was at home."

Paul didn't respond. He went about making sure that John was secure. Slowly he began to wheel the bed out of the ICU. Paul said nothing to her, so Bethany took it upon herself to follow behind. As they made their way down the corridor, Dr. Wang popped out from behind a curtain.

"Dr. Wang!" Bethany said in surprise. The orderly kept on going. "Can I speak to you for one minute?" Bethany asked as her eye moved toward Paul who seemed oblivious that she had stopped.

"Of course," Dr. Wang said.

"Just one second. I'm sorry," Bethany said holding up a finger. "Let me find out where he's taking him." As the doctor stood in place, Bethany ran toward the orderly, her pocketbook falling off her right shoulder in her rush. "Excuse me, sir?" she said loudly. Finally the orderly stopped. "I'd like to see the doctor for a moment. Where are you taking my father?"

"Third floor, room 329. It's across from the nurse's station," the orderly replied.

"Okay, thanks." She quickly turned and looked at her father. "I'll speak to Dr. Wang. I'll be up in a minute," Bethany said.

"Good. See what you can find out," he said.

"I will." Bethany ran back to the doctor while the orderly continued on. "I see the effects of the medication have worn off," she began when she reached the doctor.

"Yes," Dr. Wang answered as he adjusted his large glasses. "He's lucid and seems much more relaxed. He had been quite irritated."

"Yes, I know," Bethany said as she pulled her pocketbook back up on her shoulder.

"His infection has cleared up," Dr. Wang stated, holding his clipboard to his chest. "Right now we're still trying to get the edema to come down more. He's also very weak." He paused for a moment. "He's having trouble with fine motor skills, like holding a fork or picking up a cup. His neurologist will have to evaluate him in another week or so to see how much damage was done. Hopefully some of it will come back."

"It could just change like that? Overnight?"

"I'm afraid so."

Bethany frowned. "What about everything else? Can he walk at all or even stand?"

"Not at this time. I can't say whether he'll be getting around on his own or not. His aide told me he'd been struggling before he came here. He was in a wheelchair most of the time?"

"That's correct. Occasionally, though, he could use the walker to take a few steps. To the bathroom for instance, with assistance of course, but he could definitely stand."

"Again, that is something his neurologist will have to evaluate. He'll have to spend a few days in rehab where they'll work him and try to build up his strength. How much of it comes back remains to be seen."

"I understand," Bethany said, trying not to sound discouraged.

"As I mentioned yesterday, his tests all came back negative and his vitals are good. His blood pressure has lowered also. These are very good signs. The infection is completely out of his system. Once we get the edema under control he'll be sent to the rehab. Hopefully that will be in another day or so. It's taking a bit longer because he's been inactive. That's why the rehabilitation will be good for him. He needs someone to work and move the muscles."

"How long do you think he'll be in rehab? Do you think he'll be home for Thanksgiving?"

"That's really not for me to say," the doctor said.

Bethany was silent.

"I'll check on him again tomorrow and see if we can get things moving," Dr. Wang said, seeing the frustration in Bethany's face.

"I'd really appreciate that, Doctor. Thank you."

Dr. Wang smiled and nodded as he walked away.

None of Bethany's questions were completely answered as she had hoped, but there was really nothing she could do about it. It would be what it would be. As she headed toward the elevators, the door to one of them opened, and Bethany saw Rob standing inside.

"They just moved him," Bethany said as he stepped out. "Room 329. Third floor."

"Oh, okay good." He spun around quickly and held the elevator door open while he hopped back in with Bethany.

Bethany filled him in on her conversation with Dr. Wang on the way up to the third floor. Rob did not seem surprised.

"We'll deal with whatever we have to deal with," Rob said. "We've done it before."

"I know," Bethany said.

The elevator doors opened and the two found their way to John's room. When they entered, Paul was being assisted by a second orderly who was helping to transfer John into another bed. In one quick swoop the two muscular men lifted John's body with ease. Once John was situated and comfortable, they moved the transfer bed into the hallway, and they were quickly on their way.

"It's nice to be able to look outside," John remarked as he turned his head toward the window. "What did the doctor say?"

Bethany filled her father in on the brief discussion. He listened intently and didn't ask any questions. He simply nodded and accepted whatever fate would bestow him. When she was through, he asked Bethany if she could stay a while.

"Of course," she said, relieved her father was back. "I'm caught up at the bakery, and Alison has everything under control."

"Why don't I go down and get you some lunch?" Rob asked. "I just saw someone coming around with the food cart for the patients. Beth can eat with you if you like."

"Sounds good to me," John replied. "Will they let you bring food up here?"

"I don't see why not," said Rob. "The ICU won't allow it, but up here it's okay. What do you want, Beth?" he said turning toward her.

"Oh, I don't know," she said. "Do they have a wrap or something? Just make sure it's fresh, whatever you get. And I'll have a bottle of water with it."

"Will do," Rob said as he headed out the door.

"I was hoping to get you alone," John said softly to Bethany. "I wanted to tell you about something...something strange."

Bethany pulled over a chair and sat down. She wondered if perhaps her father was starting to remember what had happened to him as far as the hallucinations were concerned.

"I told you I really don't remember a lot from the past two days," he began. "I know I was sick and very weak and out of it, and I know I wasn't quite myself...but there is something I *do* remember because it was very real, and I wanted to tell you about it."

"What is it, Daddy?" Bethany asked. She was quite interested in what he had to say.

"Well, the beginning part is a little fuzzy so bear with me." He squinted his eyes in thought, trying to remember. "I'm pretty sure you were there...it was late yesterday...maybe in the evening."

"I was here with you last night, Daddy. That's right."

"I recall being upset about something—but just what, I have no idea—when all of a sudden he came. He appeared," John said, his brow furrowed.

"Who appeared?" Bethany asked, puzzled.

John turned and looked into his daughters' eyes. "Padre Pio," he said.

Twenty-Eight

Tell me what you remember, Daddy," Bethany said, pulling her chair closer to her father.

"It was so real, Bethany. I can't explain. It wasn't a dream. It was too real to be a dream. I've never experienced anything like it before. It was vivid. I don't know how else to explain it," he said as he looked at his daughter.

"Go on," said Bethany.

Her father took a breath and paused. Bethany studied his face while she waited for him to continue. The way his eyebrows scrunched and came together, Bethany knew he was thinking and trying to remember it all. Finally he began to speak.

"I was upset about something. I don't know what. You were here," her father said, looking at Bethany. "I felt like I was angry or something. I don't really remember. After that it all became clear though. I can remember everything." He paused.

"I remember you were looking at me," he continued, "but you weren't saying anything. All of a sudden, right next to you was Padre Pio. He was standing there...in between us. He looked down at me in the bed. He raised his hand and placed it over my head. He told me to be still, and I felt calm. I was no longer upset. I wanted to tell you what was happening then, but somehow I couldn't. He looked just like he did on the prayer card. Maybe a little younger. He wore a brown cassock, which was tied at the waist. His hands were wrapped, like in the photographs. I felt such energy go through me when he placed his hand on top of my head. He told me then to close my eyes. He wanted to take me somewhere. In my head I told him I didn't want to go. I figured I must be dying, and I didn't want to go yet. He told me I wasn't dying...he said he wanted to talk to me."

Bethany's eyes welled up with tears. "Are you okay?" her father asked. "I don't have to continue."

"I'm fine," Bethany said, catching a stray tear. "I want to hear everything." She smiled.

Her father studied her for a moment. "Everything seemed to go black for a split second. Next thing, I was not in this hospital. I was in a beautiful field with tons of wildflowers...and I was walking, Bethany...I was walking with Padre Pio. I was well."

The tears fell freely now as Bethany listened to her father's amazing account. She couldn't help but think about Jimmy and all the terrible things she had said to him. Suddenly, she realized that Padre Pio must have been in the hospital room with her the day before. It was all making sense now. She remembered shivering and rubbing her arms, having the feeling that someone was standing next to her. It was then that her father stared out into the distance and became calm. He was *seeing* Padre Pio. Padre Pio had been in the room, just like her father had said, and Pio had calmed him. While her father appeared to be sleeping, he had temporarily left his body and gone off with Padre Pio. Everything Jimmy had told her began to make sense now. Her heart ached for her friend. She needed to apologize, but how could she reach him?

As Bethany waited for her father to go on with his story, John slowly moved his left arm across the bed. He could not lift his arm, but he did his best to wiggle his fingers to catch Bethany's attention. When he did, she stopped wiping her eyes, sniffled, and held her father's hand. It felt soft and weak in hers. So very different from the firm, protective grip he once had when she was a little girl. She rubbed the top of his hand gently with her thumb.

"Are you sure you're okay?" he asked again softly.

Bethany nodded yes. "It's just unbelievable that this happened to you, that's all."

"It was wonderful, Bethany. It felt wonderful to walk again. I felt so free. I asked Padre Pio if I had died. He said I hadn't. He told me this is what it will be like one day. This is how I will always feel. I'll have no pain."

Bethany was both overwhelmed and moved.

"We walked together in this beautiful field and we talked the whole way. He told me how proud of you he was, and how happy he was that you came back to God. He told me you were a good daughter and that you've taken very good care of me. Of course I told him I knew that. I told him how lucky I've been. He then apologized for everything we had to go through, but it was all part of the plan I had worked out with God. He assured me everything would be fine, and he explained how difficult his own life had been."

Bethany's father looked at her to make sure she was alright. When he saw that she was, he continued. "He told me lots of things. Things I wish I could remember. He did tell me that I wouldn't remember everything."

"Why is that?" Bethany asked.

"Padre Pio told me I wasn't supposed to remember," John said looking a bit puzzled. "I know it must sound crazy to you."

"Dad, a mobster angel visits me, for Pete's sake." Bethany laughed and then thought of Jimmy. She wondered if he was okay. "Can you remember anything else?"

"Yes, I can remember what was happening for the most part, but I can't remember a lot of the conversation."

"So what happened next?"

"Well, we seemed to be walking in this field for quite some time, and we were talking when we ran into another man." John paused and his eyes welled up. Bethany had no idea what her father was going to say. She wondered what was causing him to get upset. "Padre Pio told me he wanted to introduce me to this person," he managed to say. "It turns out, Bethany...this person was Jesus Christ."

A tear began to roll down John's cheek, and Bethany clearly knew this had not been a dream. How it could possibly have happened bewildered her, but somehow she knew her father had gone on this incredible journey. For a short period of time, his soul had left him. Bethany cried, too, as she squeezed her father's weak hand.

"Go on," she said softly through her tears.

"I couldn't believe I was meeting Jesus. He was so kind. He talked to me, too, and he said that everything was going to be fine...that everything was happening the way it should. He told me there were good things to come. He then pointed to a lone tree in the middle of the field. On the tree was a plain wooden swing. On the swing sat your mother, Bethany."

More tears fell between the two of them. Bethany wiped hers away with the back of her sleeve. She found a box of tissues on the windowsill and grabbed a few, which she used to wipe away her father's tears. John's lip quivered as he tried to speak again. Somehow the words just couldn't come out yet. He was clearly overwhelmed.

"Take your time," Bethany whispered. "It's okay, Daddy. It's okay."

"I didn't realize how much it affected me until I started talking about it. I'm telling you, Bethany, this was real. It was not a dream. I know it wasn't. I don't know or understand how this can be possible, but it happened. I was allowed a glimpse of heaven." Her father's lip quivered again, and Bethany's tears just kept coming. They took a breath together before he continued to speak.

"So there she was...your beautiful mother. Victoria. She was so young and she was smiling and waving at me. I wanted to run to her, but my legs were stuck. I couldn't move them. Jesus and Padre Pio said it was time to go. When I looked again, the swing was moving slowly and she was gone."

"How did you feel then?" Bethany asked.

"Oddly enough I felt okay. I wasn't sad. I didn't quite feel anything, come to think of it. It was strange. They assured me I would see her again and that everything would be fine. I asked about you. I asked what would happen to you when I came back to this place. Was this okay to ask them, Bethany?" He looked at her with concern.

"Yes, Daddy. It was okay to ask them. Do you remember what they said?"

"That I do. They said they had someone looking out for you and that you would get past everything. You would get past the pain."

Bethany curled her lips while her father studied her face.

"Jimmy," Bethany could barely get the words out.

"They wouldn't tell me who it was, but I think that's who they meant," her father whispered.

Bethany turned away and looked out the window from the chair. She wiped away her tears and watched as the trees outside gently swayed back and forth. This was heavy stuff. It was a lot for Bethany to digest. In her heart she truly believed that Padre Pio and Jesus were preparing her father to die. Just how long he had, she didn't know. *Everyone's gonna die,* she recalled Jimmy saying to her.

"Are you sure you're okay?" John asked concerned. "Maybe I shouldn't have told you. I don't want you to be scared. I'm not dying now, obviously."

"I know." Bethany nodded. "I'm glad you shared this with me, Daddy. Please know that. It's just a lot to take in, that's all."

"It will be our secret," he said.

Bethany nodded. "Yes, Daddy. It will."

Twenty-Nine

A Spanish woman in a peach-colored, striped uniform stopped at the entrance to John's room with the food cart, which by now was almost empty. She lifted one of the few remaining trays and carried it off into the room.

"Ready lunch?" She smiled. "Forgive my English."

She looked at Bethany, then at her father. Her smile faded. The woman could obviously see that they had been crying. Quickly she placed the food on the mayo stand and left without saying another word.

"Let me get that for you," Bethany said, rising from her chair. She watched as her father tried to lift his right arm but couldn't. Bethany walked around the bed and pulled the stand over his lap. She then took the bed controls and raised the back of the bed up slightly so her father could have a better angle from which to eat. She took off the lid, which was sitting on top of a plate, only to reveal the most unappetizing of foods. Bethany scrunched her face together in disgust and her father laughed. The plastic dish contained a gray piece of thin meatloaf, an over-microwaved baked potato, and dull looking corn, which sat in a pool of water.

"I'm sorry," she said, laughing herself. "I'm a chef...a food snob. What can I say? And you're a food snob too." She pointed a finger at her father playfully.

"Only because you've spoiled me," he said.

Bethany sighed. "Well, you have to eat."

"I suppose," he answered.

All of the sudden it dawned on Bethany, how exactly *was* he going to eat? He couldn't lift his arms to feed himself, and she doubted he could hold a fork anyway. She looked at the sterilized utensils in their wrapper. Slowly she picked them up and opened the packaging.

"I'll help you eat," Bethany said softly.

"Okay," her father replied. "I'm sorry I can't do it myself."

Bethany sat back down and moved her chair closer to the bed and to her father. She started by cutting the meat into small pieces.

"You don't have to cut them that small," he announced.

She looked down at the plate. She had been cutting bites for a small child. She wondered if somewhere in her there were motherly instincts, despite the fact that she never had a child. She cut the remaining pieces larger, and then, piercing a piece of meat with the fork, she held it up to her father's mouth. He opened his mouth awkwardly, and Bethany carefully placed the food inside. In her head she reminded herself to breathe. She was holding her breath because she suddenly felt very anxious.

Bethany continued to feed her father. Neither of them spoke during the process but Bethany's mind wandered. She thought about the times she had spent with Sarah when her children were very young and in high chairs. Bethany would go over to her house to visit and catch up, and she would watch how quickly Sarah would shove baby food into her child's mouth. The happy child was all too eager to eat, so it made things even easier and faster for Sarah. She could carry on one of her long-winded conversations while her hand worked fluently and skillfully to feed her baby. There was something so right and so natural about a mother feeding her child.

A daughter feeding her father was another thing completely. It was possibly the most humbling thing Bethany had ever done.

Somehow, at the same time it also strengthened the bond between them.

Bethany wondered these things while she slowly fed John. Sometimes a piece of food would fall or drip from his mouth. Gently, Bethany would wipe it away with a napkin. Inside she felt so emotional she just wanted to cry. She held it in because she didn't want her father to know just how difficult this was for her.

Thankfully, Rob came bolting into the room.

"Sorry I was gone so long," he said loudly. "It was crazy down there. There were all kinds of people plus a bunch of doctors. Everyone must be on break. I had to wait on a long line to pay for this." He lifted the bag he carried. "They let all the doctors cut the line."

Rob dragged another chair over and sat down. Making room on the mayo stand, he placed Bethany's bottle of water on it. He went about straightening up and taking the food he had just purchased out of the bag. He didn't seem to notice Bethany feeding her father, or if he did, he hadn't found anything unusual about the situation. Everything was normal to Rob though. He looked at life like "you do what you have to do" to get things done.

Rob rambled on about what he had encountered on his travels through the hospital, and it made the time for Bethany go quickly. Before long, most of her father's food had been eaten.

"I think I've had enough, Bethany. Thank you," he said.

Bethany wiped his mouth with a napkin and then brought a cup of juice up to his mouth.

"I've never had orange juice with meatloaf before." Her father sighed. "I miss my wine, although it would be a sin to have wine with this meal," he said.

"Oh, John Fitzpatrick! What are we to do with you?" Rob laughed.

"Well it's true!" he answered.

"Of course it's true," Bethany added, giving Rob a look.

"What? Don't look at me!" said Rob. "I'll eat anything you put in front of me. I don't complain." He laughed. "I'm sure Beth can bring up some of her culinary treasures tomorrow. Beef Wellington perhaps?" Bethany couldn't help but laugh.

"Maybe not beef Wellington," she said, "but definitely something better than this. Don't count on any wine though. I'll get thrown out for sure."

"Hospitals are no fun," John announced.

"Except when you're having a baby," Bethany added. "Do you remember when Sarah had her second child, Daddy?"

He smiled and nodded.

"You've got to hear this story, Rob," Bethany said. "The first night of visiting hours her room was packed. She was all done up with makeup and she was walking around the room entertaining."

"You're kidding?" asked Rob.

"She and her husband converted the mayo stand into a bar. Her husband brought glasses from home and several bottles of wine. I think they went through three bottles that night. That's how many guests they had. They also had an antipasto platter catered by the Mr. Sausage Italian store in Huntington. Can you imagine? They kept the door to the room closed. I don't think the security guard was too thrilled. I think he knew what was going on there."

Bethany continued. "The best part was after everyone left. Sarah got back into bed and finished her glass of wine, which she wasn't supposed to be having. She put the empty glass down while her husband went to the bathroom. Well, one of the mean nurses came in. A very large, robust kind of woman." Bethany laughed. "She was not happy. She looked at the glass, and then looked at Sarah and said, 'You weren't drinking, were you? I won't give you your pain medication if you were.' Sarah immediately denied it was hers. 'Whose is it then?' the nurse asked. Sarah told her it was her husband's and that he was in the bathroom. Double whammy! The nurse was angry that *he* was drinking, and even angrier still that he was in her bathroom!" Bethany laughed out loud, and Rob and John joined her. "Apparently it is absolutely forbidden that anyone, even your own husband, cannot under any circumstance use the bathroom of a woman who has just delivered. Isn't that crazy? It's a bit extreme if you ask me."

"Wow," Rob said. "I never knew what a party was going on up there in maternity."

The story had surely lightened the moment and it took the edge off Bethany. She managed to eat her lunch while John and Rob talked about all kinds of things. She watched her father while she ate and she was so happy that he no longer had hallucinations. Even more, she was elated that he had no recollection of the terrible things he had said. Bethany vowed never to tell him. He would feel so upset knowing he said things beyond his control. It was much better that he recalled the extraordinary experience of his journey with Padre Pio.

As Rob fed John a very sad looking fruit cocktail, surely from a can, Bethany looked at the silver medal which hung from John's neck. How one medal had given them such strength was a miracle in itself.

Thirty

John remained in the hospital another few days and then went on to rehab. During this time, Bethany was still feeling horrible about how she'd acted towards Jimmy. She hadn't seen him since the day she'd snapped, and she'd had no way of contacting him. Finally, one afternoon at the bakery when she went out back to take a break, there he was, sitting on her bench.

"Jimmy," she said, letting out a sigh.

He sat there like a lost puppy, with his head down and his hands folded in his lap. He looked up when he heard her, but didn't say anything.

Bethany slowly walked over. "Do you mind if I sit down?" she asked.

He moved over. "I was debatin' whether or not to come in."

"I'm sorry, Jimmy...I truly am."

When he didn't say anything, she started to cry. He put his arm around her as she sobbed into his shoulder.

"It's okay, kid. I understand you were havin' a bad day."

"I shouldn't have taken it out on you. I was so wrong. You've done nothing but help me, Jimmy. Please forgive me?" She broke away from him, and his blue eyes pierced through her tearful ones.

"He's gonna get through this, Beth. I'm tellin' you. Do you believe me?" he asked.

Bethany took a tissue from her jacket pocket and wiped her eyes while nodding.

"It was horrible, Jimmy. Really horrible. My father didn't know what he was saying. He was hallucinating from the medication they gave him. He said terrible things. He accused me of wanting to kill him."

"Listen to me," Jimmy said. "Your father ain't goin' nowhere. No matter what crazy stuff he said, he's still in here..." He tapped his finger on his chest. "Nothin's gonna take that away. It's his soul. It's who he is. Do you know what I'm sayin'? It's his soul. As long as you know that, you'll get through. You and your father are connected. You always will be even after he's gone one day. I'm tellin' you. Knowing that will help you get through...that and prayin' to Padre Pio."

"I don't know what I would do without you, Jimmy."

"You'd do fine. There'll come a time when you don't need me no more. You'll have the strength."

"Don't say that, Jimmy. I'll always need you. You're my friend," Bethany said.

Jimmy looked at her without speaking, a hint of sadness in his eyes.

"Besides...who would I share cannolis with?" Bethany added.

Jimmy chuckled. "Keep prayin'," he said. "He's gonna come out of this. Be strong. He has the medal on?"

"Yes. I made sure they didn't take it off him."

"Good. You look at the medal when you're with him, you understand? That medal is for the both of you, you know. It's just as much for you as it for him. It'll give you strength. Look what Padre Pio went through in his lifetime. You'll get past this. He'll help you."

"I believe you, Jimmy. I really do. It may have taken me a while, but I believe."

"Alright then. I'll be around if you need me, kid." Jimmy stood up, and Bethany watched as he walked away.

It was either his willingness to come home, Padre Pio, or a little bit of both which enabled John to be released from the rehabilitation center the day before Thanksgiving. He and Bethany were overjoyed.

With all that had been going on, Bethany couldn't fathom how she was still right on schedule with filling all her orders for the holiday. Despite the difficult circumstances, she managed to keep her wits about her. She stayed calm and focused, whether she was helping her father or working at the bakery. She was proud of her ability to keep it together this time around, and she felt she owed a lot of it to Jimmy, who couldn't have been more encouraging during those few weeks.

"So he's comin' home for Thanksgivin'!" Jimmy happily remarked as he took a bite of a cannoli while standing in the kitchen of Giovanni's. "I told ya," he mumbled between bites. "You gotta believe."

"Okay, so you're right again," Bethany replied as she attached a whisk to her KitchenAid mixer.

"Whataya makin' now?" Jimmy asked, watching her. "You got a lot of pies here."

"Well, people like pie on Thanksgiving. I actually only have a few more to go and they'll all be ready for pickup tomorrow. If I don't finish today I can always come in really early tomorrow to do it, but I think I'll be okay." She added egg whites to the mixer and turned the machine on. "Oh, lemon meringue pie. Not your typical Thanksgiving pie in my opinion, but I'll do anything my customers ask." She turned on the mixer while Jimmy took the last bite of his cannoli.

"I'm not crazy about lemon meringue. Too much lemon for me. Now these over here," he said pointing to a grouping of ten pies. "These are more like it."

Bethany laughed as she watched Jimmy salivate over an assortment of apple, pumpkin, and chocolate cream pies. "You sure you don't want to join us for Thanksgiving dinner?" she asked over her shoulder while she raised the head of the mixer.

"Yeah, I'm sure," Jimmy replied, still looking over the pies. "I have stuff to do."

"For your work?"

"You could kinda say that," Jimmy said. He began wandering around the kitchen looking at things as if to avoid the conversation.

Bethany removed the finished egg whites from the mixer and carefully piled them on top of a pie crust filled with lemon curd. "Don't you have any family that you can see?"

"Nah, not really. They all live too far away, you know? It's okay, though. I'm fine. It's just another day, is all. Whataya do with that now?" he asked, pointing to the lemon meringue pie.

"I put it in the oven so the top can brown and caramelize," Bethany said.

Jimmy watched closely as she carefully put the pie in the oven.

Sensing he was a bit uncomfortable with the conversation, Bethany changed the subject.

"So anyway, I can come in tomorrow to finish a pie or two, but I'd rather not. That way I can just concentrate on getting my father home. I have some extra girls coming in to help Alison, so I'm pretty covered."

"That's good," Jimmy said.

"As for cooking at home, I don't have too much to do. It's just me, my dad, and Rob. Rob's family lives upstate. I'm glad he's spending Thanksgiving with us. I don't know what I would do without him." Bethany bent down, opened the door to the oven, and peered in at the pie.

"What will you make then?" Jimmy asked as Bethany closed the oven door.

"I was going to make a turkey breast since it's just the three of us, but then I decided against it. I was able to get a small bird, and I thought that having leftovers for my dad and Rob, and even for Cherie for lunch, would be good, although she does bring her own food most of the time. Then I'll make carrots, string beans, mashed potatoes, stuffing, and turnips. The usual fare," said Bethany as she leaned up against the counter. "Are you sure I can't convince you?" she asked one last time.

"I'm sure," Jimmy said. "But thanks for askin'. Nobody's ever invited me to Thanksgivin' before."

Bethany gave him a smile and then checked on the pie again. It had sufficiently browned, so she grabbed a potholder and removed it from the oven.

"Nice," Jimmy said, looking at the pie. "Real nice."

"The key is to add a lot of egg whites. Most cooks at home follow the recipe and add the amount of egg whites listed. It's never enough, though. They don't get this kind of height, and also it tends to pull away from the crust after it sets. Common problems with lemon meringue pie," Bethany said.

"Well, you're the expert. I could never do somethin' like this. You know what I'm sayin'? I had a hard enough time stuffin' those cannolis." Jimmy laughed.

Bethany went around the kitchen cleaning up the mixer and other items while Jimmy watched silently. After a few minutes Bethany said to Jimmy, "Can I ask you something?" She turned toward him.

"Sure," he answered. "What's up?"

"You didn't say much the other day when I told you about my father's dream. When Padre Pio came to visit him in the hospital? Do you remember?"

"Of course I do. Whataya want to know?"

"Well, it wasn't a dream. I believe my father; that it really happened."

"Yeah? So what's the problem?"

"It's just that you didn't say one way or another what you thought. *Did* he actually appear to my father?" Bethany asked.

"I didn't say anything 'cause I was listenin' to what you were tellin' me, you know? I wanted to hear what *you* thought about it. Come to your own conclusions, if you know what I'm sayin'. I'm not the one who needs convincin', you are, Beth. I already know it's true," said Jimmy.

Bethany stopped cleaning and leaned up against the counter contemplating this for a moment.

"So it is true?" she asked again.

Jimmy said nothing and just stared at her. Finally he said, "You need to start believin' based on your faith, Beth. Not because I tell you. Do *you* really believe it? Based on all the stuff I've been tellin' you all this time...do *you* believe it?"

Bethany looked him in the eye. "I believe it, Jimmy. I know, without a doubt, that my father was with Padre Pio; that he went on some kind of incredible journey with him. I don't know how this could be, but it was."

"So whataya need me tellin' *you* then? You're stronger than you think, Beth. Don't second guess yourself."

"I just need to know I'm on the right track."

"You don't know that by now?" asked Jimmy, folding his arms.

Bethany shrugged not quite sure how to answer.

"I told you about Padre Pio having the bilocation, didn't I? Did you believe me then?"

She nodded.

"Well this is the same kinda thing."

"But he's dead this time."

"It don't matter. It still happens. What about that woman you told me about? The woman who had breast cancer down by the beach. Padre Pio was dead then too."

"I know that. I guess what I'm trying to say...that woman stayed where she was. She was right there next to her car hoping a tow truck would come by. *She* never left. Her body didn't pick up and go somewhere with Padre Pio." Bethany paused. "My father on the other hand...he did. He left his body, Jimmy. He went away with Padre Pio, all while I was looking right at him. There's a difference."

"I understand what you're sayin'. It's all part of the mystery. Let me tell you another story. I don't think I told you this one yet. Stop me if I did. Here, sit down," Jimmy said as he pulled her work stool over. "Sit."

Bethany did as she was told. When she was situated, Jimmy, like a teacher, stood over her and began to speak.

"Did I ever tell you about the very first time Padre Pio experienced bilocation?"

"Was that the story when he was in Germany and in Italy at the same time during the war?"

"Nah. Not that one. This happened way before that. Listen to me. This incident, what I'm gonna tell you, happened while he was a seminarian. It was way before the war. It was 1905," Jimmy began, settling himself against the counter. "Padre Pio was studyin' philosophy at this place called the Capuchin Convent of St. Elia a Pianisi. One night around eleven he was in the choir with one of the brothers. All of a sudden, he wasn't there no more. His body was there, but somehow he was also in some palace somewhere...the home of some wealthy family. He was there because the man who owned the palace was about to die. At the same time, the man's wife was about to give birth to a premature baby girl. You followin' what I'm sayin' here?"

"I think so," she answered. She loved watching Jimmy tell one of his stories. He acted out every part, and would become more and more excited, stressing every point using hand gestures like only Italians can do. She waited for him to continue.

"Now, before the woman gave birth she seen the figure of a Capuchin Friar leave her husband's room. Okay? This was impossible. There couldn't have been no Capuchin Friar. The guy who was dyin' was a Mason. The Mason's don't believe in confession or last rites. They were told some friar was tryin' to get in to give the guy last rites and hear his confession. So the others in the household, in this palace here, don't let him in. Someone says 'Wait a minute! You can't deny this friar entry. Lady so-and-so just gave birth to a premature baby. It needs to be baptized right away in case it dies.' So they let him in. It was Padre Pio. Well, Padre Pio went immediately to the dying man who did confess to him after all," said Jimmy.

"Now," he said, "You remember when I told you that Padre Pio had this thing with the Blessed Mother? Okay. Roll the clock back. The Blessed Mother comes to this palace and tells Padre Pio, 'This lady's husband is gonna die and she's gonna give birth to this little girl,' you know? Well, the Blessed Mother tells Padre Pio that she's entrusting the spiritual care of this little girl to him."

"What? How could that be?" Bethany asked.

"I'll tell you," Jimmy said as he leaned forward. "Even Padre Pio questioned the Blessed Mother. He looks at her and says, 'Who me? How can I do that? I'm not even a priest yet?' She says, 'Don't worry. She will come to you at the Basilica of St. Peter's in Rome.' So Padre Pio does his thing at the palace, and before you know it, Padre Pio

was back in the choir. He was no longer in the palace. You gettin'
this so far?"

"Yes," Bethany replied.

"Years go by, you know? Everything happened exactly like the
Blessed Mother had said. The guy dies, the woman gives
birth...everything. Now...listen carefully. The little baby grows up.
This is all well documented by the way. It's all written down at the
Vatican somewhere. So this girl grows up. She knows nothin' about
Padre Pio. Never even heard of him. Has no idea that there is this
divine plan worked out with her and Padre Pio. You followin' me,
kid?"

Bethany smiled. "Yes, Jimmy. I think I've got it so far."

"Good," he said. "So anyways, by the time the girl was in high
school her faith was tested because her teachers did not believe in
God. So what does she do? She starts to lose faith. She starts to
doubt. She feels guilty about this so she goes to St. Peter's to confess
just like the Blessed Mother said. It's now 1922. There's no priests
around anywhere. What is she gonna do? She runs into a custodian
who tells her to come back tomorra. She don't have time for this. She
don't wanna wait. She decides to look around; see if she could find a
priest, you know? All of a sudden she sees this young Capuchin Friar
walkin' towards her...Padre Pio. But she don't know this yet, you
know what I'm sayin'? She begs him to listen to her and to absolve
her sins. He says okay and they go into the confessional. He clears
everything up for her and she feels so much better. She's relieved,
you know? He explains the mystery of the Holy Trinity; the whole
nine yards. Explains everything. She has no doubts now. So it comes
time to leave. 'Thank you, Father.' You gettin' this here?"

"Yes," said Bethany.

"Okay, she runs into the same custodian from before, right
outside the confessional. He tells her she has to leave because the
church is closin'. She needs to come back tomorra. She tells him she
don't need to come back. She just gave her confession to the
Capuchin father. The custodian is confused. There were no priests
there. She tells him to see for himself, so he looks in. Ain't nobody
there, Beth...gone. He ain't in there. Padre Pio's gone. The girl's in

shock. She knew he was in there. She confessed her sins to him. Confused, she went home.

"A year later now...1923, the girl goes with her aunt and a friend to San Giovanni Rotondo. It's her first time. They're gonna see some priest named Padre Pio." Jimmy smiled. "Okay? You get where this is goin' here?" Jimmy did not wait for Beth to answer. Instead he continued on in an animated fashion.

"So they get there, right? Mobs of people. Everyone's comin' to see Padre Pio, 'cause by now everyone knows about him. So she's comin' down a hallway when all of a sudden, past these mobs of people, here comes Padre Pio walking right towards her. He stops and says to her, 'I know you.' She says, 'You don't know me. I've never met you before.' He says to her, 'You were born the same day your father died.' He blesses her and walks away. The next day the aunt tells her to go to his confessional. The aunt's already seen him. So the girl stands on a line to go to his confessional. As soon as she gets there he says to her, 'My daughter, you have finally come.' She don't know what's goin' on. He tells her he's been waiting for her for years. She says to him, 'Father, you don't know me. We've never met. This is the first time I've been to San Giovanni Rotondo. You must have mistaken me for somebody else.' This is what she's sayin' to him. You followin' me?"

Bethany nodded once again.

"Okay. Now," he said loudly as he clapped his hands together. "Padre Pio says to her, 'No, I do know you and you know me. Last year at the Basilica you came up to me and I gave you confession. I was the Capuchin Friar.' Well the woman almost fell out of the confessional. So Padre Pio explains the whole thing to her...how the Blessed Mother came, how he knew the father was gonna die, how the girl was gonna be put into his spiritual care...it's somethin' isn't it?

"So she says to him, 'Father, what am I supposed to do? Am I supposed to be a nun?' He tells her no. All he wants her to do is to come frequently to San Giovanni Rotondo and he will guide her. So she's cryin' and everything. She just can't believe any of this. She tells nobody about what happened. Not even her aunt.

"On one of the girl's visits to Padre Pio, he says he wants her to be called Sister Jacopa even though she's not a nun. This is just between the two of them. She don't like the name. Asks if she can be called Sister Clare or somethin'. Padre Pio says no. She must be called Sister Jacopa because it was the name of a noble Roman lady who St. Francis called 'the beloved mother of our order.' This lady's name was Jacopa de'Settesoli. She was a very generous lady who looked out for the Franciscans. She protected them. So Padre Pio says, 'Just as she was there to witness the death of St. Francis, you will be there to witness mine.' This woman's like, 'What? What are you talkin' about?'

"The years go on. The woman gets married, raises a nice Christian family, and she always kept her promise to visit Padre Pio for guidance. She gets older. It becomes harder and harder for her to get to San Giovanni Rotondo. She's old now, you know? Been goin' back and forth for years. One day when she's there, Padre Pio says to her, 'Come again soon because I'm goin' away. If you wait too long I will be gone and you'll miss me.' She listened to what he said. She arrives again just four days before Padre Pio dies. He gives her confession. Then he says to her, 'This will be the last time you will come to my confessional,' and he absolves her of all the sins she had ever committed. She questions him and says, 'But Father, where are you going? Why can't I confess to you anymore?' He tells her again, 'I'm goin' away.' It's then that she realizes he's gonna die," Jimmy said softly.

"On the night of September 22, 1968," he continued, "Padre Pio gave his last blessing to the crowds at San Giovanni Rotondo. It was the fiftieth anniversary of his stigmata, can you believe it? He goes back to his cell to die. He knows he's gonna die. All of a sudden, the woman finds herself miraculously in the cell with him. She could see everything but no one could see her. She saw Padre Pio confess his sins to Padre Pellegrino, she saw him suffer, she saw him pray. She saw the doctors looking out for him and attending to him and she watched him get last rites. She watched as he died," Jimmy said softly again.

Then Jimmy raised his voice and said, "She screams, 'Padre Pio's dead, Padre Pio's dead!' but she's not in his cell no more. She is back in her hotel room. Her friend who had come with her on the trip said she was only dreamin'. It was a dream. The woman didn't believe her, so she quickly got dressed and ran over to the convent. A small crowd had already gathered there. She arrived just as a Capuchin Friar was announcing the death of Padre Pio."

Bethany sat stunned. "Did anyone believe her story?" Bethany asked.

Jimmy answered, "She went to see a man by the name of Padre Alberto. She described to him in detail what she had seen in Padre Pio's cell. He knew this was impossible. Nobody, especially not a woman, had ever been allowed in Padre Pio's cell. There were never any photographs of the cell taken either. There was no way she could have known. She testified to the authorities and the story went on record as being the truth."

"That's really amazing, Jimmy. It's quite a story," Bethany said.

"So...to answer your question, Beth...yes...your father, for just a short time, was given the gift of bilocation."

Thirty-One

Despite the care and physical therapy he had been given in the rehab, John was definitely not the same when he arrived home. Rob told Bethany not to concern herself too much, and to just enjoy the fact that they could spend Thanksgiving together, as difficult as it was. John still needed help feeding himself, although he was able to bring a fork to his mouth once in a while. He was completely confined to the wheelchair, and he needed to start wearing bladder control underwear, which upset him to no end. It was just one more freedom that was taken away from him.

Rob believed that over time John would grow strong again. Bethany however, believed otherwise. She didn't think that she was being negative in regards to her father's situation, she simply believed, or sensed, that whatever had happened to him on the last trip to the hospital was irreversible. The doctor who had been taking care of him had reminded her of the possibility of this fact. Still, Bethany remained strong and focused and determined to get through anything that came her way. Her father required much more care, but between Bethany, Rob, and Cherie, Bethany knew they would make it work.

December, like November, was a busy month at the bakery as people got ready for holiday parties and gatherings. Everyone wanted a cake to bring, and then there were those busy mothers who came in to cheat, buying Bethany's cookies instead of making their own. When she was at the bakery, Bethany did her best to concentrate on her work rather than to dwell on what was going on at home. She knew Rob was fully capable of taking care of John, and she also knew that somewhere and somehow Padre Pio stayed close by. Bethany continued to pray, to light candles at church and to speak to Jimmy about everything. Through it all however, a growing sense of dread seemed to consume her no matter how hard she tried to fight it off.

Sometime during mid-December, Bethany was feeling down and worried. She just couldn't help herself. So one day while Jimmy was in the kitchen, she asked him point blank, "Do you think he's going to die soon?" She popped a chocolate cake in the oven while waiting for him to reply. She could tell by the look on his face that she had caught him off guard by her question.

"Why you sayin' that, Beth?" he asked after a long pause.

"I don't know," she replied, shutting the oven door and then folding her arms over her chef's coat. She propped herself against the counter. "It's just a feeling. I hate it. I don't want to think this way. I can't shake it, though." Bethany looked at Jimmy for an answer. She wondered if he was an angel of some kind, would he have the answer to that question. And if he did know, would he even tell her? She studied his face while Jimmy gathered his thoughts.

"I don't want you thinkin' like that. You hear?" Jimmy said as he pointed to her, obviously avoiding the question. "Come on. You've been doin' great. Don't start thinkin' he's gonna die."

"I'm not thinking it exactly," she tried to explain. "It's just a feeling. I'm scared it could be a premonition, Jimmy. That's all."

He sighed and put his head down slightly as he looked at the floor and then back to Bethany. "I don't know what to tell you on this one," Jimmy said. "It's up to God, Beth. I've told you that before, but no matta what, Padre Pio's with the both of yous."

Bethany unfolded her arms and nodded, wishing he could have told her...what? She wasn't quite sure.

"Just keep focusin' and prayin'. Keep doin' what you've been doin' and everything will be okay. You believe me?" he said, walking over to her.

Jimmy put his hand on Bethany's shoulder. She was looking down.

"Hey. You listenin' to me?" he asked as he gently lifted her chin up to look at him. "You'll get through, Beth. That much I do know, whatever happens. You understand?"

Through her tears she looked into Jimmy's comforting blue eyes. She nodded again and said, "I know. I believe you. I'm just scared, Jimmy. I'm going to be all alone when he goes. I've gotten used to this strange existence I have. It's not normal, I know, but it has become normal to me. Taking care of him, living with him, dealing with all of this. Will I know how to live again? I don't know how to live *my* life. Who am I? I only know how to be an obedient daughter and a caretaker. I only know working. I can't relate to my friends, I don't date. I have no idea what it's like to have fun, to be free from all the struggles. I don't know what I'll do."

"Let me ask you this," Jimmy said. "When the time comes, and I'm not sayin' it's happenin' anytime soon, you don't think your father will still be there? You don't think he can help you from the other side? What about Padre Pio? Do you think he'll just abandon you because your father died? It ain't happenin'. You've got to trust me on this, hun. You got it?" He lifted her chin up again. "I want you to go home tonight and sit with your father. Take a look at that medal I gave him. Get strength from it. It's all gonna work out the way it's supposed to. Don't be scared. It's okay."

"I've been doing so well. I don't know what happened. I don't know why I'm feeling this way. It's been building up," Bethany said as she wiped her eyes.

"It happens. You're human. You can have a bad day every now and then. Besides, it's Christmastime. Everyone's always more emotional this time of year. You know what I'm sayin'?" Jimmy asked.

Bethany thought about that for a moment. "You're probably right. I miss my mom so much this time of year. I miss what we once had as a family. I can't even tell you how perfect it was. Why did it all have to change?"

"Things happen, Bethany. You will find out the answer someday though."

Bethany sighed. "I suppose. It will all become clear when I die one day. Is that it?"

"Yes, it is as a matter of fact."

Bethany smiled at Jimmy, not knowing what else to say.

"Let me get goin'," Jimmy said stepping away. "You alright now? You have stuff to do here. Concentrate on your cakes. It's smellin' good already." He pointed to the oven as he smiled. "I'm gonna get me a cannoli to go from Alison. I'll see you around, Beth. Okay? Okay."

He turned and left the kitchen. Bethany folded shook her head. "Jimmy," she said quietly. "What would I do without you?"

Bethany did her best to get through the month. She avoided anything that could possibly upset her, from listening to sad Christmas songs to hearing Sarah complain on how stressed out she was because of all she had to do for the holiday. "At least you have something to celebrate," Bethany had said to her on the phone one day. Sarah was at a loss for words.

Bethany concentrated on work and took care of her father. She debated not putting up a Christmas tree, but she didn't want to upset him. He'd always loved Christmas.

When Bethany and Steven were young, Victoria and John would drive out to Long Island's North Fork where they would traipse through the Christmas tree farm in search of the perfect tree. After finding it, Victoria would take countless photos of the kids in front of the tree. Then John, with his old bow saw in hand, would crouch down and lay under the tree on the ice cold ground. Sometimes it would take him a while, depending on how thick the trunk was, but John was always determined to cut the tree down the old fashioned way. Bethany would sometimes cry thinking how they killed the tree that had taken so long to grow. Her mother would kneel on the cold ground and comfort her, telling her that the trees at the farm were different. They were special and were grown to be Christmas trees.

Some of the trees would wait for years for someone to pick them, for they longed to be brought inside and adorned by a special family who would love them. Soon Bethany would begin to feel better. Her mother could always make her feel better, so could the cup of hot chocolate that she and Steven would get while the tree was being wrapped and tied to the roof of the car.

How beautiful and simple it all had been. Bethany couldn't remember the last time she was at a Christmas tree farm. Instead, this year she had instructed Rob to go down to the local Home Depot and pick one off the lot.

Her father never asked where the tree had come from, but he did enjoy watching Bethany decorate it.

"Look at that one," John said, referring to an ornament of a lighthouse with a Christmas wreath around it. "That's the one we got the summer you were twelve, when we took the boat up to Cape Cod. What a great time we had."

Bethany took a deep breath and hung the ornament on the tree.

"Oh, look. Over there," John said, pointing to a snowflake ornament which contained a family photo from a ski trip. "May I see it before you hang it?"

Bethany passed it to him and John stared at it with a big smile on his face.

"Look at how beautiful your mother looks. She loved that coat."

Each ornament seemed to hold years' worth of memories, and as Bethany placed each one upon the tree, her pain grew. She wondered if this would be her father's last Christmas. She tried to push the thought aside but it haunted her nonetheless.

An hour or so later when she was finally done decorating the tree, she made them each a hot cocoa. Her father had trouble holding the heavy mug, so Bethany brought it to his lips each time he wanted a sip. His nose hit the whipped cream brimming from the steaming mug, and Bethany couldn't help but laugh. Her laughter quickly turned to sadness as she took a napkin and gently wiped her father's nose. How childlike and helpless he had become. It was so very sad to her.

She tried to keep the conversation light, but he was in the mood for reminiscing, to Bethany's dismay.

"When you were little, the church formed a caroling group and they all came up the hill in the snow to sing Christmas songs. It was so delightful...like something out of an old movie. Your mother, the entertainer that she was, had them all come in afterwards and warm up by the fire. She searched the house for every Christmas mug she had and made hot cocoa for everyone."

Bethany offered a sad smile.

"This house does look beautiful in the snow," he continued. "You and Steven took the sleds down the hill hundreds of times...you never got tired. Your mother had to beg you to come in. And what about the snowmen family we made? Do you remember that, Bethany?"

"Yes, Daddy," she said softly. "I remember all of it. Those were great times."

As the fire crackled in the hearth, John continued to speak of Christmases past, and it took all Bethany had to keep herself together. Her father seemed so happy in his thoughts and so accepting of his present situation. Bethany could just not comprehend it all. After a while she could see him beginning to fade and she called Rob.

She looked at the medal around his neck, and she kissed her father goodnight as Rob wheeled him away. Bethany brought the empty boxes which had held the ornaments back down to the basement. She then returned to pick up the empty mugs of hot cocoa. *The First Noel* was gently playing on the stereo while the fire burned to cinders. Holding the mugs, she turned to look at the newly decorated tree before leaving the room. The pain was just too great, and the tears came rolling down her face.

"I hate Christmas," she said softly.

Thirty-Two

January had arrived and Bethany was relieved that both Christmas and New Years were over. The entire month had been a difficult one for her; with her emotions running the gamut. She did her best trying not to forecast the year ahead, and she vowed to take things as they came. It wasn't even two weeks into the New Year, however, when her father started not to feel well.

"He doesn't seem right to me, Rob," Bethany said early one morning when she met Rob down the long hallway of the house.

"He does seem a little bit out of it, I agree, and he looks a little swollen. I think the edema may be coming back." Rob scratched his head as if wondering what to do. "I'd say we should bring him to the doctor but he doesn't have any other symptoms. I checked his temperature. He doesn't have a fever. He's weak, but he's had bad days before. I'm just afraid that if I bring him to the doctor, he'll catch something. The flu is rampant right now, and he has no immunity to fight it off. I don't need him in a waiting room next to all those people who have God-knows-what."

Bethany, with her hands on her hips, stood with Rob in the hallway discussing the situation and trying to figure out what to do.

"Maybe you could call the doctor and just mention what's going on," Bethany said. "He's really been inactive so maybe that's why he's swelling up."

"I don't know. I really think something else is going on here. I'll keep a close eye on him throughout the day. I'll call the doctor."

"Please let me know if anything changes. Call me."

Rob promised, but Bethany went off to work feeling a little uneasy. The feeling stayed with her throughout the day. At four the phone rang and it was Rob.

"Bethany, he's starting to run a fever now and he hasn't eaten much either. He's just not right. It's your call. Do you want me to take him somewhere or do you want me to treat the fever and wait it out? The doctor's office is swamped. They wouldn't even let me speak to him. I called hours ago and they told me he'd call back, but I haven't heard anything."

Bethany didn't know what to do. She knew the risks if they took him to the doctor, and she also knew he would be dead weight because of the fever. They would really have their hands full even if the doctor had agreed to see them. She wasn't sure they could manage him. Bethany paced up and down in the bakery's kitchen, one hand on the cordless phone, the other gripping her forehead.

"Have you given him anything?" she asked.

"Motrin and his usual medication. That's it," he replied.

"How long ago?"

"About an hour ago."

Bethany continued to pace the floor and then she looked up at the clock.

"Listen, it's slow here. Alison should be able to close up for me. It's almost time to go anyway. I'd rather come home and see for myself."

Within fifteen minutes Bethany was pulling up the driveway, and she ran inside. Without taking her coat off, she tossed her bag on the kitchen counter and went directly to her father's room. Rob was in there with him.

"What's going on, Daddy?" Bethany asked. She unraveled her scarf. When her father didn't answer, she looked at Rob.

"I just took his temperature again. It's going up instead of going down. I don't want to be an alarmist here, but I think we need to get him to the hospital. Look at his legs." Rob pulled the covers off the lower portion of the bed and exposed John's very swollen legs. "This isn't good. Look at his chest and neck. He's retaining water or fluid and he seems to be struggling to breathe. That just started maybe twenty minutes ago. Not long after I got off the phone with you. I don't think we should mess around with this."

Bethany stared down at her father, her mind racing. She really didn't want to go through the whole hospital ordeal again, but deep down she knew she had no other choice.

"Okay," she said softly. "Call the ambulance."

John had pneumonia. He was in ICU for days and his condition did not seem to be improving. Most times he slept and was unresponsive. Other times he would awaken and was extremely confused and agitated just like he had been back in November. As each day went on he grew older and older looking. His body was retaining water, and his arms, neck, chest, face, and legs were completely swollen.

Bethany was sitting beside her father one afternoon when Dr. Wang entered the room.

"His condition obviously is much worse than when he was in here in the fall. The pneumonia has complicated matters, and even with the high dosages of medication, his body is not responding as well as it should be. His body offers no support or immunity in fighting against it. Unfortunately we cannot keep him here in ICU. We have to bring him upstairs to a room because we need the space down here. I have arranged for him to have his own room and he will be monitored very closely. We'll continue the same regimen and see if there are any changes."

Bethany nodded but said nothing. The doctor looked her in the eyes, and while doing so, he adjusted his glasses and then folded his arms over the chart that was pressed up against his chest. Bethany sensed there was more and her body grew instantly stiff while her heart began to pound quicker.

The doctor took a deep breath and said, "I see on his chart that John is Catholic."

"Yes, that's correct," Bethany answered nervously.

"It may be in his and your best interests if he is anointed."

"Anointed?" Bethany said in surprise. "The Sacrament of the Sick?" Bethany's mind went wild. Anyone who is ill can have Anointing of the Sick at any time, but most people considered it to be the final sacrament given right before a person dies. "He's not going to make it, is he?"

"Although anything can change," he said, "as it appears now, it's not looking very good. That's another reason I'd like him upstairs. It's quieter and I think it will be more comfortable for him, as well as for you, if he should pass."

Bethany turned away from the doctor, her right hand covering her mouth. She paced a step or two.

"I know this is difficult," Dr. Wang said. "Your father is a very sick man and he has been for quite some time. I want you to know that we are not giving up on him. We are treating him to the best of our abilities, but there is only so much we can do."

"I understand," Bethany said, barely audible.

"If you have any other family that may need to see him, I suggest you take care of that as well."

"How much time do you think he has?" she asked. "My brother lives in Colorado. He'll need to fly in."

"It could be a couple of days, a week maybe. It's hard to tell."

"I see," Bethany said, putting her head down.

"I know it's hard, but try to take care of yourself. You'll need your strength."

The doctor put his hand on Bethany's shoulder, and she made a small effort to smile. The doctor nodded and left the room.

Thirty-Three

Bethany called her brother, and then Father Michael. That evening, John received the very last of the Catholic sacraments, while Steven made immediate plans to come to New York. All Bethany could do was wait.

Bethany had a restless sleep that night, tossing and turning, half expecting the phone to ring in the wee hours with news that her father had passed away. She awoke at five o'clock to begin her day. Having not received a phone call, she took a deep breath knowing her father was still alive. She quickly showered and dressed and headed down to the bakery. She'd work for just a few hours before heading to the hospital.

The back and forth was taking a toll on her, and she was concerned how it may be affecting her business. She knew there was no other way, however. This was her life right now and she was doing the best that she could. Alison had a good handle on things, and Bethany couldn't have been more grateful.

As she worked her way around the kitchen making rolls, scones and bread, her thoughts had turned to Jimmy. Where was he? It must have been at least two weeks since she had last seen him. She missed him and she hoped that everything was alright.

At nine-thirty in the morning Rob called. He was up at the hospital and John's condition was the same; not better and not worse. He said he had gotten to the hospital at eight and that John had been sleeping the whole time. He told Bethany to take her time and not to rush, that everything was fine and he'd stay until she arrived.

Relieved that her father hadn't gotten worse, Bethany was able to concentrate on completing a cake she was making. Once the bakery cases were filled, she felt free to go. She took off her chef's coat and put on her winter jacket. Before leaving Bethany talked to Alison for a few minutes and promised to call her in the event anything should change and she couldn't make it back.

Bethany left Giovanni's and instead of going straight to the hospital, she took a detour and drove down Main Street to church. Like she had been doing every single week at various times, Bethany made her way over to the Padre Pio statue and the image of the Divine Mercy. She knelt down around them, but before doing so she lit a candle for her father, which was her usual routine.

No one was in the church. She began to say her prayers. Then, looking up toward Padre Pio and to the image of Christ, she said, "Please help my father. Please give him some more time. I know that's really selfish on my part. I know it is, but I'm not ready to let him go. Not this way." The tears began to flow and Bethany wiped them away. "I want to be able to have one last conversation with him. I don't want him to die in the hospital. I understand there is no other way, but if you could help him...if you could help me...please, please, I am begging you...help him. Don't let him die yet."

She propped her elbows up against the top of the kneeler and covered her face with her hands while she sobbed. A few minutes later, she felt calmer. She looked up at the statue of Padre Pio, which seemed to be looking upon her. Her eyes then turned to the image of Jesus pointing to his pierced heart. "Please help him...and me."

Not long after, Bethany left the church and then drove to the hospital. Her thoughts turned to Jimmy. Maybe when she returned to the bakery later, he would be there. Perhaps he had come recently and she missed him. With so much going on, maybe Alison had forgotten to tell her that he had been around looking for her. She just wanted to see him and to talk to him. The thought of him in her bakery eating a cannoli brought a smile to her face as she continued on toward the hospital.

As always, once there Bethany had difficulty finding a parking spot in the crowded lot. She tried not to get frustrated. Someone had his brake lights on and appeared as if he was going to back up. Bethany stopped and waited for them to pull out. It seemed endless.

"Come on already," she yelled out inside her car. "Are you going or what?" The car started to back up slowly and then it stopped. The person was obviously having a difficult time.

"Oh, my gosh," Bethany said as she put her forehead over her hands on the top of the steering wheel. "Can anything in my life not be difficult?"

Finally the person managed to pull out and drive away. Bethany quickly pulled in. She walked swiftly down the path toward the hospital. The looming building stood before her and she considered it a type of prison. She kept her thoughts at bay and continued on. She ran into Rob in the lobby.

"Oh, hi, Beth," he said, walking toward her. "He's still sleeping. I just came down to get something to eat."

"I'm here now. Why don't you go home and eat there? I don't know how you keep forcing down the food here," she said.

"It's not too bad." Rob smiled.

"Please," Bethany said.

"Oh, you chefs are too picky. You should have seen what I grew up eating."

"Spare me," Bethany said and laughed. "Really, go home. There's some food I made in the refrigerator. I'll call you later when I'm ready to go back. No sense in us both being here. If something should change with him, I'll let you know.

"Are you sure? What time is your brother getting in?"

"That's a whole other story," Bethany said. "He called me on my cell this morning while I was at work. He was at the airport and his flight was delayed. The airport is literally shut down. They're having a snowstorm and no one can get out."

"Jeez! That's Colorado for you. What timing, though. So what are they telling him?" Rob asked.

"The storm's supposed to end sometime this afternoon," Bethany said. "They hope to get the flights going by evening. Who knows? Steven thinks it's going to be a really late night. He may not get in until after two. He said he'll get a room at one of the hotels near JFK. He doesn't want us coming out at that time. Would you be okay with picking him up tomorrow?"

"Of course. I told you I would. It's no problem at all," Rob answered.

"I really appreciate that. Just say a prayer that my father doesn't die before he gets here."

"There's really been no change. I haven't seen any doctors around, but he seems pretty stable. I think we have some time."

"Okay, that's good news, I guess," Bethany said. "Now go. Go home and get something to eat, walk the dogs, get some downtime, even if it's only for a little while."

"Will do," he said and was on his way.

Bethany walked her usual path to the elevators and waited for the doors to open. As the elevator reached her father's floor, she stepped out and something in the distance caught her attention. She saw the back of a man with a long, brown robe and gray hair leave her father's room. Her eyes grew wide and she started picking up her pace. The man kept walking. Bethany pulled her pocketbook up over her shoulder and quickened her pace. "Hey," she yelled out.

Oblivious to her, the man kept walking. Bethany never took her eyes off him. As she got closer, she happened to see his hands as they moved back and forth with the rhythm of his gait. Bethany gasped and covered her mouth.

"Wait!" she yelled. "Please!" She began to run. "Wait!" No one else seemed to be around. The hallway was an endless journey. As she ran the tears began to fall and her heart was pounding in her chest. It seemed impossible, of course, but the man she was chasing was clearly Padre Pio, for when she looked down at his hands as he walked, they were partially covered by dark, fingerless gloves.

Bethany's thoughts were racing. Why was he here? Did her father die? Did he cure him? Oddly enough she didn't even bother looking into her father's room as she ran past. She was afraid to let Padre Pio out of her sight. She had almost caught up to him when he reached the end of the corridor. He turned left and Bethany quickly followed. As she turned the corner, he was gone. Frantic, she looked around, and then spun around again. She popped her head in a room and then in another. She was desperate.

"Have you seen a man with a long brown robe? Like a priest, a holy man?" Bethany pleaded to several women at the nurses' station. They glanced up at her from beneath their paperwork and computers and shook their heads. Bethany spun around again and put her hand on top of her forehead. She was out of breath and confused, when suddenly she remembered her father.

"Oh, my God...Daddy!" She turned the corner and ran back down to her father's room, not knowing if she would find him dead or alive?

"Please, Padre Pio. Please don't have taken him yet," she said softly as she reached the entrance to her father's room. With her heart racing, she took a deep breath and ventured in. The curtain around her father's bed, which was usually open, was drawn shut. Underneath it she could see a pair of black shoes and black pants. They were men's shoes, and by the look of the pants, the man clearly was not a doctor.

Who's in here now? she wondered as she held her breath. In one swift movement, she pulled the curtain around and found Jimmy standing over her father.

Thirty-Four

Bethany was in utter disbelief and confusion. "Jimmy!" she exclaimed. "Daddy..." She went running over to her father's bedside uncertain what she would find. "Is he dead?"

"He's gonna be just fine, kid," Jimmy said.

"Fine like how?" Bethany asked.

"He ain't gonna die yet," he said, looking into Bethany's eyes.

Bethany stared into his eyes wondering, like she had so many times before, who exactly he was.

"How do you know this, Jimmy? How do you know?" she repeated softly, looking at him for an answer.

"'Cause I know things."

Bethany nodded and looked away. "Okay. Okay, Jimmy. If you say so."

Jimmy paused for a moment and said, "I know so. It ain't his time to die. Not this way."

"Then when? And how?" Bethany asked. "Do you have any idea how difficult this is for me? He had last rites last night, and my brother is stuck at an airport in Colorado trying to get here so he can see our father for the last time. I don't want him to die, Jimmy. I really don't, but I have mentally been preparing myself for this, as hard as it is. The doctors said it would only be a few days...a week maybe."

Jimmy stood there staring at Bethany from over her father's bed. "Let me ask ya somethin'. Why are you giving up?"

"Giving up? I haven't given up."

"You've given up on him."

"I've given up on my father?"

"No...in Padre Pio."

Bethany remained silent. She didn't yet want to bring up the fact that she may have just seen the man. She thought for a moment before replying.

"Jimmy, I believe in Padre Pio. You have to know that I do. It's just...I think my father's time has come. I'm trying to accept it if that's the case. You yourself said that he may not be cured if it's God's will to let him go. The doctors can't help him anymore."

"But Padre Pio can. He doesn't have to die like this. In this hospital."

"But the doctors..."

"The doctors don't know shit."

Bethany raised her eyebrows.

"Who do you trust?" Jimmy asked. "Me...or them?" He nodded toward the door.

She thought about that for a minute. She looked down at her father lying there with his eyes shut. She wondered if he could hear any of their conversation. Her eyes moved down to the silver medal around her father's neck and she studied it. A tear ran down her face and she quickly wiped it away. When she looked up, Jimmy was staring at her.

"I don't know why, but I trust you, Jimmy. I believe you."

Jimmy nodded, seemingly satisfied with her answer. He then looked at John. Bethany followed his gaze.

"Why are you here, Jimmy?" she said very quietly. "Why now? Why did you never come any other time I asked you to meet my father? The times he was at the house and could have spoken to you?"

Jimmy looked up at her and then slowly turned around. He folded his hands behind him and looked out the window. His back was facing Bethany and he did not speak.

"It's complicated," he finally said, not turning around.

"Why can't you tell me?" Bethany asked. "Why can't you tell me who you are?"

Jimmy sighed. "'Cause I can't, Beth. And I wish you'd stop askin' me so many personal questions."

With his hands still folded and his back turned toward Bethany, Jimmy continued to look out the window. Bethany scrunched her eyebrows and tilted her head, a little hurt by his words.

"I'm sorry," she simply said. "I'm just trying to understand."

"You just need to believe, Beth. Some things are not meant to be understood." Jimmy turned around and walked back over to the bed. Looking Bethany in the eye and pointing to her he said, "Go with your heart...go with your gut, and just know that I won't let anything happen to you. I'm here to help."

Bethany stared into his crystal blue eyes. What else could she say? She broke the gaze, looked down, and nodded. Bethany sighed. Looking back up to Jimmy, she asked cautiously, "Can I ask you one more question? It's not about you...it's nothing personal..."

When he didn't answer, Bethany took that to be a yes. "He was here...wasn't he?" she asked. "Padre Pio was here...in this room...just a few minutes ago."

Jimmy looked at her and nodded yes.

Bethany took a deep breath, trying to understand how this could be possible. She went over to a nearby chair and sat down while Jimmy remained at her father's side.

Finally she asked, "You could see him? He was here...in this room with you?"

Jimmy answered, "Yes."

"And then I saw him. I saw him leave this room. Could anybody else see him?"

Jimmy shook his head no.

"I see..." Bethany said, putting her head back down. She folded her arms. "What was he doing here?"

"He was helpin' your father."

"What happens next then?"

"Your father's gonna get better. Keep prayin' at church, keep askin' for help. Continue to light the candles for him. He should be outta here in a few days. He'll go to rehab. He'll be home soon," Jimmy replied.

Bethany looked down at her father. It seemed completely impossible; completely unreal. Jimmy moved closer in toward her father. He put his hand over her father's forehead. As he did so, he began to speak so quietly he could barely be heard at all. However, what Bethany did hear was something she had only heard one other time in her life; something she recognized immediately. Jimmy was speaking in tongues. Watching his movements and listening to him speaking over her father brought Bethany to tears as she quietly remained in the chair. Through her tears she noticed a bright glow surrounding her father's head. She wondered if she was imagining the vision, or if in fact it was an aura she was seeing. Whatever was happening, she was so completely overwhelmed by the entire experience...seeing a mystical, holy man, who was clearly dead, roaming the hospital corridors, finding Jimmy at her dying father's bedside, the conversation with Jimmy, the certainty that John would get better, and now a moment so touching she couldn't breathe. It felt as if all her breath was taken to bring energy and life to this moment. As long as she lived, she would never forget this experience.

As Jimmy removed his hands from John's forehead, the aura seemed to disappear. Without saying another word, Jimmy stared down at John, seemingly oblivious to Bethany's presence in the room. With his left hand, he reached over and carefully picked up the silver medal. Jimmy seemed to study it before he raised it to his lips and kissed it. He then carefully placed it down again on John's chest. He stood back up and looked at Bethany, who could not take her eyes off of him. There were no words that could be said.

Jimmy slowly walked around the bed and made his way over to Bethany who seemed immobilized in the chair. He put his right hand on her shoulder and gave it a squeeze. Bethany lifted her left hand over his in thanks. She could not speak and she hoped Jimmy would understand the gesture and know just how grateful she was.

Without saying another word, Jimmy quietly left John's room while Bethany sat motionless and exhausted. She had no idea how much time had passed. Time seemed irrelevant now. All that she knew was that she was tired; so very, very tired.

Bethany quietly moved the chair toward her father and sat as close to him as she could. She stared at his face and then at the medal. She didn't know what would happen, but she knew it was out of her hands. She knew without a doubt it was in the hands of God.

Bethany put her right arm across her father's abdomen as she lowered her head against his body. His gentle breathing and the rise and fall of his chest comforted and soothed her. The even rhythm and the dull sound of the monitor beeping drifted Bethany off to sleep.

She dreamed of Padre Pio and Jimmy. She was with them both in a beautiful garden. The most beautiful garden she had ever seen. They were talking to her, but she could not hear what they were saying. In her dream she smiled at them and then grew tired, resting her head on a soft, mossy log. She remembered being woken by Jimmy's hand brushing back and forth across her head. However, she was no longer in the garden. Padre Pio and Jimmy were nowhere to be found. Instead she heard the steady beep of the hospital monitor, and when she opened her eyes, it was her father's hand who had been brushing softly against her head; a hand that had previously been too weak to rise. She looked up in shock and met her father's eyes that were now wide open.

"Daddy," she said softly.

"I'm back, Bethany," he said and smiled lovingly at his daughter.

Thirty-Five

J ohn had defied all odds of surviving, and his doctors were left speechless. No matter how many times they reviewed John's chart and went over his tests and progress, there was simply no explanation as to his recovery. The pneumonia was gone. His lungs and chest were completely clear. He'd come out of his catatonic state. The doctors just could not explain it, but for Bethany, she knew that a miracle had taken place.

She eagerly awaited Steven's arrival in the hospital lobby the next day. He had called her from his hotel room at seven that morning to arrange for Rob to come and pick him up. When Bethany told him of the news, he was both elated and shocked. Steven's biggest fear had been that he was too late; that John had died sometime during the night and that he had lost his chance to say goodbye. He was overwhelmed with the fact that his father was alive and was continuing to improve. It wasn't until he saw his father that he broke down in tears.

"It was a miracle," Bethany told him, and later that night back at the house, they sat in the parlor by a warm fire and she told her brother all that had transpired. She told him everything...about Jimmy, about Padre Pio, and about the medal. She thought it was time her brother knew what she had been going through and what she had experienced. Steven had been mesmerized by her story, and to Bethany's delight he had also believed her.

"Why didn't you tell me these things sooner?" Steven asked as he set his almost empty glass of merlot on the marble-topped, side table beside him.

Bethany studied him before answering. The likeness to her father in his younger, healthier days was uncanny. Steven was tall and lanky; same blue eyes as their dad's, and his features were soft and gentle against his dark, full hair. "I was afraid you'd think I lost it," she said. "It didn't help that you turned away from God when things got bad. You lost your faith. It happens though, Steven. It happened to me."

"You're so strong now," he said. "It's changed you...you seem...older somehow."

"Well thanks a lot," Bethany said playfully as she took a sip of her own red wine.

"That's not what I mean. You know that. I guess the word would be...grown up."

"I've grown up alright. This whole thing has aged me, tremendously." Bethany tucked her legs up comfortably into the oversized chair. "More than I wish it did."

"I'm sorry, Beth...I'm so...very...sorry. I'm sorry I wasn't here to help you all these years. I'm sorry if I seemed aloof, or indifferent to things when we spoke on the phone. I don't know why, but I couldn't handle it. I couldn't handle watching him shrivel away...I couldn't watch him die."

Bethany nodded.

"I guess by separating myself from the situation, I thought I could run from it...that it somehow would go away. Some example I set as big brother."

"It did bother me for a long time, Steven, but I've come to realize how everyone handles things differently. It's accepting it all in the end that counts. It's dealing with the present...moving forward...learning from it."

Steven picked up his wine glass and took another sip as the fire crackled between them.

"I'm proud of you, you know that?"

Bethany smiled.

"I just never thought I'd be getting advice from my little sister." He smiled back. "When the time does come...for Dad, I mean...I want us to stay close. I know we have a physical distance between us, but I want us talk more, visit more, keep in touch."

"I'd like that."

"Are you going to be okay? When the time comes?"

Bethany pondered his question for a moment. "Maybe not initially...but yes...over time? I think so."

Steven nodded.

"What about you? Will you be okay?"

Steven shrugged. "It's hard to say. I can't take back the years. I guess I'll always have regrets. "

Bethany knew there was nothing she could say, and she felt badly for her brother. His face looked sad, and she searched for something to say which would make him feel better. "Steven, you're a wonderful, caring husband to Karen. You've really been there for her throughout all the difficulties with trying to get pregnant, the fertility treatments, the disappointments. You can't take care of everyone. Maybe God wanted me to take care of Dad, and you to take care of Karen."

"Maybe," he said, looking into his glass. "You're alright...you know that?"

"So many compliments tonight." Bethany smiled.

"I just want you to know how grateful I am...and that I'm sorry."

Steven did not yet have a return ticket to Colorado. He wanted to stick around a while and spend as much time with his father as he could, and this made Bethany very happy.

As for Jimmy, he had been right. He was always right. Four days after the visitation from Padre Pio, John was released from the hospital and was on his way to the rehabilitation center. Steven was there every step of the way, helping Bethany with all the arrangements for the rehab and attending to his father's every need. As for John, despite his incredible weakness, his determination to live was extraordinary. When Bethany told her father everything that had happened on that miraculous day, he wasn't overly surprised, for his own faith had been strong. Bethany asked him if he recalled anything during the episodes in which he had drifted away in an unresponsive state. He revealed that he had been given the opportunity to take a peek at heaven once again. He recalled strolling through the most beautiful meadows with Padre Pio and with Jesus, and seeing in the distance, the most precious of all, his beloved Victoria.

He told Bethany and Steven how he was being prepared to die and how easy the actual journey would be once he left his body, for there would be no pain, only happiness.

There was no doubt in Bethany's mind that this indeed was what was happening. She felt a lump in her throat when her father told the story because so much of her just wanted to go with him into this perfect place. She did not want to be left alone in a world so full of difficulties and heartache, a world without either of her parents.

As she stood over her father's bed, Steven's hand reached for hers. The simple gesture had meant so much to her. From his bed, her father took Bethany's other hand.

"It wasn't quite my time yet, Bethany, but I can honestly say I don't know how much time I have left. I'll miss you both so much. Please know that, but I am not afraid, and I am ready when God calls me. I truly am," her father stated.

"We love you, Dad," Steven said.

Bethany nodded and wiped away her tears.

Part of the reason Bethany had believed that her father was given a second chance was because of Steven. They desperately needed to have time together, especially if this was going to be the last time Steven would see his father. Bethany turned and left the room. She paused and stood outside the cracked door, unable to resist a bit of eavesdropping.

"Karen's upset she couldn't come to see you," Steven said. "With the treatments she's undergoing, she's not supposed to travel right now."

"Please tell her not to worry, Steven. I understand. I only wish I could live long enough to see my grandchild. And she *will* conceive a child...of that, I'm certain."

Steven took a deep breath.

"I'm sorry, Dad. I wish I could have been here more to help...to spend time with you."

"We will all be together again one day. You'll see. For now, you have to live *your* life. And that life happens to be in Colorado. Don't think I've held that against you."

"Yeah, but Bethany..."

"It's been hard on her, I know, but for whatever reason, her place was here."

Bethany's eyes filled with tears.

"I'll never forget everything you've done for me," Steven said. "Growing up you were always there to talk to when I had a problem. You'd drop everything for me and Bethany."

"That's what fathers are for," said John.

Steven chuckled. "Thanks for helping me with my homework, and for never missing my baseball games." A tear rolled down Bethany's cheek.

"It's going to be alright, Steven. I promise."

Thirty-Six

B ethany had not seen Jimmy in days and she was desperately wishing he would come in and say hello. It wasn't until four days into John's stay at the rehab that Jimmy finally showed up Giovanni's.

"Jimmy!" Bethany exclaimed as he made his way into the kitchen from the back door. "I was hoping you would come soon." She gave him a big hug and he smiled.

"How you doin' kid? You look good. You look better. Less stressed," he said.

"I am better."

"And Pop?"

"He's good, Jimmy, he really is. Just like you said."

"I told ya," he said, while he pulled over a nearby stool. "He's in rehab now, yeah?"

"Yes, he is," Bethany said, taking some eggs out of the refrigerator. "My brother's in from Colorado. We had a really good talk the other night. We talked about my father, how we both have dealt with his illness differently. That kind of thing." Bethany started cracking the eggs in a bowl and then began whisking them. "I told him about you," she said, looking over at Jimmy, "and about Padre

Pio too. I didn't know how open he would be about it. I think he understood, though."

"That's great," Jimmy replied.

"And now he's spending some much needed time with Daddy. It's allowed me to get caught up here. It's been a bit overwhelming trying to juggle it all..."

"I'm sure it is," said Jimmy as he watched Bethany mix egg yolks into melted dark chocolate. "What are you makin' over there?"

"A flourless chocolate cake. It's one of my favorites. It's one of my dad's favorites too." In another bowl, Bethany beat egg whites with sugar until soft peaks formed. While she did so, she tried to figure out how she could ask Jimmy more about the week before.

"You're quiet all of a sudden," Jimmy stated as if he knew she had been thinking. "You okay?"

Bethany carefully folded the egg whites into the chocolate mixture and then poured the contents into a cake pan. She shrugged. "I'm okay, I guess. I just have questions." She paused. "Questions about what happened last week." She turned and looked at him for a reaction.

"What about?" he simply asked.

Bethany placed the cake into the oven and then she cleaned her hands on a towel. Pulling up a stool next to him and sitting down, she asked, "How did you know to come? Did you know Padre Pio would come?"

Jimmy stared at her a moment before speaking. "I have a big devotion to Padre Pio as you know. He's kinda like my friend, if you know what I'm sayin'. I can't explain it really, but I guess because I talk about him so much and I tell all his stories, maybe he thinks he's my friend too."

"Okay..." Bethany said, not quite sure where this was going.

"What I'm tryin' to say," Jimmy said, "is that because I know so much about him and talk about him, he comes to me sometimes."

Bethany studied Jimmy's face. "So you've seen him? You've seen Padre Pio...before last week?" she asked.

"Yeah. I seen him."

"How come you've never told me that? With everything you've told me? I mean, that's pretty big, don't you think?"

"I don't like to talk about myself much."

"Only about Padre Pio?"

"Yeah."

Bethany nodded and folded her arms together. "Where did you learn to speak in tongues?"

"It just happened one day. One day while I was prayin'."

"It's quite a gift," Bethany said. "You didn't tell me that either, especially after I told you how I heard it for the first time at that church in Oyster Bay. Why?"

"'Cause I knew you'd find out one day. I don't like to go 'round braggin' about it."

"I see."

"I do a lot of prayin'. I wanted to come up and see your father. I wanted to pray for him. The tongues...it happens a lot when I pray."

Bethany considered this for a moment. "It really meant a lot to me that you came to see my dad...that you were praying like that. I needed it. My dad needed it. When I saw Padre Pio, I thought my father was dead. Did Padre Pio pray over him too?"

Jimmy nodded yes.

"During the time my father was not coherent he told me he was with Padre Pio and with Jesus too. He said he saw my mom. Did this happen? Was it a dream?"

"It was no dream, Beth. Padre Pio let your father see what it's like over there. So he wouldn't be scared one day, you know?"

"That's what my father believes."

"And you? What do you believe, Beth?"

She hesitated before answering. "I believe God has given me a great gift, a second chance. I believe he gave me you so I would understand everything...so I wouldn't give up hope and faith. So yes, Jimmy...I believe anything is possible. Anything at all, no matter how utterly impossible it may seem. And I have you to thank for that."

Jimmy smiled. "You done good, kid. Pretty soon you ain't gonna need me no more."

"Don't say that. I hate when you say that," Bethany said. "I'll always need you, Jimmy. You're my friend. I've told you that."

There was something suddenly sad in Jimmy's expression, which caused Bethany to feel momentarily uneasy, like something was wrong.

Perhaps sensing her uncertainty, Jimmy said, "I'll always be around some way or another. Always know that...no matta what. You hear?" He rose from his stool. "I'm just sayin'...you're strong now." Jimmy put his hand on Bethany's shoulder. "I know I've been there for you, but you're a strong woman. You know how to handle things. Me bein' here or not has nothin' to do with it. Even if I'm not here, I'm in here." He pointed to Bethany's head. "And in here," he said, pointing to her heart. "Always...you understand?"

"Always," Bethany replied.

Thirty-Seven

When it came time for Steven to go back to Colorado, it took all Bethany had in her to not get completely hysterical. Watching her brother say goodbye to their father, knowing this may be the last time he would see him, was almost more than she could bear. She left the room to regain her composure, but as soon as Steven left his father's side and joined Bethany in the kitchen, they hugged each other and sobbed, mourning the inevitable.

"I can't believe this is the last time I'm going to see Dad," Steven said as he wiped away a tear. "We're not going to have parents anymore, Beth. It's hard to imagine."

Bethany rubbed her brother's arm as her tears flowed freely. "I know. It seems impossible...unfair. We'll get through somehow...we will."

Neither of them had anything left to say, so Bethany watched as Steven loaded his things in the trunk of Rob's car, and then they slowly drove away. Cherie, coming up from the basement with John's freshly washed clothes, put down the laundry, went over to Bethany, and held her tightly while she cried. No words were spoken. Just the comfort of being held was all Bethany needed and she soon began to calm down.

In the days that followed, Bethany spent more time at church, going almost daily to the Padre Pio statue and the image of the Divine Mercy. Bethany would light a candle for her father at the beginning of every week, and she would kneel and pray and ask God every day to make her father well and to give her strength. She knew ultimately her father was dying, but she begged anyway to spare him.

As the days and weeks wore on, she felt like she was aging rapidly. Except for work, she saw no one. Bethany wondered if there was anyone else in the world who had to endure what she had over the years. She knew there must be others like herself, but where were they? Who were they?

By the end of February, her father was getting weaker and weaker yet he was not sick. The MS was affecting just about every single part of his body. He had difficulty seeing, swallowing, and even speaking at times. His arms and legs had become completely useless. He had to be fed, changed, and medicated. There was very little he could do, yet he was always happy. It was as if he knew this was all temporary, and that he'd soon be relieved from the burden of his own body.

When Bethany was not at work or church she spent every waking minute with her father. He became childlike to her, as if he was oblivious to all that was happening to him. She didn't mind, though, as long as he was happy and peaceful.

The neurologist tried his best to convince Bethany to send her father to a nursing home, saying the burden of taking care of him was much too great, but Bethany wanted nothing to do with that, no matter how difficult the situation got. She and Rob had talked about it at length, and he had felt the same way as she did. They felt they owed it to John to let him live his life at home, and they were going to do whatever was needed to allow for this to happen. Between the two of them and Cherie, they believed they could manage and they would, no matter what. The only thing they did agree on was to have an outside nurse from the neurologist's office come in once a week to evaluate John and to take his vitals. Since it would be impossible to get him to the doctor, the nurse would bring back her findings.

One evening Bethany was in her father's bedroom feeding him dinner. Everything she made for him now had to be cut extremely small and had to be very soft. He would smile at her often, but he usually didn't say much. On this particular day, however, he made an extra effort.

"You've...been...so...good...to me...Bethany," he began slowly. "I want you to know...that everything is okay...when God calls me...I am ready...I have been...ready. He won't take me...yet...though, but that's okay...because I get to spend...more time with...you."

"I know you're ready, Daddy, and I know you'll be fine," Bethany said. "I guess it's me. I'm the one who's not ready to let you go. I'm so sorry." Tears began to well up in her eyes.

Her father smiled. "Don't...don't cry...and don't be sorry. I understand...it's okay. Life...life will be easier for you...it will...be...better."

"How could it be better without you in it?" Bethany asked.

"Because...you can't...keep going on like...this...taking care of...me. It isn't fair...you need to live...your life...my dear daughter."

Bethany picked up his hand, which was like dead weight in her own, and she held it tight. She had no idea what to say. Her father lay there looking at her and smiling.

"You won't...have to worry...about anything either...you can stay in...the house...you'll be fine...it's a gift from me...I have already...told your brother...he is fine with it."

Bethany nodded and wiped her nose with a tissue.

"Everything else...as far as my arrangements...is taken care of and paid for. Call...George when the time comes...he will know what...to do."

George was John's longtime attorney and friend, and Bethany had no doubt that everything was in order. That's the way her father was.

Bethany slowly lifted his hand and kissed it. "I love you so much, Daddy. I always will. Say hello to mom for me when you get there."

"I will...she is proud...of you."

Bethany nodded again and wiped her eyes.

"Padre Pio has...helped us...both of us...you know that...don't you?"

"I do know that, Daddy, without a doubt. I think that's why you didn't die that day in the hospital. You were given a second chance. You were supposed to have time with Steven."

"You are...right. I wanted to be...at home...when the time comes."

"I know you do."

"You and Rob...and Cherie...have made that possible...I am...grateful. I...love...you." Her father smiled, but Bethany saw a tear come down his face. "Thank you," he said.

Bethany was overcome with emotion, and she had to turn away for a moment. She held his hand tightly in hers.

When she looked back at her father, his eyes were closed as he drifted off to sleep. She carefully placed his hand back down on the bed.

"You're welcome, Daddy," she said. "I would do anything for you. Forever."

As he lay quietly, the silver medal around her father's neck shone like a beacon of faith.

Thirty-Eight

John continued to hold on in the weeks that followed. Rob and Bethany did everything they could to keep him happy and comfortable no matter how exhausting it was. The early days of spring had arrived, and on one particular Monday, the day was warm and spectacular. Bethany went into the bakery early to catch up on some paperwork, but was home by ten-thirty to spend the day with her father, who had mentioned a special request.

"I...would like to go outside," he said weakly. "One more time...by the Adirondack chairs."

The weather had been cold for weeks and he hadn't been outside at all. Bethany knew that going out to his favorite spot would do wonders for him.

"Let me get Rob," she said.

It took them a while, but together Bethany and Rob were able to get John out of his bed and into the wheelchair. Bethany took a spare blanket and put it over her father's legs, and then Rob slowly wheeled him out of his room, onto the back porch, and down the handicap ramp.

"What a...glorious...day," John announced within minutes of getting outside. "Thank...you...Rob."

"It's my pleasure, John. It's good you're getting out and getting some fresh air for a change.

"Look...at the flowers...blooming," John said.

The one thing Bethany had learned throughout her father's illness was just how important all the little things that so often get overlooked meant to him. There were so many things humanity as a whole took for granted, like being able to get out of bed in the morning, or being able to walk, or being able to feed oneself; seeing flowers grow and hearing birds sing. Bethany vowed to herself never to take anything for granted ever again in her life, because everything, no matter how small it may be, is a gift. She could see this now through her father's eyes.

"I'm glad you're happy, Daddy," she said, following behind Rob. "It is beautiful out, isn't it?"

"Yes...it is," he replied.

Rob wheeled the chair over the grass and headed toward the Adirondack chairs while John bumped along.

"You okay there, John?" Rob asked. "Sorry for the bumpy ride."

"It's fun...actually."

When they reached the Adirondack chairs Rob said, "It's not going to be too easy to get you in and out of this chair, John." Rob knew it was next to impossible, actually.

"That's fine. I'll...be good...just sitting in this."

"Very wise choice." Rob smiled while he applied the brake on the wheelchair.

"Thanks for doing this," Bethany whispered to Rob before she sat down next to her father.

"It's no problem at all. This is good for him. We'll worry about how we'll get him back into his bed later," he said. "You need anything else, John? If not I'll let you spend some time with your daughter."

"Oh...I'm just fine...Rob...thank you," John answered.

As Rob walked back to the house, Bethany studied her father's face as his eyes moved around looking at everything.

"This place...it gets more and more...beautiful all the time," he said.

"That it does," Bethany said as she put her feet up on the ottoman.

"We were...very fortunate to get this place," he said. "Your mother...she loved it here...she loved the views...the flowers..."

"We are lucky," replied Bethany. "We're very blessed with all that we've been given. I'll make you a promise that I will make more time for myself and I'll spend it out here."

"Good...I want you...to do that. Appreciate...every day."

Bethany looked out over the water. "Look at that. There are already a few boats on the moorings. Now that's a sign that summer is coming."

"Remember...our boat? How much fun...we all had."

"Those were great days." Bethany smiled. "Remember our trips to Sand City? That place was wonderful. All the boats anchored off this little deserted island. Remember the shoe tree that was there? That small dead tree with all the lost summer shoes on it?" Bethany turned in her chair to look at her father.

He chuckled. "I lost mine...in the muck at low tide. Sucked right off...my foot...disappeared."

"We searched and searched, and every time we came back to Sand City we looked again. Steven and I would look at every shoe hanging from that tree to see if it washed up each year, hoping someone had hung it up."

"No...such...luck."

"What about when we had the bottle of wine and no cork screw? Mom was so mad that you had forgotten it. We had all this great food and you had no wine."

"But...you saved...the day," he remembered.

"I did," Bethany said proudly. "I swam over to the next boat and we borrowed their corkscrew. As soon as you had the bottle open, I swam back and returned it. You let me have a few sips of your wine as a reward."

"It was...great." Her father smiled.

"And what about at the end of the day when we'd go tubing? Steven was crazy. He was a madman on that thing. I just remember holding on for dear life."

Her father nodded slowly. "Such fun...we had. These are the things...I want you to hold onto...These are...the things...I want you to...remember...not the hard times. Not your mother's...death. Not my...illness. Okay?"

"I think it will make me too sad to remember."

"It won't...over time...it will make you...happy."

"I hope so, Daddy. Why don't I make us some iced tea? It will only take a minute to brew and I'll get it chilled fast with lots of ice."

"Sounds...good."

Bethany stood. "Will you be okay out here by yourself for a minute or two?"

"Yes...in fact...it will be nice...to have some time...alone here," he replied. "I want to...take it all in."

"Okay, then. I'll be back."

Bethany made her way to the kitchen and began brewing some tea when Cherie entered.

"I changed the sheets on your daddy's bed so they'd be fresh for him," she began. "I straightened up the room too." She attempted to slick back some loose strands from her coarse black hair, and she repositioned her hair clip above her round, dark face.

"Thanks so much, Cherie. That's great. I really appreciate it," said Bethany as she reached in the cabinet for some tall glasses and some straws. "Would you like some fresh tea?"

"That would be nice. Thank you. You can cool it down that fast?" Cherie asked.

"This is my quick method. Ideally the tea should steep for a while and then be brought to room temperature and then chilled, but we don't live in an ideal world, do we?" Bethany asked with a sad smile.

"No ma'am, that's for sure. Especially not in this household." Cherie chuckled as she gave Bethany her wide, Jamaican grin.

"So it will have to do," said Bethany as she continued preparing the tea.

They made small talk for a few minutes, and while Bethany was pouring the tea into the glasses, Cherie walked over to the windowsill and leaned over to see John. "Your daddy's so happy to be outside, I'm sure. What a day. Who's that man with him?"

Bethany was pulling a third glass out of the cabinet when she stopped dead. "What man?"

"The man out there. The man in the robe," Cherie said, turning back toward Bethany.

Bethany's eyes grew wide as she put down the glass and hurried over to the window.

"See?" Cherie said, pointing.

"Oh, my God!" Bethany said quietly. She put her hand over her mouth in disbelief.

"What is it, girl? You don't know that man? What's wrong?"

Bethany just kept staring out the window at the man who was talking to her father. Finally she said, "Yes, Cherie...I do know that man. The only thing is...he's been dead since 1968."

Bethany rushed down the hallway so she could get to the main porch without having to go around the handicap ramp off the kitchen. Opening the huge doors, she raced outside, and by the time she got to the edge of the porch, Padre Pio was gone. She spun around wildly in search of him, and then she jumped off the porch, ran past her father from behind, and headed toward the path which led down to the street. When she got there she looked down the curving stone path surrounded by Hostas. No one was there. Moving quickly, she made her way down the steps. When she reached the street she ran in circles, desperately searching for Padre Pio. He was nowhere to be found.

"I just don't believe this," she said, slowly making her way back up the stone steps.

She walked to her father and when she arrived at his side, tears were coming down his face. Concerned, she knelt down next to his wheelchair and she put her hand on his upper right arm.

"Daddy, Daddy! What is it? What's happening?"

"Padre Pio...he came...he came to visit me...Bethany."

"I saw him!" Bethany said. "He was talking to you. What did he say, Daddy? Please tell me!"

"He...he came up the path," he said slowly. "I couldn't...I couldn't believe what I was seeing. I...wasn't sleeping...or dreaming this time...when it happened."

"No, Daddy, you weren't. I saw it for myself. He was here. He was talking to you. What did he say?"

"He said...he said this would be his last visit. He said...not to be afraid. He said...the next time I see him...he...he..." Her father's lips began to quiver and a tear rolled down his face. Bethany held on to his every word as she gazed into her father's eyes. Suddenly a smile came over his face and his eyes moved over the horizon.

"Daddy, please!" Bethany pleaded.

He looked back at his daughter. "He said...he would be back...to take me to...the kingdom of heaven."

Tears streamed down Bethany's face as she placed her hands on the side of the wheelchair and rested her forehead on them. She cried for the experience and she cried because she knew it was only a matter of time for her father.

"Don't cry...Bethany...I am at peace. Padre Pio said something else...he told me you will be fine...he will take care of you."

Bethany sobbed louder. "I'm sorry, Daddy, I'm sorry."

"Don't worry...I understand you're scared...and sad too. But we've had this journey together...this amazing...beautiful journey...it was a gift...a gift of faith...to make us strong...for our next journey. Not everyone is given...this opportunity. He has prepared a path for us...he is with us both."

Bethany lifted her head and looked up at her father who seemed to have an angelic glow about him that instantly comforted her. She saw that he was trying to lift his hand. She reached for his hand and held it tightly.

"Please say that you understand...this...Bethany. Take comfort...in what we have...experienced...what we have been told...what we have come to believe. It's been...an incredible journey."

Bethany nodded as she wiped away her tears. She leaned over and gently kissed her father on the cheek.

"I'll miss you, Daddy. I will always love you."

"We will find...we will find a way to be...together...I promise."

Thirty-Nine

The day Bethany and her father saw Padre Pio was the last time John was outside. He grew weaker and weaker with each passing day, and the disease was taking over every inch of his body. A few days after Easter, the visiting nurse came to Bethany suggesting that she re-think her decision to put John in a nursing home where he could get professional care.

"He doesn't want to go," Bethany told the nurse, "and I'm willing to do whatever it takes to allow him to stay here. It's not like I don't have help."

The short, stocky nurse gave Bethany a look as if she were crazy. It was quite easy for the nurse to write John off and send him on his way. *What did she care? After all, it wasn't her father.*

Bethany looked down on the woman and waited for her to reply.

"There are different things they can do for him, medications he could be on after he's evaluated," the nurse said.

"He doesn't want to be on any more medications and he certainly doesn't want to be treated like some kind of guinea pig either. Nothing they do is going to save him. My father is dying. It will simply prolong his death in an unfamiliar place. I won't allow it,"

Bethany said firmly. "My father is going to die the way he wants to...with dignity and with his family."

"So you would deny him care then?" the nurse asked.

"Deny him care?" Bethany said, raising her voice, "You have to be kidding me! For years he has gotten the best care he could possibly get, and he got it from me and his private aide who would do anything for him. Don't you dare say that I am denying him care. You don't know anything!"

"I will have to report this back to his doctor," said the nurse.

"You do that!" shouted Bethany, "because he will also be hearing from me. I don't want you in my house again."

"His throat is closing up," the nurse continued. "If in a week's time it's gotten worse he'll need to have feeding tubes put in. You will have no choice then."

"Get out! Get out of my house!" Bethany walked over to the massive kitchen door and opened it, signaling her to leave.

Hastily the woman gathered her things and marched through the door.

Bethany slammed the door and walked away. She headed towards her father's room, her heart racing from anger.

"Hello, Daddy," she said softly as she came into the room.

"I...heard...yelling," he said, just barely able to get the words out.

"Apparently the nurse and I don't see eye to eye, that's all," Bethany answered.

"Don't...let them...take...me."

"I won't, Daddy. I promise."

"I...I...want to...die...here..."

"I know," Bethany said taking his hand in hers.

"I...am...fine."

"You're not going anywhere so don't get yourself upset about it. Just rest. Everything is fine, Daddy. Just rest."

He closed his eyes and Bethany studied him for a moment. While she did so, she thought about her mother and wondered how she would have handled all of this if she were still alive. She believed that her mother would have made the same decision for her husband.

When Rob came back from the store, Bethany filled him in on all that had transpired with the visiting nurse, and he had agreed with Bethany 100 percent.

"He's better off here," Rob stated. "And once he got into the system...forget it. We'd never get him back."

Bethany knew that to be true and she was satisfied with her decision. That evening she invited Father Michael to come by the house for dinner and to give her father another blessing.

Although Bethany's father couldn't say much, she knew that the visit meant a lot to him and that he took comfort in Father Michael being there and praying over him. Father Michael left John's room, and once they were in the kitchen, he turned to Bethany.

"How are you holding up?" Father Michael asked her.

"I'm doing okay. As best as I can be, I guess."

"My doors are always open. Come by any time if you need to talk. I'm very proud of you. You've come along way. Your faith and trust has been renewed."

Bethany gave a slight smile. "I'm trying."

"I'm doing the twelve-thirty on Sunday. It's Divine Mercy Sunday. Do you think you can break away from the bakery? I would love to see you at my Mass," he said.

"I will definitely do my best. I'd like to come. If I get in early enough, I don't see why I won't be able to swing by. As long as everything's okay here, of course."

"Yes, of course," he answered taking both her hands in his. Smiling at her, Father Michael said, "God bless you, Bethany. Your reward will be great in heaven."

"Thank you, Father...I hope so." She smiled.

By the time the end of the week came around, John could barely speak anymore. The few words he did say were slurred and difficult to understand. Rob kept him as comfortable as possible, and John slept most of the time.

Bethany was determined to attend Mass on Sunday so she got to the bakery very early as planned. Business was slower now that Easter was over, so she had no problem getting everything done. She arrived at church with just a few minutes to spare. The image of

Christ as Divine Mercy was prominently displayed on the side of the altar in celebration. During most of the Mass, Bethany found herself staring at the image and taking comfort from it. When Father Michael stood at the pulpit and began to read the Gospel and speak the homily, Bethany's attention turned toward him.

"In today's reading by John, he writes: 'You believe in me, Thomas, because you have seen me,' says the Lord. 'Blessed are they who have not seen me, but still believe,'" Father Michael began. "This statement is a very powerful testament as to who Thomas was as a person. He was a follower of the Lord, but he was not perfect. He had doubts; he had questions; he had fears." He paused. "It was these doubts, questions, and fears which ultimately lead him to a deeper faith. The same could be said about our own lives. Do we doubt God? Do we question what his plan is for us? Do we get angry with God?" Father Michael paused and looked around at the congregation. "Just because we cannot understand, doesn't mean that we should give up our faith. When Jesus was taken away on Good Friday, his loyal disciples believed in him. They knew with all their hearts that he was not a criminal; that no crime had been committed despite the accusations against him. Why did they continue to follow him? Faith. Faith teaches us to believe in what we cannot comprehend. There are times in each of our lives when things happen which do not make sense to us. As Jesus said to Thomas, 'You can have deep love and still question.' To have true faith..." Father Michael paused and pointed to the crowd. "It does not mean we have all the answers. It is okay to turn and question, 'Why me? Why now?' It is this doubting and questioning which leads us, like Thomas, to a deeper faith. When things happen in your own lives, and you are feeling lost and confused as to why...do not lose your faith...God has a plan...God has a purpose...and in time, just like the resurrected Lord appeared to his disciples, God's vision and plan will become clear and visible to each of us. It is then, when we truly will understand the meaning of faith."

It was after that Mass that Bethany knew what she had to do. After saying hello to Father Michael who was happy to see her, she waited for the parishioners to clear out from the church before she approached the statue of Padre Pio.

"You have been good to me, and you have been good to my father," Bethany said as she knelt on the kneeler in front of the statue. "I want you to know that I understand that my father's time has come. I am asking you to stay with him through the process, to help him on his journey...and Padre Pio? I am asking you not to forget about me. Please stay with me, and help me to go on." Bethany bowed her head in prayer as a tear fell from her eye. As she got up, she kissed her fingertips and gently touched the statue. "Thank you," she said softly.

Bethany then made her way over to the image of the Divine Mercy and knelt down on the edge of the altar. Her heart began to pound as she prepared herself for the words she never thought she would say. For months she prayed and begged God to save her father and to make him well. It was now that her prayers had changed. Looking up at Christ's face she said, "As hard as this is for me to say...I am going to say it. Please, Jesus...please take my father with you...he is ready. I do not want to see him suffer this way anymore, and I realize it has been selfish of me to continue asking you to keep him here...with me." Bethany's tears began to flow freely. "It's okay...you can take him now...he can die and he can join you in your kingdom." Bethany covered her eyes with her hands and sobbed while the vision of Jesus's face looked down upon her.

Forty

Monday came and Bethany did not go to the bakery at all. She stayed by her father's side and read to him, played him his favorite music, and did anything else which made him happy and content. She felt anxious and stressed, but she made sure her father knew nothing of her feelings. It had become more and more difficult for him to eat, and Bethany feared that if he continued to hang on, she would be forced to make the decision about feeding tubes. She knew her father did not want them put in, and as she cared for him that day, she thought about the request she had made to Jesus the day before.

That night she slept on the floor next to her father in a makeshift bed. Rob pleaded with her to go to her room and get a good night's sleep, but Bethany wouldn't listen. She would not leave her father's side.

She awoke the next morning, and her father was still alive and somewhat responsive, although he could not talk. It killed her to have to go into work and she asked God not to take him while she was there.

"Rob, you have to call me immediately if there is the slightest change in him," Bethany pleaded before heading off to the bakery on

Tuesday morning. "I will drop everything and come back. Do you promise?"

"I won't leave his side. Cherie will be here in a little while to help so I can spend time with him," Rob stated.

"Read to him, if you don't mind. Anything, but just read to him, tell him stories and play Tommy Dorsey for him," Bethany said as she made her way around the kitchen and collected her things.

"He'll be in good hands," said Rob. "And I'll call if anything at all changes."

"Okay, great," she said as she headed to the door with her keys. "I'll talk to you later then."

"You got it," said Rob.

Bethany felt sick to her stomach as she left the house; a general sense of uneasiness seemed to fill the air around her. She wasn't exactly sure how she would be able to work, but she had no choice. Luckily it was a weekday, so it wouldn't be that demanding, but she still had several items to prepare and she was already exhausted.

She arrived at the bakery by seven and moved around the kitchen swiftly. By ten she had already called Rob twice. She just could not believe how unsettled she felt, and as she cooked, she prayed for help.

By eleven o'clock she heard the voice of the only person who could make her feel better.

"Hey, kid," Jimmy said as he came through the back door. "How's it goin'?"

She threw down the pot she was cleaning, went over to him, and hugged him.

"What is it, Beth?" he asked. Bethany began to cry on his shoulder. He waited for her to calm down. "Hey...it's okay. It's gonna be okay...here...let's sit down." Jimmy pulled over two stools and then handed Bethany a tissue to wipe her eyes.

Bethany sat down and collected herself. "It's time, Jimmy...it's time. I've asked Jesus and Padre Pio to take him. I can't watch him suffer anymore."

Jimmy put his hand on her shoulder. "Remember everything I taught you. Remember all that we talked about it. We knew there would come a time, Beth...you know what I'm sayin'?"

Bethany nodded. "I do, but I'm scared...I'm so scared. I feel like I'm not part of this world, like I'm living in some non-existent world separate from everyone and everything. My father is dying, yet the world still goes on, but my world doesn't. Does that make any sense to you?"

"It makes perfect sense. It will change, you hear me? You're not gonna feel like this forever. You gotta believe me. You've made it this far. You just got a little ways to go. You'll find peace. I'm tellin' you."

"I'm not going to have any parents, Jimmy. I just can't imagine this. I don't want to imagine it. Some of my friends, they have everything. I feel like I have nothing. I am losing everything."

"You have more than you know, Beth, and you will be given more than you know. You've just got to hang in there. Over time, you will see."

Bethany blew her nose and took a deep breath. "I always feel better when you're around. You've helped me so much, Jimmy. I know I've told you before, but I don't know how to thank you...for everything."

"That's what I'm here for, kid. Everything's gonna be just fine. You gotta believe me. Is your father still wearin' the medal?"

"Yes, he is. It helps to keep me calm and focused too."

"That relic that's inside there. It's very powerful and it's right there next to your father, just like Padre Pio's right there with him."

With all that had gone on in the past few weeks, it dawned on Bethany that she hadn't seen Jimmy since before the appearance of Padre Pio in the backyard with her father. She remained seated and told Jimmy the entire story, and just the retelling of it seemed to calm her down. Jimmy listened intently and did not seem surprised by anything she had said. When she was through, he pointed to her and said, "I told ya...see what I'm sayin'? You have nothin' to be scared about. Nothin', Beth, no matta what happens. You understand me?"

Bethany nodded and looked away.

Jimmy stood up and took her face in his hands. "Look at me," he said softly. "No matta what happens Beth...no matta what...have faith."

Bethany looked up into Jimmy's blue eyes. He almost sounded as if he was pleading with her. She didn't quite understand where this was coming from.

"Please, Beth. Just believe and have faith and the answers will one day be revealed to you."

"Of course I will, Jimmy. I promise you," Bethany said softly.

Jimmy turned away, and if Bethany didn't know better, it looked as if his eyes were welling up. She had never seen him filled with such emotion.

"Jimmy, are you okay?" Bethany asked as she rose from her stool and touched his arm.

Jimmy waved her away. "Yeah, yeah, kid. I'm fine. You okay now?"

"Yeah, Jimmy. I'm okay. I really am..."

"Well I'm gonna get me one of those cannolis of yours, if you don't mind. I'm gonna get a seat and have a cappuccino too. Okay?"

"You do that," Bethany answered. "Tell Alison it's on me." She smiled.

"I'll do that...thanks."

Bethany leaned in the doorway of the kitchen. She watched as Jimmy bent over and looked at the pastries laid out on the trays behind the glass of the counter. She smiled as she contemplated how childlike he became when it came to her cannolis.

"I'll take that one," Bethany heard him say to Alison. Jimmy always picked just the right one. "Yeah, that one back there. That's it. And the boss said it's on her."

Bethany chuckled and headed back into the kitchen. She started cleaning up, satisfied with what she had accomplished. If she could, she was hoping to go home sometime between two and three o'clock, leaving Alison to close up. The day had been slow. Even now, it was only Alison, Jimmy, and Bethany who remained in Giovanni's. Bethany was putting the last of the washed cake tins away when Alison came running inside.

"Bethany, come quick!" Alison raced back out of the kitchen with Bethany right behind her.

Nothing could have prepared Bethany for the scene before her eyes. Her whole body became stiff and frozen while her heart beat at an incredible pace. She ran out from behind the counter into the main part of the bakery with her right hand covering her mouth in complete shock.

"What's going on here? What's happening?" Bethany screamed as she watched two police officers in uniform handcuffing Jimmy. "No, no, you can't do this. Jimmy! What's happening? No, please!"

Bethany ran toward him but one of the police officers blocked her path. "Jimmy!" She tried to push herself through while Jimmy just stared at her blankly.

"I'm sorry, ma'am, but you're interfering with official police business."

"What did he do? You have to tell me! He's my friend!" she demanded, still trying to push her way past the police officer. She watched helplessly as Jimmy was read his rights, his hands already cuffed together behind his back.

"No, no, don't take him! You can't take him! I'm begging you! He didn't do anything, you must be mistaken!" Bethany continued to scream.

"Ma'am, there has been a warrant out for this man's arrest," the police officer who was restraining her said. "He's charged with leaving the scene of an accident in which a seven-year-old girl was killed."

"What!!!" Bethany pulled away from the officer. Her eyes were in a wild panic. "You cannot be serious! There is no way this man is capable of doing anything like that! He's innocent! I'm telling you! He is! You have the wrong guy!"

Jimmy stood there stone-faced and calm, as he allowed the officers to handcuff him.

Bethany struggled to get to Jimmy. The officer restrained her again.

"Let go of me!" she screamed.

"If you don't get a hold of yourself, ma'am, we're going to have to take you in as well for reckless conduct and interfering with a police investigation."

"No, no," Bethany sobbed as she stopped struggling and backed away. "Jimmy!"

The police officer who had been holding her back joined the other officer as they began to lead Jimmy away.

"Jimmy!" she cried. "You can't leave me!"

Before they made it to the door, Jimmy managed to turn his head around.

"Beth, remember everything I've told you. Think about it, Beth, and be strong. You'll manage without me. You will."

"Jimmy, don't go." Bethany fell to her knees. "Please tell me this is a mistake!"

As they headed out the door, Jimmy managed to swing his head around one last time. "Beth," he shouted, "I'll see ya around, kid, I will..."

Bethany cried in anguish as Alison stood in silence. The phone began to ring and Alison ran to answer it.

Bethany paced the room and then turned to look at the table where Jimmy had sat only a few minutes before. His half eaten cannoli and cappuccino remained. Bethany cried harder and sat down.

Alison hung up the phone and came back to Bethany. Putting her arms around her she looked into her eyes sympathetically. "Beth," she began. "I don't know how to tell you this, but that was Rob on the phone. He thinks your father doesn't have much time. He needs you to come home."

Forty-One

Bethany arrived at the house within seconds and ran to her father's bedroom in a state of shock. She saw Rob standing over her father with tears falling down his face.

"Oh no, Rob! Please don't tell me I'm too late!" Bethany said as she raced to her father's side.

"He's still with us, but he's in a catatonic state and his breathing is shallow. I called his doctor and told him I didn't think it would be long. Then I called you right away."

Bethany sat in the chair next to her father and looked down at him while she rubbed his forehead gently. "I'm here, Daddy, it's me, Bethany. I hope you can hear me. I'm here with you." More tears began to flow down her cheeks.

"I've said my goodbyes to him, Beth," Rob said. "You need to spend time with him now. I'll be down the hall in the kitchen or in the parlor. Call me if you need me."

"I will," Bethany said softly. Rob turned and left the room wiping his eyes.

"Oh, Daddy, I can't believe you're leaving me, but I want you to know..." Bethany trembled and tried to compose herself. With a shaky voice she continued, "I want you to know it's...okay, Daddy. It's okay to go now, do you understand?"

She continued to caress his head.

"I had a nice talk with Jesus on Sunday. I told him...I told him it was okay to take you now. No more suffering. I...I wanted you to be set free. You can go see Mom now...and of course, Padre Pio too. Won't that be great, Daddy?"

Her father lay completely still without speaking and stared into space. If it wasn't for the slight rise and fall of his chest, it would almost appear as if he were already dead. Bethany placed her hand over his chest and felt how it moved ever so slowly up and down. It was the last bit of life he had in him. Bethany stared at the silver Padre Pio medal as it, too, rose and fell with every breath. She thought about the last words Jimmy had spoken to her. *Be strong, you'll manage without me. You will...*

Right now Bethany could barely get through the minutes, let alone the rest of her life. She doubted she would ever make it through, now that the two people she loved the most were gone. She flipped the medal over and looked at the relic. *Jimmy would want me to be strong. He'd want me to continue to pray to Padre Pio and to have faith. I can't let him or my father down...but how?*

She placed the medal back on her father's chest and continued to stare at it while she prayed aloud to Padre Pio. When she was done, Bethany looked into her father's face which had aged beyond his years, and a lifetime of memories flooded through her. She pictured herself as a little girl learning how to walk; how she held the large, strong hands of her father for balance. She thought about summers on the boat, holidays, the camping trip that her father had taken her and Steven on, and most of all she recollected the times he had spent with her mother, holding hands and enjoying life on the Adirondack chairs. Despite all the hardships, Bethany realized she did have a wonderful life after all, no matter how difficult it may have turned out. Even through his illness, she had a relationship with her father that was beyond compare. Everyone should be so lucky.

"Daddy, I hope you can hear me, because I want to tell you how proud I am of you. You were the best father any man could be. You were a giving, faith-filled person who loved his family more than life. Everything was important and special to you...a gift...and I can only hope to be as strong and wonderful as you some day." Bethany wiped away her tears. "Throughout your entire life you've been strong and accepting of what life threw you—Mom's accident and death, your debilitating illness. You remained upbeat and accepting of it all. The whole word should live by your example."

Bethany lowered her head and sobbed before continuing through a trembling voice. "I'll never forget our time together, Daddy, our talks, our meals...I was so fortunate to have spent that time with you and I have no regrets for the sacrifices I made to do it. Sometimes you need to give up things in order to gain, and to live each day to the fullest. You've taught me so much, Daddy. I will never forget any of it."

Bethany sat quietly for an hour, watching her father and looking at the medal. Rob was finally able to get a hold of her brother, and for what it was worth, Bethany held the phone next to her father's ear while Steven spoke his final goodbyes. She could hear Steven through the receiver and her heart went out to him that he couldn't be there in person. Her only hope was that their father could hear him. After a few minutes Steven stopped speaking and Bethany could hear him crying on the other end. She brought the phone to her own ear and spoke to her brother, trying to calm him down. While she listened to him she said a prayer to her mother to help them all.

She was completely drained after the phone call. She called Rob to stay with her father for a moment while she went upstairs to her room to get her rosary beads. She knew to recite the Chaplet of the Divine Mercy in the presence of someone who was dying, to ask for God's mercy and forgiveness, and to help them on the next stage of the journey. She wanted to do this sacred act of prayer for her father.

Bethany returned to her father's room and Rob quietly left. Sitting back down in the chair, she folded her hands in prayer over the rail of the bed and held the rosary beads tightly as the crucifix gently dangled over her father. She began to pray the Chaplet and found that in doing so, it comforted her.

When she was done, she read poetry to her father and played soft music for him. She had no idea how long it would take for him to die. She'd never experienced anything like this in her life, and it seemed almost surreal. All she knew was that she was afraid to leave her father's side, and she wondered if there was some other unseen presence in the room, perhaps Padre Pio himself, who was watching over them both.

Day turned into night and the hours dragged along. Rob relieved Bethany only long enough for her to go to the bathroom or stretch her legs. She would return within minutes and she would sit back down again.

"Daddy...there is one more thing I need to ask you," Bethany said. "You have always been there for me. I want you to still be there for me from wherever you are. Please, Daddy...please...if you can hear me, please find a way to communicate with me when you're gone."

By ten-thirty that night, Bethany could barely keep her eyes open. She lowered the rail of the bed and gently placed her head on her father's chest, taking comfort in his soft breathing. She fell asleep to the quiet music and the gentle movement of his chest.

Bethany had no idea how long she had been asleep when suddenly something felt different. She woke, and opening her eyes, she realized she no longer felt the movement of her father's chest on her cheek. Startled, she quickly lifted her head. When she looked at her father's face, she knew immediately.

"Rob! Rob!"

Within seconds Rob was at her side.

"He's gone, Rob...he's gone," Bethany cried.

Rob pulled Bethany's head toward his stomach and comforted her while she remained in the chair next to her father and cried. Rob led Bethany out of the room and into the parlor. Bethany knew that he was going to get John's body ready for her to say goodbye one last time before he called the coroner.

Ten minutes later he called Bethany inside. Her father looked peaceful and his eyes were now closed as if he were sleeping. Bethany continued to cry as she approached him. Rob stayed close by her.

"Goodbye, Daddy," she said through her tears. She kissed him on his forehead and then said, "I love you."

Rob led her out of the room and helped her shaky body to a comfortable chair while he went ahead and made the necessary calls. Within a few minutes the house was filled with hustle and bustle as they prepared to take her father's body away.

Suddenly Bethany remembered and jumped quickly from her chair. "Rob, come quick!" she yelled out to him. In a second he was there. "The medal, you've got to get me the medal around his neck. Please...hurry!"

Bethany paced back and forth waiting for him to return. When he did, she held her hand out. Rob placed the medal and chain in her palm. She closed her hand over it immediately and clutched it.

Rob left the room to assist with John, and Bethany went back over to the chair and sat down. She opened her hand to look at the medal which felt warm in her grip. When she looked down upon it, she could not register what she was seeing. She rubbed her tired eyes and looked at it again. Her eyes grew wide.

"How is this possible?" she asked.

Bethany carefully pulled the silver chain slowly upwards until the Padre Pio medal dangled in the air. She held it up to the light to get a better look as it delicately swayed back and forth on the silver chain. To Bethany's complete and utter amazement, the silver medal, which had hung around her father's neck, had turned to gold.

PART III

Forty-Two

A year and three months later...

It was a hot and sweltering, mid-July day in Northport and Bethany was busy making lemon meringue and key lime pies in Giovanni's Bakery. While she prepared them, she thought about the weekend ahead. It was Friday, and that evening she was headed down to the gazebo in town for a summer series concert by the water with an old friend from culinary school. Afterwards they'd go for drinks and appetizers at the little bistro located on Main Street.

After work on Saturday Bethany would hit the five o'clock Mass at St. Francis, and then she had invited Sarah and Cassandra and their husbands over for dinner at the house. Bethany was hoping the sea breeze would help to cool things off so they could at least enjoy appetizers on the porch. She had been planning the meal for days and she had already prepared a cooling gazpacho soup for a first course along with her homemade croutons.

Sunday night she was meeting a friend in Huntington to take in a movie, and on Monday morning she was seeing Rob in town for breakfast. Even though he was no longer living in the Northport house, he had found an apartment nearby. He and Bethany had remained good friends and saw each other at least once a month.

The thing Bethany was most looking forward to was time alone to sit on the beach and read on Monday afternoon. She was all caught up on orders and bills. She had so much time to read now that she was constantly picking up more books.

Bethany was amazed at how well she had adjusted to losing both her father and Jimmy. It hadn't been easy, of course. She felt as if she had been to hell and back, but she was okay, just like Jimmy had said she would be. Bethany missed them both terribly but she tried not to dwell on the loss. She kept herself busy and took advantage of her new freedom to have fun and enjoy life for a change. On occasion she even went out on a few dates, but she wasn't quite ready to settle into a new relationship just yet. She needed time to sort out her life and to recover from all that had been thrown her way.

In the beginning of March she closed the bakery for a few days and took a vacation out to Colorado to see Steven and Karen who were celebrating the birth of their new baby boy, whom they named John, after his grandfather. The fertility treatments had finally worked and they couldn't have been more thrilled. Bethany was now not only an aunt, but a godmother as well. She was overwhelmed with love for the tiny baby the very first time she held him and she realized that no matter what, life does continue and people move on. It was nice to have something happy and positive happening for a change, and it was as if they were all given a new lease on life.

As for Jimmy, Bethany did think of him quite often. She prayed to Padre Pio, asking him to help Jimmy and to make sure that he was okay. She still wondered about Jimmy; who or what he was, and she knew that she would probably never know the answer, but to her he would always be her angel.

The biggest hole left in her life had been her father and there were still nights when she'd cry herself to sleep longing for him. The house was big and empty, but every once in a while something would happen that would make Bethany wonder if her father was indeed around. The stereo in the parlor would suddenly play John's Tommy Dorsey CD, which had been left in the carousel, or lights would flicker in whatever room Bethany entered. Instead of being frightened, moments like that would bring her comfort, as well as the memories, just like her father had told her. She would look back at his life before his illness, and these were the things she would remember—that and all their special talks together. She knew her parents were united again, so what more could she ask for?

The two collies, JJ and Max, were all Bethany had left in the big rambling home, and she was thankful for the comfort they brought her. She missed Cherie and her wonderful smile. Cherie had found a new family to work for, where she took care of a middle aged woman who was going through chemotherapy. Every once in a while Bethany and Cherie spoke over the phone, and they always reminisced about John.

Yes, she was thankful for the people who had been there for her, Bethany thought one hot afternoon while putting the final touches on some pies. Alison came into the kitchen just as Bethany slid the last of the meringues into the oven.

"Beth, do you have a moment? There's some guy out here who says he wants to speak to you," Alison said.

Who is he?" asked Bethany.

"I don't know. I've never seen him before. He's definitely not a customer and he certainly doesn't look like he's from around here."

Bethany gave Alison a puzzled look.

"You'll see," said Alison as she headed back into the bakery.

Bethany finished up what she was doing and placed the pies carefully into the refrigerator. Cleaning off her hands on a towel, she made her way out into the bakery. It was empty with the exception of a tall, thin man, perhaps in his late twenties, whose arms were completely covered in tattoos. He had bleached blond hair and he wore several earrings in one ear. He had on jeans and a plain white tee shirt. Bethany had never seen him before.

As she approached him, he said, "Bethany Fitzpatrick?"

"Yes...that's me. Can I help with something?" Bethany asked.

"Would you mind if we sat down?" the man asked. "I have a few things I'd like to talk to you about."

Bethany walked over to one of the tables as he followed behind. They were both sitting down before he began to speak.

"My name is Mark. I know you don't know me, but someone you *do* know sent me to find you," he began as he folded his hands on the table.

"Someone is looking for me?" Bethany asked.

"Yes. He said he's a friend of yours. He's a friend of mine too." Looking into Bethany's eyes, he said, "Jimmy sent me."

Bethany sat up straight and her eyes grew wide. "Jimmy?"

"Yes," Mark answered. "The Italian guy."

Bethany instinctively touched the gold medal hanging around her neck. "Where is he?"

"We did time together," Mark began. "Don't worry, I'm harmless. I was brought in for petty stuff...kid's stuff...I had a lot of growing up to do. Anyway, I got out on parole about a month ago. I've been getting my life together, you know? I made a promise to Jimmy that I would come and see you. He wanted me to give you this." The man reached into the front of his jean's pocket and took out a small, wrapped, circular gift. "I don't know what it is," he said sliding it across the table, "but he made me swear I'd give it to you. He said you should open it alone."

Bethany picked up the small wrapped gift and held it tightly in her hand. She could not believe this was happening. "Is he still in prison? What happened to him?"

"It's kind of a sad story," Mark said.

Bethany swallowed hard. "Tell me...I need to know." She leaned over the table.

"There was this little girl...run down in a hit and run accident. The girl died; the family was distraught, as you can imagine. Well, the police looked for a while for the guy who did it. They were given some misinformation apparently. The whole case was crazy..."

"And what happened?" Bethany interrupted.

"Well, it turns out they brought Jimmy in. Locked him away." Mark paused. "Turns out...he was the wrong guy."

"I knew it!"

"Sad, isn't it?" Mark replied.

"How could this have happened? He's been in jail this whole time?"

"Yeah, I'm telling you. The case was crazy, man."

Of course he was innocent. "Where is he now?" she asked, hopeful.

"He got out a week before I did. Sometime around Memorial Day, I think."

"Well, where is he? Where did he go? Why didn't he come to see me himself?" Bethany asked excitedly.

"I asked him that same thing," Mark replied. "He said something about his work...social work, I think it was."

Bethany didn't know what to say. She stared at Mark blankly.

"He said he had some new assignment or something," Mark continued.

A million memories came flooding back to Bethany, from the moment when she first met Jimmy to the day he was taken away, to everything he had told her and all that she had learned. She started to put two and two together. *But if he was an angel, why on earth was he carted off to jail?*

"You mentioned he was your friend," Bethany said. "What kind of a relationship did he have with you and the other inmates? What kind of person was he?"

"He was a great guy," Mark said. "I wish I could see him again but I don't know where he is. He didn't like to talk about himself very much. He was more concerned with how everyone else was doing. And all he talked about was this Italian friar named Padre Pio. I see you have a medal too." He nodded his chin toward Bethany's necklace.

"Yes, I do," Bethany said in surprise as she touched the medal again.

"He gave me this," said Mark. He pulled a silver medal similar to Bethany's from underneath his tee shirt. "I've never seen a gold one before," he said. "The ones he gave out to the guys were all silver."

I don't even believe this. "He gave out medals to the men in prison?"

"Yeah, he changed lives."

"What do you mean?"

"He changed us...he changed me. All the guys I were with...it was like we were transformed or something. Jimmy gave us something to believe in, something to give us hope. He made us realize we weren't the only ones struggling in the world. He taught us to forgive ourselves and ask God for forgiveness for the things we had done in life. I'm telling you...he changed everyone; made a difference in our lives forever."

Bethany listened intently.

"I never met a guy like him," Mark continued. "I don't think I ever will again. I knew all along that he couldn't have committed a crime like that. He never even talked about it, and he didn't complain either. He's a remarkable guy."

"He is," Bethany said.

If it were true that he changed all these people's lives in prison, was it possible that Jimmy knew all along what was going to happen? Was that why he didn't put up a fight the day the police came and arrested him? He had accepted his fate as his new assignment. How else could people in prison change and find God unless someone was placed there right with them? Jesus Christ was taken away a prisoner on Good Friday, accused of blasphemy, beaten and nailed to a cross, yet still, his disciples followed him and believed without a doubt that Jesus was the son of God.

Everything began to make complete sense to Bethany now. "I can't get over any of this," she said leaning back in her chair.

"Tell me about it," Mark said. "What he did for me? It was a miracle. No one on earth could get through to me, but he did. I'm starting fresh now. No more mistakes."

"I'm so happy to hear about how much he helped you and made a difference. Thank you for sharing that with me, and for coming here as well."

"I made a promise to Jimmy that I would do this. I wouldn't let him down. He said that when I got here that I really should try one of your cannolis." Mark smiled.

Bethany's eyes filled up with tears and she had to look away and compose herself.

"Are you okay, Miss?"

"Yes," Bethany said as she nodded and wiped her eyes. "It's just...cannolis were his absolute favorite. I'll be happy to give you one. It's on me." She smiled.

"Thank you," Mark said. "Well, I guess I better be going. I start a new job tomorrow and I have to get ready for it. It's a good job too." He stood to leave.

Bethany stood as well. Extending her hand to him, she said, "I'm so happy for you. I wish you the best of luck. And thank you...thanks for stopping by. It means more than you know."

Mark nodded and shook her hand. "It was nice meeting you too," he said.

Bethany wrapped a cannoli up and he took it with him. She watched as he walked out the front door.

"Wow, what was that about?" asked Alison.

"He was innocent...just like I thought," said Bethany as she held the gold medal around her neck. "Jimmy was innocent."

She turned and walked back to the kitchen and then headed out the back door. She went over to her spot on the bench where she and Jimmy had many a conversation. Bethany sat down and pulled the small, wrapped gift out of her chef's coat pocket. Slowly and carefully she unwrapped it.

When she opened it she saw that it was blue in color and it was round and smooth. It was a glass rock with white lettering on it. As she brought it up to her face to get a better look, a tear rolled down her cheek.

BELIEVE IN ANGELS FOR THEY ARE THE MESSENGERS
OF MIRACLES.

A Readers Guide to

THE MEDAL

><(❖)><

A Note from the Author

On June 16, 2002, Pope John Paul II declared Padre Pio a saint after seven years of investigations. Over three hundred thousand people attended the canonization ceremony, which was held in Rome, Italy.

Two years later, on July 1, 2004, Pope John Paul II dedicated the Padre Pio Pilgrimage Church in San Giovanni Rotondo in memory of Saint Pio of Pietrelcina.

Saint Pio has become one of the world's most popular saints, and it is said that more Italian Catholics pray to Saint Pio than any other saint in history. Hundreds of books have been written in several languages about the life of Padre Pio.

It is estimated that more than 3,000 Padre Pio prayer groups exist throughout the world, with a membership of over three million.

September 23 has been declared the Feast Day for Saint Pio.

The third and final miracle that was needed for the canonization of Padre Pio involved an eight-year-old boy from San Giovanni Rotondo. The boy had been stricken with meningitis on January 20, 2001. The boy's father, who was a doctor, brought his son to the Home for the Relief of Suffering, a hospital founded by Padre Pio. The boy was examined and placed in the intensive care unit. Nine of his internal organs had shut down.

The doctors had given up hope. That night, the boy's mother and several Capuchin Friars of Padre Pio's monastery attended a prayer vigil. The boy's condition suddenly improved. He woke up from the coma as if nothing had ever happened to him. The doctors had no explanation as to his recovery. The boy told his family that while he was asleep, he saw an elderly man with a white beard and a long, brown habit. The man said to him, "Don't worry, you will soon be cured."

A Conversation with the Author

Interview by Jean Cody

JC: What was your inspiration for *The Medal*?

KFB: My father had multiple sclerosis for sixteen long years. It was a very difficult time for me and my family. By telling this story, I'm hoping to help or comfort those who may be in a similar situation.

JC: How did you become interested in Padre Pio?

KFB: Just like Bethany, I had met someone who told me about Padre Pio. I had never heard of him before. I was given a medal to give to my father, and I started praying to him.

JC: Do you feel that Padre Pio helped you through your journey or encouraged you in some way?

KFB: Most definitely. Padre Pio helped me during a time when I was losing my own faith, and I believe in some way he's encouraged me to write this book as well. He definitely had a huge impact on my life.

JC: What makes this book unique compared to other books written about Padre Pio?

KFB: As far as I know, there's not another book out there that features Padre Pio in a work of fiction. Although there are tons of books on Padre Pio, they're all non-fiction, and a lot of them are written by religious people – theologians and priests. So *The Medal* is unique in that I brought Padre Pio into the mainstream.

JC: Do you see any connection between *The Medal* and your earlier published works in the areas of local history, the paranormal and cooking?

KFB: Actually yes, in all of them. I'm a local historian, and I did the historical research on Padre Pio for this book. The paranormal aspect would be all the different gifts that Padre Pio had including bilocation, psychic sensitivity, and prophecy. As far as the cooking, I have written a cookbook (co-authored), and I love to cook. It obviously played a role in this book, with Bethany being a pastry chef. So all my interests kind of came together. You write about what you know.

JC: Were any of Bethany's recipes pulled from your own files?

KFB: Yes. At the very end of the book Bethany was having her friends over and she made gazpacho soup. That's something that I make. And in the bakery, she advertises her homemade croutons. I make croutons all the time. There was a cake or two that I make also. Maybe I should consider putting some of the recipes on the website.

JC: Besides your common interest in food, are there any other similarities between you and Bethany? How was the character developed?

KFB: Again, they say to write what you know. The character of Bethany was conceived from the experiences I had during my father's illness, as well as what I watched my mother go through. I didn't want to have two strong female characters in the book, so that's why I had to unfortunately kill the mother off. But I took what my mother went through and what she experienced, and what I experienced, and sort of melded them to create one character.

JC: How did you conceive of the character of Jimmy?

KFB: I had a lot of fun with him. I know a lot of Italians, and the person who gave me my medal is similar in some ways. It was fun to develop him and his language. He brings a bit of intrigue to the story, but also some humor. And since Padre Pio is Italian, Jimmy's character is in keeping with that theme. It just worked.

JC: Have you ever actually made cannolis? (I hear they're difficult to make correctly.)

KFB: It's funny you bring up the cannolis, because one of my favorite scenes in the book is when Bethany is showing Jimmy how to make cannolis. No, I have not made cannolis before, but they have played a part in my life. When I was pregnant, I had a craving for cannolis, and people from my husband's office starting bringing cannolis from all over the place – Staten Island, New Jersey, New York City and Brooklyn. I became sort of a connoisseur of the cannoli. The book is very serious, but the whole cannoli thing added a little lightheartedness to it.

JC: Writers sometimes talk about how their stories or characters seemed to take on lives of their own. Did this happen at any point during the writing of *The Medal?*

KFB: I'm very attuned to things like that because of my work in the paranormal. Especially in this book, I do think that I have gotten some help, whether from spirit guides or even from Padre Pio. In some parts of the book, I didn't realize until after I had written it that there was a deeper meaning. The character of Jimmy almost wrote himself. Out of all the characters in the book, he really came alive to me.

JC: Were there any parts that were difficult to write?

KFB: The most difficult part to write was the death scene, by far. It was very realistic. When you're writing a book, you have to constantly be reading it and revising. It never changed – every time I read it I had a difficult time. The other scene that was difficult was the chapter where Bethany trashes the bakery, because I remember what it was like to feel that hopeless, and to feel like you just can't go on – and how I was in that place at one point in my life and now I'm not.

JC: Talk a little bit about your involvement with the MS (Multiple Sclerosis) Society. What would you like readers to understand about this progressive, debilitating disease?

KFB: It's a very difficult disease to diagnose, first of all. It's difficult because it goes on for years and years. I watched my father's entire body deteriorate over a period of sixteen years. I felt helpless to do anything for him, so I decided to start working with the Long Island Chapter of the Multiple Sclerosis Society. I began a Ladies Tea Fundraiser that I still run every year. I created the Michael Flanagan Memorial Fund and the money goes specifically to pediatrics, to put children through a special summer camp. People don't think children can get MS, but they do.

JC: Prior to writing, your background was in photography. What led you to want to write?

KFB: I have a BFA in photography and studied under Arthur Leipzig. I specialized in photojournalism. I worked for newspapers and did photography for a while, and I did have the opportunity to do some writing. I started my own column on local history and that ultimately led to writing two books on local history. That then led to the ghost books, and it just sort of took off from there. I was always interested in both fields.

JC: Although you have several published works to your credit, *The Medal* is your first novel. Was it always your dream to become a novelist? Do you prefer writing fiction or non-fiction?

KFB: When I wrote my first book and did my first book signing and saw the response that I got, I knew that this is really what I wanted to do. I love that part of it. As far as whether I prefer fiction or non-fiction, it's kind of hard for me to tell at this point, but they are very different. The thing that I miss about writing non-fiction is being out in the world. I was always meeting new people and going on all these adventures into these unbelievable historical homes and mansions. Writing fiction is very reclusive. There is research involved but not the type that I was doing with non-fiction. But on the other hand, fiction gives me the ability to use my own creativity in actually creating characters.

JC: Are there more novels in your future? Are you working on anything right now?

KFB: I have several story ideas for future novels. I'm keeping a journal on each of them, where I just take notes as I think of things.

JC: Who are some of your favorite authors and books?

KFB: My all-time favorite author is Nicholas Sparks. I just love his characters and his stories. I do read a variety of authors just to keep current. The two best books that I've read this year have been *The Kitchen House* by Kathleen Grissom and *The Help* by Kathryn Stockett. I try to read a variety of authors, not just in women's fiction.

JC: As a practicing Catholic, how difficult is it to reconcile your religious beliefs with your interest in the paranormal? Can they coexist peacefully?

KFB: I think they totally can. When I was sixteen I started believing in reincarnation and reading Shirley MacLaine's books. I thought I was a bad Catholic, so I went to our family priest and he told me something very profound that has changed my life forever. He said the Catholic Church is like a box, and we're required to teach you what's inside that box. It's up to you to move outside of that box and find your own spiritual path. In fact, it's in the book. Jimmy says this to Bethany. It has changed my life because I realized that you can go beyond your standard religion. You can still have that but you can explore other things and it's not going against your religion. I've seen the positive impact my work has had on other people. It's all very uplifting.

JC: How do you envision Bethany's life unfolding after the story ends?

KFB: That's an interesting question. I haven't given it a lot of thought, but I would hope that she would find happiness and meet someone; that she would further the knowledge she gained through her experience with her father, with Jimmy and even with Padre Pio, and that she would use that somehow to her benefit. I have toyed with the idea of possibly writing a sequel which would include another spiritual aspect. That remains to be seen.

JC: What do you hope readers take away from *The Medal?*

KFB: I want caregivers to know that they're not alone in what they're going through. They need to have faith no matter how difficult things get. I also want them to know that life does get better even after death. It's a struggle, but our purpose on this earth is to live our own lives. You have to work to try to get past this. It can be done.

JC: What do your two grade school-aged sons think of your books and your career?

KFB: First, they are proud to say that their mom is an author, but the most intriguing and unique aspect of my career is the fact that I'm also a ghost investigator. That's a really cool thing to tell your friends – that your mom hunts for ghosts and walks around with a ghost meter.

JC: Is the life of a writer a difficult one? If you had the chance to do it all over again, would you?

KFB: I would say yes, it is a difficult career for many reasons, but if I had the chance to do it all over again, I would probably say yes. Although there have been many times in my career when I've said "I should have been a marine biologist."

Book Club Discussion Questions

Prepared by Jean Cody

1. In her devotion to her father, Bethany sacrifices her dream of becoming a high profile Manhattan pastry chef, as well as many of her most basic needs – for companionship, romance, fun and peace of mind. What effect does this have on her? Does devotion always require sacrifice?

2. Bethany's anger and despair nearly cause her to lose her faith in God. How well do you think you would cope in the role of caregiver, and in the face of great loss?

3. Food is an omnipresent theme in *The Medal*, from Bethany's intricately decorated cakes to the gourmet meals she prepares for her father, from teaching Jimmy how to fill a cannoli to hand-feeding her father in the hospital. Discuss the role that food plays in Bethany's life and relationships.

4. In contrast to the elaborate dishes Bethany creates for others, when she cooks for herself, it is simple. One breakfast consists of an egg and yogurt. Much of the time she seems to subsist on coffee, bottled water and wine. Why do you think this is, and what does this say about Bethany?

5. Why do you think Jimmy decides to take on Bethany as his "assignment?" What does he see in her? How does he know?

6. Bethany has a keen sense of order, seen in the fastidiousness of her kitchen and her management of the bakery. How does Bethany's need for order and control clash with the reality of her life? Discuss

the scene in which Bethany trashes the bakery's kitchen. How does it open the door for Jimmy's character to appear?

7. Bethany's sense of loneliness and isolation is only heightened by her dinner with her friends. Do you think Sarah and Cassandra are capable of truly understanding what Bethany is going through? How can friends support one another in the face of crisis, loss and grief?

8. What do you make of Jimmy and his apparent supernatural abilities? Is he an angel? A divinely inspired but all-too-human instrument of God? An extraordinarily compassionate and intuitive person? A socially inappropriate loner? A stalker? How suspicious would you be if a person like this showed up in your life?

9. Do you believe that angels walk among us in the world? Have you ever had an encounter with someone who you suspect might have been an angel? What was it about the encounter that made you think so?

10. Jimmy tells Bethany that the Catholic Church is in "a box" and that Padre Pio is outside that box. Why do you think the church had such a difficult time accepting the mystery of Padre Pio's life? Talk about the ways in which Bethany's story, although deeply rooted in Catholicism, ventures outside the box.

11. The words John Fitzpatrick tells his daughter, "I will never leave you Bethany. Trust me. I will always be there," echo those Jesus told his disciples: "I will not leave you as orphans; I will come to you." (John 14:18) These words speak to the very heart of human suffering – to the fear of abandonment, isolation, vulnerability and loss. Discuss how these words are also at the heart of Bethany's story, and how she makes peace with these fears.

12. Discuss the symbolic meaning of the silver medal turning to gold – the spiritual alchemy by which faith, hope and love can transform human suffering into pure gold.

13. Although a silver medal turning to gold sounds like something that could only happen in a novel, reports of similar, real-life occurrences abound, particularly of rosaries taken on pilgrimages to Medjugorje. Critics of these stories argue that faith should not need proof or "magic tricks." What effect do you think such an event would have on your faith? Would it change your life?

14. Catholicism greatly emphasizes the value of suffering as a pathway to God. As Bethany says, "Sometimes you need to give up things in order to gain." Is this just something people tell themselves to justify their losses, or do you believe that suffering serves a higher purpose?

15. Do you feel that Bethany's prayers were answered, even though her father ultimately died? How did Bethany's prayer change over the course of her father's illness?

16. When Jimmy is falsely accused and hauled off in handcuffs, he goes willingly, without a word of protest, just as Jesus went to his own torture and execution. Later, Bethany says that Jimmy "accepted his fate as his new assignment." How is this mindset at odds with a popular culture that equates faith with the ability to "manifest" one's desires through positive thinking?

17. Discuss some other ways in which Jimmy imitates Christ. For example, just before he is arrested, Jimmy seems to know what is about to happen and tells Bethany to hang on to her faith no matter what – just as Jesus did when he warned the disciples of his imminent arrest. Can you think of any other parallels?

About the Author

Thomas Decker Studio

Five-time, award winning author Kerriann Flanagan Brosky, has been featured in a number of publications including *The New York Times*, *Newsday* and *Distinction* magazine. She has appeared on CBS' Sunday Morning Show, "Ticket" with Laura Savini, News 12 Long Island, and The Writer's Dream in East Hampton, for her previously published non-fiction books. Kerriann hosts a weekly Internet radio show on Blogtalk Radio, "The Kerriann & Joe Show - Spirit Connection," and she blogs for Patch.com. Kerriann is the President of the Long Island Authors Group, and is a well-known speaker who draws standing-room-only crowds to her lectures. Kerriann lives in Huntington, Long Island, and when she's not writing she enjoys spending time at the beach with her husband Karl and their two sons. *The Medal* is her debut novel.

Visit her websites at

www.kerriannflanaganbrosky.com

www.padrepiomedal.com

CPSIA information can be obtained at www.ICGtesting.com
Printed in the USA
BVOW07s0627040913

330078BV00001B/12/P